Himmler and the Handmaid

by

Erik Martiny

River Boat Books

Himmler and the Handmaid
Copyright © 2023 by Erik Martiny

The painting adapted for the cover artwork is
titled "Freudlose Gasse" (1927) painted by Franz
Wilhelm Seiwert. German New Objectivity
painter.

Printed in the United States of America.
Published by River Boat Books, St. Paul, MN.
First printing December 15, 2023.

ISBN: 978-1-955823-16-6

Acknowledgements

Many thanks to Lisbeth Martiny, my first reader, and to Rick Gekoski and Dermot Bolger for their sterling advice and unflagging kindness. Much gratitude is also due to my indefatigable publisher, Peter Damian Bellis.

I would also like to thank the staff at Kreismuseum Wewelsburg for answering my questions and for offering to guide me so interestingly around the Castle museum.

To Rick Gekoski and Dermot Bolger

Himmler and the Handmaid

There lies the cold of winter.

—*Heinrich Heine*

CONTENTS

Prologue

It will perhaps surprise the reader—and my learned colleagues who chance upon this book—to become acquainted with what I have to announce in this somewhat wayward introduction.

Having long retired from my position as History professor at Humboldt, I no longer feel the need to maintain appearances as I did in my younger days as an academic with a pristine reputation to uphold.

You will have surmised that I am no longer even Professor emeritus. That relatively faux-prestigious status is now only tenable for a brief fifteen years for the simple fact that conference-goers tend to shy from conventions that are vetted (or even attended) by doddery old has-beens such as myself. Having thrown caution to the winds, I thus take the liberty of unmasking myself, running the risk of dismaying the starchy world of academe.

Before I disclose, let me pre-emptively dispel any uncertainty that may be lurking. I hope you

will believe me when I say that the memorabilia
from which the ensuing diary is culled in no way
reflects a covert nostalgia for war on my part.
I have always been a pacifist and hold a deep
distaste for oppression of any sort, as I trust my
disclosure will confirm, despite its somewhat
errant nature.

As some of my esteemed colleagues know,
my parents both died in the early 1940s. I hope
it is not too difficult to imagine that my partial
fetishizing of wartime souvenirs as an antic
collector of antiques stems from a desire to
recapture the period that led to the loss.

The truth will out eventually, as Shakespeare
and others once put it, and it is right it should be
so. As a historian, I have always sought to reveal
the demonstrable truth: being myself a relic of
the war, I am naturally impelled to unveil myself
in my true light. In these unprecedented times
of revelation and other comings out, I sense the
time is ripe to get this off my chest.

And yet, now that I have set myself up, I
find myself hesitate (as you can tell from the
dithering nature of these sentences, and as
I imagine Günter Grass once did before he
revealed his sugar-coated secret to the world),
and yet what needs to be said has to be uttered.
Here it is, then, in all its laughable grotesquery.
It will hopefully seem innocuous enough to you
now that I have spent so much time working up
to it.

On the side lines of my professional research area, I am what is commonly called a costume connoisseur. To put it more bluntly, I am what most people would call a clothes fetishist.

It will no doubt contribute to the mildly scandalous nature of my revelation if I add that although I am not particularly keen on cross-dressing, I do from time to time also dress up as a 1930s woman when the yearning to do so arises. Generally speaking, I tend to wear the garments that seem the most appropriate to my frame of mind on any given day.

Having read the paragraph above, I imagine you probably think I am nothing but a risible old crank with a good deal of his marbles lost on the dreadful path to dotage. A perfectly understandable response to an unusual habit. I can conceive that by ordinary standards, privately dressing up in 1940s attire is far down the neurotic road in the direction of psychosis, but strange as it seems it feels ordinary to me. It's a truism that one's own foibles feel perfectly normal, even if one is conscious that they do not follow mainstream behaviour.

There are days when I feel comfortable wearing the equivalent of what my father would have worn in 1939. At other times, I enjoy wearing what my mother would have worn up to 1941 when she was removed from her life.

In my more coquettish moods, I have sometimes daubed the colour of her lipstick on

my mouth, shielded from too much shame by
the knowledge that aristocratic men in Ancient
Rome wore lipstick too, as a sign of social
status.

On darker days, I sometimes take to wearing
concentration camp attire, both inmate, guard
and kapo.

I should say that I do this only on rare
occasions and often under the mantle of shame.
My aim is of course not to mock those who were
forced to endure the horrors of the camps but
to experience them at a safe remove, in a mild,
innocuous form.

As the only death camp survivor in my
family, I sometimes experience a need to
immerse myself in the murky waters of history.

Dressing as the Auschwitz prisoner I
once was as a child offers both respite and
chastisement in equal measure, a pretty common
paradoxical manifestation of survivor disorder.
Suffice it to say that the habit is not merely
self-punitive. I do not feel I am only a plaything
of what Freud called the death drive.

Impersonating camp inmates at this
historical distance allows me to feel I am back in
the place where I last saw my parents. With the
front and back doors securely locked and the
curtains pulled over the windows, I move about
the house in my striped pyjamas and someone
else's yellow star etched on my chest.

You may find it hard to fathom that there

might be anything comforting about indulging in this somewhat macabre fancy dress rigmarole. Believe me when I say it takes some of the sting out of my childhood memories of life in the camp. I was only four years old on January 27, 1945 when the Soviet troops released me along with the other survivors.

The reader may rest assured that I recreate only a fraction of the experience of concentration camp life. It is not as if I feel the need to bark orders at the mirror or subject myself to corporal punishment or any other forms of humiliation.

Unless I decide to go out, the rest of my day is spent enjoying the comforts that my status as a well-known Jewish intellectual have given me: a flat-screen TV, a state-of-the-art ultra-light laptop, a voice-controlled smart house, a swath of today's newspapers and magazines, freshly squeezed orange juice, butter and honey on toast for breakfast, home-delivered, smart-fridge-ordered sushi for lunch.

But enough of me and my foibles and eccentric, uncomfortable truths. Let us turn to the more disquieting circumstances in which I acquired the diary you are about to encounter.

I must admit here too that despite my advanced years there are times when I descend into the depths of the dark net to trawl for the murkiest mementoes, protected by the interlocking digital shield of my onion router. And yet I chanced upon the item with which you are about to become acquainted as I was browsing through the usual Google-curated, squeaky-clean websites.

Returning to the first webpage, I noticed an entry that had escaped my attention when I scrolled down in haste to capture something new for my collection. It wasn't exactly what you would call a proper site. The http address led to one single item and had nothing else to offer but a picture of the front cover of a notebook, a fairly summary account of its contents, and a short sample of the writing enclosed within it.

After reading a few paragraphs of the abstract, however, I was instantly hooked. It's usually that way with me. If the item manages to tap into my nerves, I simply need to possess it. The terms and conditions stipulated below suggested in somewhat vague, ineloquent terms that the price would be negotiable up to a point, usually a good sign; it didn't give a price bracket, though, usually less of a good sign. Nevertheless, the article seemed acceptably authentic. The passage quoted had an instant ring of historical truth and accuracy to it; the photograph of the cover suggested the virtually inimitable patina and tattering of time. Within seconds of discovering the item, I was rearing to go out and acquire it.

I should say I have a particular interest in

first-hand accounts of the war. Purporting to be an eye-witness account of Heinrich Himmler's sojourns at Wewelsburg Castle, this journal seemed to hold a rare promise indeed for someone with my kind of vested interest.

Little is known about what occurred during Himmler's intermittent stays at the Westphalian castle, a fact which raised my curiosity almost to fever pitch as I reread the excerpt and the promise of disclosure suggested in the abstract. Himmler's goings-on at Wewelsburg were his most closely-guarded secret.

Legend has it that Himmler treated Wewelsburg Castle as a kind of private Camelot. Some historians have gone as far as to call the keep his "personal playground", but even that was until now based almost entirely on conjecture, untrustworthy or untraceable hearsay with next to no supporting evidence.

Only the most select SS members ever entered that castle. Other occupants of the keep included those who worked in maintenance, as well as a few Niederhagen prison labourers, most of whom died in the process of rebuilding the premises from both undernourishment and exhaustion. What went on inside Wewelsburg castle from 1934 to 1945, however, has remained virtually unknown until the discovery of the momentous document you are about to read.

After Himmler took out his hundred-year lease on the castle, he enforced disciplinary measures to make sure that nothing ever came out of it. All those who entered or worked at the fortress were sworn to secrecy. Fear of retaliatory punishment has ensured that no written or recorded accounts of what went on there have survived.

Himmler was so secretive about the happenings in that most obscure of abodes that no details of its full former furnishings have ever come to light. When he fled the castle at the end of the Second World War because the American Spearhead division was gaining ground, Himmler ordered his personal assistant Heinz Macher and his Panzer brigade to destroy everything it contained and leave the castle in ruins. Although they failed to assemble enough explosives to bring the castle to the ground, they were able to reduce it to a fractured, burnt out empty shell. All furnishings and documents were lost in the blaze that ensued from the detonations triggered during this brief and partially unsuccessful operation.

The reader will have little trouble imagining how eager I was to acquire a document that promised to lift the veil on such an obscure pocket of history. What historians have conjectured for decades has now been both confirmed and qualified substantially by the document that you are about to read.

Wewelsburg castle was clearly intended to be the epicentre of the hoped for Nazi empire, in both geographical and spiritual terms. If the present document is to be trusted as a valid reflection of what went on inside its craggy walls, Wewelsburg Castle was Himmler's SS headquarters and the rituals he organized there were both myth-focused and occult.

The words "Nazi" and "spiritual" will seem mutually exclusive to the average reader (and in the usual religious meaning of the word 'spiritual' they certainly are), and yet this is what Himmler seems to have attempted: to generate a new Nazi faith, equipped with its own rituals and gods. The document you are about to read provides sometimes shocking insights into the murky deeds that took place at Wewelsburg Castle and the nearby concen- tration camp known as Niederhagen.

Without dithering or waiting for further developments, I wrote back post haste to the website manager to inquire about the prove- nance of the piece. The laconic emailed response came back to me after a minute: it read simply *"Wewelsburg"*. No seasoned collector with a modicum of experience would settle for a source containing that degree of imprecision, so I ventured to press him for more ample information.

Not receiving a reply, I decided against my better judgment to play along and venture to ask the seller for his price. We haggled a little

over the rather high estimation—let me just say
without naming the figure that it was steep,
even for that rare kind of memorabilia. But the
high price requested made me trust its authenticity, at least to some extent. It suggested that
the owner of the article was aware that he was
in possession of a genuine historical artefact of
importance, something that might be regarded
as the Rosetta stone of Nazism. And yet,
disturbingly, he did not wish to put it up for
auction, despite the fact that he probably knew
it could reach a much higher bidding price.

After half a dozen emails, we settled on
a slightly more affordable figure and agreed
to meet in Hamburg the next day. I live just
outside of Wolfsburg, some 200 kilometres
away, but with the high-speed train service we
now enjoy in Germany it didn't seem that great
a distance so I conceded without attempting to
negotiate a closer meeting point.

What I was more worried about was the time
the site manager wanted to meet at. Midnight
is never a very reassuring hour, the very word
seems dipped in murk and menace. Being
elderly and never having had much of a taste
for danger to begin with, I didn't like that one
bit and made it clear in my message, but the
owner of the manuscript proved to be inflexible
on that count.

When I wrote back suggesting 9pm at the
latest, he failed to answer. Fearing he might

demur or cancel our appointment, I wrote back offering 10.30pm. I was deeply relieved when he finally answered a whole endless twenty minutes later that the time would be acceptable. He obviously wanted it to be dark and seemed afraid of being compromised. His appended final words rang rather chillingly like something out of a crime movie: in capital letters, it read "NO FUNNY BUSINESS. You must come **ALONE**."

In humble miniscule letters, I promptly answered "yes, of course". Being so close to obtaining the coveted item, I was more than anxious not to forfeit it so I wrote one last time to confirm all our terms. There being no further messages in response, I quickly copied down the details of the meeting point and logged out guiltily as if remaining on my email account might lead to prison.

Having withdrawn the sizeable amount of money from my savings account, I proceeded to embark on the early evening train to Hamburg so that I would get there well in time. I have to say I was feeling rather nervous, as I often am when I find myself forced into this kind of assignation. I usually pay for my collectables by card or money transfer and rarely have to deal directly with brokers. I am generally thankful that I seldom have to go through the strain of having to meet sellers in the flesh.

Some of the people in the business of World

War Two collectables are pretty shady types.
Typically, they tend to be neutral at first—by
that I mean that the high-end brokers don't
generally advertise under the name of Adolf or
anything that obvious, and they don't usually
display their skinned heads, if they have one.

In fact, unless you directly broach the
subject, you can be chatting to them for up to
half an hour without actually realizing you're
talking to a neo-Nazi who says his prayers
before going to bed every night kneeling in
front of the swastika or a portrait of Hitler on
his wall. With the way things are these days,
especially in Eastern Germany, you can never be
too sure who you're dealing with.

Of the two kinds of nostalgic Nazi though
I was more worried that evening that I might
have to meet the skinhead variety in that
dark alley, the kind that is visibly disturbed,
sporting psychotic blue eyes, a knife nick on
his lip, a couple of homophobic ticks twitching
at the nerves in his cheeks, and the number
18 tattooed on his knuckles (a very mildly
encrypted numeric code, corresponding to
the first and eighth letter of the alphabet—an
obvious giveaway for A.H).

I've had to deal with a few of those types
in my time and been subjected to a number of
cold sweats, but nothing more severe. They're
generally miles away from suspecting that I'm
Jewish. I suppose I don't correspond to their

fantasy of a hooked nose and clawed, filthy, money-grubbing hands. I also think that my quest for war collectables just doesn't tally with who I am. With their thoughts trained on the money, they never bother to ask if I'm circumcised.

For the most part, they tend to settle for the intuition that I'm either a backward-looking crank with a WWII serviceman father or one of their own neo-Nazi pseudo-intelligent scumbags. I usually end up telling them I'm a historian if they ask, but I sometimes go along with what they've initially surmised, avoiding the truth lest it place me in harm's way.

The transaction itself is generally a behind-the-scenes hush-hush online affair which suits me fine. Remaining more or less incognito offers the safest cover. It also provides me with the excitement of brokering a deal in digital disguise, a little written role play I engage in to alleviate the boredom of retirement and solitude.

On those rare occasion when I have felt a little edgy before a face-to-face appointment, I generally wear my Nazi-black coat (it belonged to a former SS officer, but sports no obvious signs of party politics on the outside). I've had it treated and the sig-ornamented lapels removed, so the leather looks virtually new and incon-spicuous in a crowd, except to the expert eye. In pristine condition, it looks pretty much the way

I imagine it looked when it was first produced in the Third Reich all those years ago, minus the insignia. I find that wearing this coat tends to put the Nazi-loving sort at ease. They take one whiff of the Himmler-black leather and instantly take it for granted that I am one of their kind.

I should add that as a lecturer I've acquired an affinity for showmanship which has allowed me to avoid blowing my cover on these mercifully rare, rather stressful occasions.

And yet there was something about this assignation that I distrusted, some undefinable thing that put me slightly ill-at-ease. The dark alley, the cloak-and-dagger request for a midnight meeting suggested I was going to have to do commerce with something of a confirmed shady dealer, an underworld trader who had either illegally harvested the document from some privately-owned archive or hived it off the black market himself.

I couldn't help wondering too if I had not fallen for a deceitful piece of clickbait—rather computer savvy for one my age, I'm not entirely naïve on that count, having fallen prey to it before. Since those dark days at Auschwitz, I've developed a keen sense of paranoia which has sometimes served me in good stead, when it hasn't dogged my relationship to others. Most of the women I've courted over the years couldn't take more than a few weeks of my paranoia, however. I say this with deep regret as it has led me to end my days alone.

Although there was nothing on the site
that suggested it had been set up as a trap
for unwary Jewish browsers, I couldn't help
wondering why the advertisement had been
taken down the next time I went to have a look
at the photograph of the manuscript. Jew-bait or
not, it had vanished.

Despite being much enthused by the
prospect of possessing the manuscript and
devouring its secrets, it was with a slight sense
of foreboding that I took myself out to Hamburg
on that evening express train.

By the time I reached our meeting point,
I was a good fifty minutes ahead of schedule.
There being no one in or around the alley,
I went for a little walk to take stock of the
surroundings, keeping a wary eye trained on
the alley and circling back at regular intervals in
case my dealer happened to turn up in advance.

When he still hadn't shown up ten minutes
after the hour, I decided to venture forth into
the dreaded alley of the shadow of death in case
he was lurking somewhere inside it. To steel
myself with a modicum of hardiness, I dipped
my gloveless hand in my pocket to where I had
concealed the usual skewering screwdriver I
bring along on such occasions.

It's illegal to carry a gun or even a knife
around in Germany, but a sharpened screwdriver is generally ok—you can always adduce

that you were out to fix something for a friend in need if anyone stops you for a frisk—something which fortunately has not happened to me since the early 1940s.

A friend of mine carries a fork around in her handbag: it gave me the idea of taking the screwdriver, a tool that feels slightly more virile than a fork or a scoop spoon. I'm not a violent man by any means, but I've trained myself both psychologically and physically to lunge or stab with a screwdriver in case the need arises. Of course, at my age, it's unlikely I would be any match for a young, Jew-hating skinhead with murderous intent, but having the screwdriver in my pocket allays my unrest enough to allow me to behave more or less normally without quaking too visibly.

I was walking away from the meeting point when I heard a man's voice inquire if I happened to be "Herr Messerschmidt?" That's my alias. I call myself Herr Hermann Messerschmidt to give my profile a certain edge and to stave off any suspicions that I might be a Zion-loving pacifist.

The man in front of me was hooded. From what I could see of his face, he was in his late forties, maybe early fifties. It was impossible to tell with the hood if he was graced with cranial hair. For some reason (probably due to my mounting paranoia), I took it for granted he had the skinhead's disdain for follicles.

"Yes", I said, "Herr Bismarck?"

The site manager had called himself Otto Bismarck, with no apparent attempt to conceal the fact that the name was an alias.

"Yeah", said Bismarck. "You got the dough?"

"Of course. Here it is", I said, holding out my bag without edging a step closer to hand it over. "You have the document?"

"Naturally", came the answer.

He dipped his hands into a breast pocket and took two steps towards me. My right hand was gripped around the handle of the screwdriver deep within the holster pocket of my leather coat.

Once he had his hand safely out in the open, I released my grip on the screwdriver a little and put out my kid-leather gloved hand, still half expecting to be slashed in the wrist by an unseen knife hidden under the serviette the man was holding.

A little grudgingly, he proffered the pouch so I could take a look.

I handed him the envelope containing the money as soon as he released the serviette into my hand. We both had a look inside our respective treasures to see if everything was as it should be. As he fingered through the banknotes, I pulled the worn-out leather-bound copybook out of the serviette, flicked through it warily, inwardly quivering with barely mastered excitement. It bore that unmistakable time-weathered look that I so cherish.

Skimming through it in the dim, orangey light of the streetlamp, I saw that it contained a good two hundred pages or so of the same wiry feminine handwriting I had seen advertised on the webpage.

We were about to go our separate ways when I ventured to ask my hooded dealer the question that had been tugging at my thoughts since the beginning.

"Can I ask where you got this?"

Instantly, I realized that the phrasing of the question was too blunt.

I have never been that good at strategizing. I knew it as soon as I said it that I was going about it in the wrong manner. To make matters worse, nervousness had made my tone of voice sound somewhat brazen, as if I was demanding an answer. I sounded discourteous, as if I was about to subject him to a police interrogation. To my chagrin, it was already blurted out.

The hooded broker stiffened, but gradually eased out when he saw the almost spasmodic batting of my frightened eyelids. I imagine he was probably used to coarser requests and harsher interlocutors. He fixed me in the eye for a moment, as if weighing the pros and cons of divulging that kind of information to a stranger. He had proved to be singularly incurious about me up to then and I wanted to keep it that way.

"I got it from my grandfather."

Something in his tone suggested to my practiced ear that he was lying through his teeth.

"Your grandfather?"

"He used to live in the village of Wewelsburg."

"Are you saying your grandfather was one of the people who plundered the castle after the Nazis left?"

I heard a sharp intake of breath.

Again an obvious faux pas. "The Nazis" sounded too dismissive, too I'm-not-one-of-them. But the question had to be asked.

I could feel in his manner that he was about to give me the slip.

Herr Bismarck took a step backwards, cast a nervous, sidelong look down the alley, his eyes shifty and insecure. His voice lowered to a rough, threatening pitch when he next spoke.

"He left me the contents of a safe, ok? There were a few objects inside it. This was one of them. I don't know where or how he got them. What the fuck difference does it make?"

"I'm a historian, and it makes a great deal of difference to me. I promise anything you say will remain entirely anonymous."

"Look, man, it's like I told you. I don't know how he got them. I have to go."

"Can you tell me what the other objects were?"

"No."

Turning his back, Herr Bismarck walked back into the nineteenth century and I never saw him again. No other advertisements for the text or other items he had claimed to possess appeared again. The experience of selling the manuscript must have rattled him, or else he sold them on the dark net which I am told possesses three more layers of onion router encryption than the deep web itself. I am certain a lot of memorabilia is lost on me in such overlay networks, but my sometimes excessively cautious nature has left me disinclined to descend to such digital depths. I only go there when my usual servers have nothing to offer and I require a darker collectable.

And thus my little anecdote comes to a close in a dead end. I regret to say that I have not been able to ascertain the precise identity of the author of the diary. A number of the individuals mentioned in the document are verifiable bona fide historical figures, but the identity of the writer herself has left no trace in any record at Wewelsburg, or in her native country. Her Polish surname will, for the present at least, have to remain an unresolved conundrum.

The author of these pages refers to herself as 'Ewa' in the manuscript—this Polish equivalent of Eva is pronounced in the same way as in German and English. She went by the name of Eva Kaufmann at Wewelsburg—as the author of the diary reveals, the surname was bestowed upon her from the first day of her employment during her forced indenture at the castle.

It is likely that her employers—either Frau Elfriede Wippermann, the household manager, or the *Obergruppenfürer* of Wewelsburg Castle, Herr Siegfried Taubert—kept a ledger of the servants in their employ (the document alludes to one), but any such registration was most likely destroyed in the fire and subsequent pillaging of the castle after the Nazis vacated the premises in March 1945.

In the hope of providing a companionable presence in the margins of this frequently harrowing account of wartime hardship and endurance, I have included footnotes in various parts of the text to assist the reader's historical and lexical understanding of certain details.

The reader who prefers to enter the labyrinth unassisted is invited to ignore these editorial asides and happily forget my presence throughout the text. I have attempted to refrain from over-commenting so that the reader may immerse him or herself in the narrative. Plot spoilers within the notes have also been kept to a bare minimum.

I have worked in tandem with Artek Sniegowski, the translator of the document, to render a text that flows freely and eloquently. Though I have stepped back on occasion when Mr Sniegowski felt that I was rendering the text

too flowery by comparison with the original, I
must confess to occasionally contributing a few
additions to Ewa's lexical reach when I thought
her descriptions could have been formulated
more precisely. Her prose is for the most part
exceptionally keen and eloquent for one so
young. On certain days, however, especially
towards the end, Ewa's entries become a little
erratic (presumably because she was flustered
by events that would have taken their toll on
any sensitive being in her position).

As I have had the last say in these editorial
matters, I take full responsibility for all
perceived modifications by those who decide
to consult the original Polish (which is now
out with Iracka Press). Perhaps a later translation into English will provide a more faithful
rendering and retain all of Ewa's occasional
stylistic, syntactic lapses, even including any
breaches of logic (there are a few rare, minor
instances of this at the end).

The temptation was great to reveal the
document's historical disclosures within the
confines of this introduction, but I leave such
matters to their rightful owner, the author of
the personal, and indeed sometimes endearingly
quirky account that follows in these pages. It
is to Ewa and Ewa alone that these revelations
belong and so I entrust you to her candid prose.
The acuity of her descriptions and observations
are, as you will see, often surprisingly preco-

cious for one her age.

For those who might feel that her flair for comedic faux-naivety strikes a discordant note in what was a most harrowing period in modern history, let me just point out that the atrocities of the war years were full of tragicomic asides. One has only to think, for instance, of the fact that Hermann Göring (the man Hitler announced as his successor as early as 1941) spent his last nights in fear of being stabbed by the SS prisoners in the castle in which they were being held captive by the Allied Forces— the tragicomic irony inherent there being compounded by the fact that Göring's cell was guarded by an American sentinel with Jewish origins.

When I first chanced upon the tale you are about to read, I knew with absolute certainty that despite the utter impossibility of doing so I would have to encounter the woman who had written it.

She would have been around my mother's age at the time. I can picture her breath-taking splendour, how infinitely delectable she must have seemed to all and sundry. She was what the Preraphaelite painters called a stunner, what in my day used to be called a looker, an enchantress, and now tends to be called a knockout or drop-dead gorgeous—but more than all that, there was the resplendence of her spirit.

As though having received a shot of adren-
aline, I felt the poignant prick of irony at
being punished for this immaculate beauty
by the dooming quirks of the Fates. Although
my plumage is not anywhere close to pretty,
especially now, I too have known what it is like
to be scorned, to be branded with a tattoo, to
have a yellow star stitched to one's chest. I too
have known what it is like to be outcast, to be
deemed beyond the pale, a misfit, a scapegoat,
persona non grata.

The list of those fateful words goes on:
castoff, castaway, deadwood, untouchable,
pariah. I'm sure there are others. So many
expressions to describe the plight of those who
have been considered misshapen—or in some
cases too shapely—to be kept in the main fold
of society. The reason for this verbal prolifer-
ation is simple of course: ethnic cleansing has
occurred so repeatedly in the past that it is
bound to happen again and again before the
history of the human race has run its course.

If inordinately beautiful women can hardly
be said to suffer rejection, oppression or impris-
onment in our day (other than by their own
fame and the harassment of the popular press),
they have certainly had to endure these things
in the past. One need but bring to mind the
countless vestal virgins, geishas, courtesans,
concubines and odalisques who were enslaved

for their eye-catching features, and the fate
to which our heroine falls foul will seem an
integral part of a long-established pattern.

As a historian specialized in the period of
the Second World War, I have felt it incumbent
upon me to bring the written document translated in these pages to the attention of the
broader public. Having more than a mere
working knowledge of Polish, I oversaw the
translation of the text that you are about to read
into the German tongue. Its instant popularity
with readers in the Germanosphere prompted
my publisher to ask me to supervise and
introduce the present translation into English. I
have no doubt it will meet with the same enthusiasm it garnered in German-speaking countries
this past year.

For those few crusty critics who have put in
doubt the historical authenticity of the artefact
transcribed herein, suffice it to say that before
considering publication I delivered the original
booklet into the hands of four of my most
esteemed historian colleagues at Humboldt so
that its genuineness could be ascertained.

I have had the text examined by a panel of
three Slavonic linguists who have unanimously
concurred that the stylistic features displayed
therein are characteristic of the period to which
we believe it belongs. No lexical or stylistic
anachronisms have been detected, a fact which
corroborates our view that it is most unlikely to

be a forgery.

I have also had the document authenticated by the palaeography and graphology departments at Humboldt. Professor Dr Ania Silverberg has confirmed that, allowing for the idiosyncrasies of individual script style the handwriting evidenced in the original document is characteristic of the letter formations prevalent in Polish schools of the 1930s. Professor Silverberg has worked in tandem with the palaeography department of the University of Cracow to confirm her analysis.

Needless to say, the artefact itself has been tried and tested according to the most modern dating techniques. There is no doubt that the paper and ink used in the document go back to the interwar years.

Identifying the timeframe referenced in the text was a far less complicated affair. Although the writer of the original document includes no dates, she refers to a sequence of events spanning from late winter of 1940 to the early summer of 1941.

The kidnapping of children by Nazi officials in various parts of Europe to increase the size of the German population is a well-documented phenomenon and will require little exposition in these pages. I have myself written a book on the subject that readers may look up if they wish to expand their understanding of the practice.

To inform the lay reader, let me just point

out a few statistics to indicate the magnitude of
National Socialism's assimilationist strategy.

It is estimated that around 500,000 children
were abducted from various European countries
by the Nazis. The historical consensus amongst
certified Polish and German academics is that
around half of these kidnapped children were of
Polish origin.

As part of *Generalplan Ost* (the coloni-
zation and ethnic cleansing of Central and
Eastern Europe), the objectives of the abduction
operation were outlined by Heinrich Himmler
on 15 May 1940 in a top-secret memorandum
entitled *A Few Thoughts About the Treatment of
Racial Aliens in the East.*

In this infamous document, Himmler laid
out in the most practical terms how he planned
to implement the directives he received from
Adolf Hitler on 7 November 1939. The main
objective of the operation was to abduct children
with "racially valuable" physical traits in order
to convey them to Germany where they were
placed in family-based homes or in so-called SS
Home Schools.

The abducted children were invariably given
new Germanic-sounding names and reared as
German citizens. During the final "quality-fil-
tering process" within these education camps
and foster homes, children deemed insuffi-
ciently Germanic or incapable of assimilation
were conveyed to extermination camps around

Europe. Resistance to Germanization—or failure to adapt—was mercilessly quashed both within Germany and elsewhere: recalcitrant children were generally sent back to the Polish concentration camps from which they were culled.

According to the terms of Himmler's memorandum, an annual selection of children with racially approved features was held in all German-occupied territories. The overall aim of Generalplan Ost was thus to destroy the ethnic group known as Polish whilst expanding the scope of the German population.

It is estimated that a large number of abducted children were kidnapped at a young age so that they could be forcibly Germanized with greater ease. Falsified birth certificates were issued to German foster parents so that even they were often not made aware that the children they fostered had been abducted from Poland. As the children were renamed and under strict orders to speak no other language but German, many abducted infants grew up with, at best, a very dim recollection of ever having been Polish. Most of them have now gone to their graves without knowing the truth concerning their origins.

In accordance with the Lebensraum policy, the biological parents remaining in Poland were either executed or used as forced labour until they perished. I will refrain from going into further detail here: the horrendous conditions of this human trafficking to Germany are vividly documented in the narrative that follows.

Although the account that you are about to experience reads like a diary, it contained no date markings. It is as if the diarist lived in a kind of timeless limbo. This being said, as I have stated earlier, certain events referred to allow the reader to gain a clear enough understanding of the time frame.

The narrator of this diary was clearly one of the early victims of Himmler's mass abduction plan—judging from the events she later narrates and the spring season she evokes at the start of her account, it seems likely that she and her sister were abducted around February or March 1940.

I have taken the liberty of numbering the sections that were at times interspersed with blank pages. I believe these original blanks were intended to be filled at a later stage, or at least to allow for additions that never materialized. I realize it is probably unduly German of me to have omitted these blank passages—for those who might object to such intrusive editorial practices, please forgive this personal, or cultural, propensity.

Wolfsburg, 8 June 2022
Prof. Dr. Kaspar Blumenfeld

1

My grandmother used to tell me as a child that my looks would be my downfall. Not expecting that time would prove her right, I would shrug off the remark as just another instance of Grandma's tender teasing. Little did I realize back then that my face would indeed prove to seal my fate and that I would one day have to barter my beauty.

Although I suppose most people would say I have what is generally called 'arresting looks', I grew up without really fathoming what all the fuss was about. You might find it hard to believe that I felt genuinely puzzled by relatives and visitors gasping and gushing about what a gorgeous girl I was. I'll admit that as soon as the guests' attention had moved onto other matters, I would sometimes slip out of the dining room to snatch a look at myself in the mirror to try to fathom the outcry; all I could see was my usual face staring out. Plain ordinary me—definitely nothing to get excited about.

I don't mean I saw myself as plain as in

entirely boring to look at, but I'd gotten used to the sight of myself and didn't find the spectacle of my face anywhere near breath-taking, or even particularly interesting to contemplate for very long.

I suppose I possess what you might call particularly regular features, but certainly nothing mouth-watering. If you asked me, I'd say that my face actually lacks a little character. It's all regular lines, like a nondescript model in a book on how to sketch a harmonious-looking, slightly bland face. Anyway, the story of Narcissus has always baffled me. The idea of falling in love with your own reflection seems far-fetched at best.

The looks I got from others were the only indicators that there was anything special on display in my face—I have always been surrounded by gazers, as far back as I can remember, but you get used to people ogling you. You take it for granted and sort of fail to notice that other people don't get the same treatment.

They say life is easier for people with prepossessing looks, and I suppose I can confirm that, to some extent. I've noticed that people tend to like you more. They certainly try to woo and curry favour with you, I presume mostly in the misguided hope that some of your looks and aura will rub off onto them. If truth be told, though, my experience of physical appearance up to now has made it more of a burden to shoulder than anything else.

This was true even before they came to take me away. I used to get a lot of unsolicited attention at school, a lot of people eager to be my friend, so many bumbling boys wishing me to be their girlfriend, and I have to say that being in such demand is a drag most of the time. Having to divide your attention equally between rivals, always having to be careful not to alienate one, or spite another without meaning to, unwittingly eliciting jealousy and the whole gamut of petty revenge.

I'm not saying that beauty is like a rock you have to push up a hill every day. It does have its advantages. But for the most part, it has given me a less than commendable assortment of fair-face friends, cumbersome enthusiasts who worshipped the ground I walked on and had little to offer in the way of conversation.

On the whole, being admired for something so shallow has always made me feel undeserving. How many times have I craved to be courted solely for my inner qualities, for the content of my thoughts, not the chance arrangement of bone and the skin on my face?

I know it sounds a little ungrateful and that many people would be delighted to swap features with me if they could, but how would you like your whole personality reduced to a few square centimetres of facial skin?

Who am I talking to? I don't know why I'm even bothering to write all this. Am I really that nostalgic for a period in my life that was for the most part pretty irksome?

Anyway, all my beauty ever managed to achieve was to turn even well-behaved boys into jittery bugbears. Some were so nervous they reminded me of shaky new-born foals floundering about for a stable foot to rest on, instead of being concerned by how to engage me with more than desultory small talk. I've seen boys sent into spasms of awkward fawning and forwardness.

When they made so bold as to come up and ask me out, they were often so tongue-tied I practically had to say their lines for them. All the eloquence they might have possessed had been flushed down their throats by the time they got anywhere near me.

Now that I think back, how tedious it was to have to humour that kind of ineffectual chit-chat, to have to bring them down gradually and tactfully refuse their advances after they got round to stuttering their piece.

And then there were the ones who thought that pinching, prodding or thumping me would do the trick. I generally avoided scoffing or indulging in giggles of course, not wanting to hurt anyone's feelings. I also learned to steer well clear of angering the spiteful.

The most vindictive brute I ever encountered

back in those forlorn schooldays went by the name of Paweł. I don't think I'll forget that lout in a hurry, though really I should. The chunky, thickset school bullyboy. I recall his features very clearly. His uncouth, stony face is unfortunately etched into my mind. Unfortunately, he managed to earn himself a place on the wall of my soul.

When I declined Paweł's generous offer of a kiss on the mouth behind the oak trees at the back of the schoolyard down near the great wall, he exacted most painful revenge by jabbing me repeatedly in the buttock with a compass under the desk the next day when I was least expecting it.

He seemed delighted to see the tears well up in my eyes as I turned around to seethe at him as I bit down the pain. I could see from the lingering expression on his face that he had relished the sharp intake of breath when the tip of the spike sank deep into my flesh. I looked around to see what had stung me, and there he was gloating, bastardly braggadocio, almost smouldering with bliss.

After enduring the second and third jabs on two successive days, I asked the teacher if I could be moved up closer to the blackboard, claiming I couldn't see her writing properly. I knew that denouncing Paweł's behaviour would only lead to more exactions on his part.

Despite the six bench rows separating us

then, Paweł managed to find a way to slither
and snake his way up under the desks to
torment me in the days that followed. Always
fawning and good at ingratiating himself with
the teacher, he was able to have himself placed
at the top of the class right behind me so he
was able to hector and taunt me as much as he
pleased.

Seeing he was not about to relent, I finally
put my hand up to tell the teacher what he
was up to, but she was already so annoyed by
my yelping every time Paweł stuck the tip of
the compass into me that she merely slammed
my desk with her hand and told me to stop
whining.

When I told my parents, they were furious at
both Paweł and my careless teacher, especially
mama. My mother could be a real battle
axe-wielding ice queen when you got her goat.
Even my papa stood in awe of her when she
flew into a fury.

In no uncertain terms, she told me I was to
get back at Paweł without dithering.

As usual, my father muttered agreement,
nodded and spread his feet in that slightly
belligerent way of his. Prompted by mother, he
added gruffly that I should definitely retaliate
immediately, striking any offender ten times
harder so they wouldn't be tempted to start
again. I'll never forget the blaze in his eye, the
indignation soaring in his voice when he said

ten times harder.

When I argued that hitting Paweł would just make him angrier and more vindictive, my mother said she would accompany me to school and make sure the creepy twerp got his comeuppance.

The very next day, she came to fetch me. I pointed Paweł out as soon as he stepped into the corridor. Sticking a firm hand on his chest, she stopped him in his tracks.

He looked at us both uncomprehendingly, not quite intuiting what was in store, faintly curious, only slightly perplexed. As soon as the other kids had deserted the corridor, my mother shunted him forwards by the arm.

Looking wide-eyed, but hardly crestfallen, Paweł let himself be led by the arm like a tethered, horn-spiked bullock to the disused former cloakroom.

As soon as we were in, my mother closed the door behind the three of us. Without any beating about the bush, she launched her usual tight-lipped interrogation:

"Ewa tells me you've been hurting her."

Paweł just stared at us, awkwardly shifting his foot, his eyes ablaze with defiance.

"I want you to say sorry to my daughter. Tell her you'll never harm her again and then get down on your knees and kiss her shoes."

I wasn't expecting that and couldn't help but pull in a sharp breath of disagreement with what my mother was suggesting. She was going too far.

Paweł gave us both a disbelieving, scornful look, smirking right up to his brow, striking a bellicose pose, all devil-may-care.

"You must be fucking joking," he muttered, putting his hands on his hips. He let out a snort of derision.

"Do I look as if I'm joking?"

"I'm not going to kiss her shoes."

"You better do it, if you know what's good for you."

My eyes kept shifting from one to the other as if I was watching a tennis match at the courts. I could hardly believe what my mother had just said. The whole situation was horribly embarrassing.

Paweł kept casting venomous glances at me as if to say *how can you be letting this happen? You know what I'll do to you.*

"Get down on your knees."

"Whore."

My mother's face looked as if he had just slapped her.

"Excuse me, what did you say?!"

I was shocked. I didn't think even a brute like Paweł would dare to call my mother a prostitute. I sensed her seething inside, and I half-guessed what was coming. I knew that whatever happened in the next few seconds Paweł would end up regretting that misplaced word for a long time.

I wasn't expecting her to say what she said next, though. It left me lost for words for once and quite unable to act.

I have never been able to summon much violence, even when slapped, even in a fight. I suppose I'm what you call gentle-natured and soft-spoken, or perhaps just phlegmatic. Whatever my defining trait may be, I was dumbstruck when she gave me the order.

"Kick him hard."

"*What*?"

We both stared at her, wide-eyed in disbelief that an adult could organize a painful kicking session as if it was some kind of yogic exercise.

Paweł gazed back at me in scornful amusement, a snide ironic smile playing over his features. His nostrils were pumping and flaring as if he was about to burst out laughing.

"Ewa. I said kick him. You do it now. For your mother if you can't do it for yourself."

"But, mama—"

"You have to learn to fend for yourself. If you don't do it now, you never will."

"But ... I ... I can't—"

"We will wait here until you do it. Paweł is in no hurry. No one will leave this room until he gets what he deserves."

The swashbuckling brute stood there in front of me, daring me, smirking in an open-mouthed leer of disbelief, laughing at my inability to do my mother's bidding, and yet I couldn't summon any anger, not even resentment over the pain he had caused me.

"Wipe that smirk off your face, boy," barked my mother. "If you kick her back when she kicks you, I'll knock your head against the wall until there's a circle of blood on the paint."

That did the trick. The smile was wiped from his face.

"Now, kick him. He just called me a whore. Are you going to let that stand?"

"Mama—"

"Do it NOW!"

She had that deadly look in her incandescent eye. The look that used to make me lower my eyes and do what I was told.

But for some reason I couldn't quite fathom, kicking Paweł was one of the hardest things I'd ever done up to then. Just lifting my foot off the ground took all the willpower I possessed.

But I did it in the end, I gave Paweł a kick.

A kick on the leg, a half-hearted blow, but still. A kick in the shin. A palpable hit.

Paweł just stared at me. He looked so taken aback he didn't even bother to flinch as I kicked him. He had a gawking expression on his face, as if he hadn't yet come to grips with the fact that I was kicking him, he, the local tough guy, kicked in the legs by Ewa the sweet, gorgeous girl.

"Kick him harder! I will only let you go

when he has endured enough pain. Kick him in the shins again where it hurts."

I kicked him in the leg again, a bit harder this time, trying to aim for his shins.

"HARDER!" came my mother's steely voice.

I managed to kick Paweł hard enough for him to lift one of his legs back.

"HARDER."

Paweł was squirming up against the wall now, bracing himself for my kicks, trying to shelter his legs, though reluctant to kick me back under the threat of my Fury of a mother, still not quite believing what was happening.

I pretended to kick a ball this time and gave it all I had. He even let out a grunt of pain after that one. I couldn't kick him any harder though and could feel my leg tremble and weaken.

"Ok, that's enough. Let me just show you something you need to know about men for future reference."

She gave Paweł a swift, pointed kick of her boot straight between the legs.

The effect it had on the poor wretch was amazing. The congested look that stole over Paweł's flailing features reminded me of a toad that's been half rolled over by a car and is still looking up in the hope that it won't happen a second time—I once witnessed a toad like that, agonizing on the road, it kept looking up at me with the lower part its body plastered to the road, as though straining towards me for help.

"That's where you should aim if any other male gives you trouble. As you can see, it's the place that works best. It's their weak point. Their Achilles heel, if you like."

I have always had a soft spot for mythology and knew exactly what she meant, though I was only eight years old back then.

Paweł had slunk to the ground by the time my mother had finished instructing me in the art of mortal combat with boys. Groaning mutely, his cheek dribbling onto the ground, he nursed the battered apparatus between his legs. I had previously noticed that his skin tended to flush, but on this occasion his face looked positively engorged. He looked like someone who has run a mile and can't catch his breath.

Kilting her dress, my mother leant down beside Paweł.

"You use that compass on my daughter again, I'll shove it so far up your bottom you won't be able to sit down on a hard chair ever again. Do we have an understanding?"

Paweł just looked at her, aghast.

"I said *DO WE HAVE AN UNDERSTANDING?!*"

Paweł managed to breathe out a whimper and grunted, nodded his head in mortal fear.

"Good, now be a good boy and nothing bad will happen."

2

How strange to be writing again. The stick
of graphite still feels a little foreign in my hand,
like an unfamiliar tool. But what a relief to
be able to inscribe all these words in my own
native language for the first time in months. I've
decided to get a few pages written before I go to
bed, in the short space of free time they allot us,
which means I have to disobey orders and burn
the midnight oil.

The handmaids have been teaching me to
gargle German, a tongue I find so ungainly,
so miserable, so dry, so terribly throaty, brisk
and unmelodious. Uttering its words feels like
chewing a piece of gristle, taut and nervy and
impossible to swallow.

The household deities have stipulated that
they do not see a need for me to read or write
the language. They say it would be a waste of
time and only get in the way of my duties.

I've heard they're setting up a library at the
heart of the castle. Unfortunately, it is to be
a scientific library, stocked with nothing but

forbidding tautological treaties. It is designed to
be used only by recruits and the more confirmed,
high-ranking officers. But if I could get my hands
on even one meagre science manual I'm sure it
would feel like fresh poetry to my print-deprived
eyes. Would I be able to decipher any of it? I
practise reading in secret every time I come across
a scrap of paper, or the occasional signs they put
up like *Achtung!*— one of their favourites. They
seem to love that word and have it pasted up as
often as they can. Instead of a "fresh paint" sign,
for instance, you see *Achtung!* I've managed to
determine from hearing them speak to each other
that the 'ch' in that word is the guttural sound
you produce when you're clearing your throat to
hawk up a piece of phlegm in the winter. We have
roughly the same sound in Polish, but it seems so
much softer. I wonder who borrowed it off who.

Whether out of a lack of interest or because
even she is disbarred from availing of the library
herself, Frau Wippermann never goes there, as
far as I know. At least that is what she led me to
understand when I enquired.

I'd give so much to be able to just take a quick
peek inside the place, just to feast my eyes on
the beautifully-bound tomes all neatly lined up.
To be able to inhale the smell of newly tanned
leather yoked to a ream of freshly cut paper. The
hide on new books feels so alive it's like holding a
sleeping creature in the palm of your hand.

Although the books are all in German, I

imagine entering that library would be like
stepping into Ali Baba's cave. I've always
viewed books with the gluttonous gaze that
others experience when placed in the proximity
of multi-tiered chocolate boxes.

But of course nothing is better than being
able to read and write in your own native
tongue. And though I only have Russian
and French to compare with, I have always
felt Polish to be infinitely more supple and
sensuous. A structure so delightfully yeasty
and malleable. Each Polish word feels like a
morsel of moist, soft, springy bread crumb in
your mouth. I have always felt that writing in
French, for instance, is like aligning a rigid set
of building blocks on a narrow strip of carpet.

Writing in Polish by contrast is like aggre-
gating coloured bits of clay. You can twist and
press words into any shape you like. There's
even a special version of every word, a language
within the language that you can use with
children.

Germans are proud of their tongue because
it allows them to juxtapose small words to form
bigger ones, but that is still only like adding
adhesive mortar to the rigid French building
blocks. Polish can add any number of suffixes
and prefixes to modify the inflection and
meaning of each word.

What a blessing I don't have to write this
in German. I have at least been spared the

indignity of that and can burrow with my own tongue.

I know it's subjective and probably unfair to find their language so incisive and harsh, but there it is. I cannot help feeling that German is as callous as a sharp slap on the ear. It all sounds so clinical, as if people are talking around an operating table instead of exchanging pleasant twittering chit-chat around a meal. Most sentences sound like they're saying "swab! pincers! handsaw! lancet! *bitte!*"

Only once so far have I heard German gently spoken with any charm, but that was mostly because the speaker was a child who came to the castle to sell flowers. I happened to be shaking the linen in one of the rooms out the window when she wandered through the gate, her mother running after her in tow. I heard the child almost sing-speak. A little piccolo of gorgeous voice. She and her mother were sent packing so gruffly by the bark of the compound guards that it's unlikely they'll ever venture in here again.

Everything estranges me in this place, even the clothes they have given me feel alien and awkward.

I must not let myself be dragged into despondency. Let me count blessings. I was able to acquire this lovely copybook thanks to Anna, one of the only genuinely kindly handmaids. She regularly asks me if there is anything I need. Anna is in contact with a boy from the village who can procure her more or less anything she requires. She's the handmaids' secret operator and very popular thanks to this role. She seems universally liked, which is more than can be said for me.

Handmaids are only allowed to leave the castle under the express orders of Frau Wippermann, when they go about her errands in the village. She chooses two different helps each week to venture forth beyond the compound and carry shopping baskets back to the castle.

Handmaids are under strict orders not to converse too much with shopkeepers or other customers queuing in the shops. Under no circumstances are we to mention the castle or discuss its affairs.

Not that it would make much difference to me. For some reason, Frau Wippermann has so far refused to consider my willingness to be taken into town on these already rare occasions. I do not know exactly why. Perhaps she thinks I would try to escape. It may be that she has been given the directive to keep me indoors at all times. Being the only Pole around here makes me the only foreigner on the staff. Although I am considered a handmaid, I am also their prisoner.

It is of course possible that Frau Wippermann is only following orders herself.

She's the kind of woman who takes pride
and pleasure in fulfilling the demands of her
superiors. I have seen her in their company, as
eager to please as she is keen to have me kept in
my place.

I regularly get the feeling that Frau
Wippermann disapproves of my presence here,
especially in those moments when I am granted
private audience.

She has the most exacting standards of
etiquette and expects her orders to be obeyed on
the instant under her attentive gaze. She rules
over the roost without demur.

With her steady steel eyes and downturned
icy mouth, the woman has such a glacial
manner the very temperature in the room
seems to drop a few degrees when she makes
an appearance. Like a land surveyor, she paces
towards us in measured steps. She reminds
me of a glacier moving through a valley, her
tonnage of ice grinding down any residual
mirth and chatter remaining in the room, any
excitement that may have brewed up in the air.

She has had me punished on more than
one occasion. There are times when I feel like
telling her to give herself a sound whipping.[1] I

---

[1] Translator's note: the narrator of this text makes a
partially untranslatable pun that associates the start of Frau
Wippermann's surname with the first two syllables of the
Polish expletive *wypierdalać*. Having no equivalent, I have
resorted to the most obvious pun in English.

suppose she must sense it from the look in my eye when I'm thinking such ungentle thoughts.

I am in no doubt that she disregards me because I am nothing but a Polish blot in this neat Aryan stronghold. And yet there are times when I get the distinct impression that she can't help liking me. I see a look steal into her eyes at times that suggests her suppressed self sees something else in me. It's as if her mouth says one thing and her eyes another.

It may merely be that she approves of the irreproachable regularity of my features, but I think there might be more than that. My hunch is that although she finds me little more than a disputatious foreign contrarian, the resistance within me to her counsel is something which she secretly admires.

Part of her reticence concerning me no doubt comes from the fact that I am the only handmaid that she has not personally vetted. The other castle handmaids have all been culled from various corners of the region. Not too far afield, nothing too foreign. Being herself from the Ruhr, Frau Wippermann has a liking for the character and demeanour of demure Ruhr-bred girls. With my current lowly standing, I can hardly accuse her of playing favourites.

Although many of Frau Wippermann's handmaids are for the most part not honey-haired or particularly Aryan-looking, her selection is humoured because Heinrich Himmler (the official leaser of the castle) has condoned it.

I have not yet seen Herr Himmler with my own eyes. I am told he comes to the castle only three or four times a year. The handmaids (who have been here since last spring) say that being in his presence is a nerve-wracking experience.

The stories you hear about him are sometimes terrible. I have heard it said that he is the kind of blindly loyal man who would have his own mother shot if he suspected it would be pleasing to the Führer. I'm told his nationwide nickname is Heinrich the Faithful, but I've heard one of the officers call him *Reichsheini*, allegedly because Himmler loves to say the word 'Reich'.

I am the only handmaid forced to stay here indefinitely. The other girls will go, at least that is what I have been led to believe. The entire staff of maids is destined to be renewed on an annual basis, though having only been here for three months I have yet to see it happen.

Our duties at the castle involve making beds, setting tables, arranging furniture, cleaning silverware, copperware, scrubbing the masonry, collecting and washing clothes, hanging them out to dry, that kind of thing.

But that is not the only function of the handmaids.

Anna and others have told me that the

principal reason for their presence in this castle
is to be groomed as brides for the SS Officers
who sojourn here intermittently. Much to my
relief, Frau Wippermann has told me that it is
unlikely that I will meet the same fate.

And thus I am darkling. I have no idea what
purpose I serve other than to wait in the wings
and busy myself with churlish chores.

Those who are not singled out during the SS
ballroom festivities will return to their native
villages and towns at the end of the spring
or early summer at the latest. They will be
replaced by a fresh batch of maidens, carefully
handpicked by Frau Wippermann, our stern and
stolid manageress.

I have been given to understand that in
May of every year Lady Wippermann leaves
the castle for a period of two weeks only to
come back in June with a fresh load of twelve
more or less lookalike maidens. The remaining
handmaids who have not been auctioned off to
officers by that time are told to pack their bags
and leave.

I shudder to think that I might one day
be given away to one of those slick upstarts.
Thankfully, Frau Wippermann has informed me
that while I have been assigned indefinitely to
the castle, my tainted Polish blood makes me
unsuitable for marriage to a German officer,
especially one of SS rank. She has told me that

my slavish Slavic genes make me unfit, not to mention unhygienic.

When I asked her why I had been placed here in the first place, she answered that she had not been informed of the reason. The decision has come from above.

"Herr Taubert?" I inquired. "Higher", came the answer.

I am to remain in the castle until further notice and keep my questions to myself.

My position here is thus strangely absurd. Most of the time, I feel utterly out of place. Like a transplanted sapling placed in inhospitable soil.

Why then have I been moved here? I can only surmise that my looks have something to do with it. I must serve some decorative purpose, the spoils of war, a useful trophy maiden, plundered flesh, ornamental booty set on display for all and sundry to behold.

Whenever a dignitary of the regime arrives at the castle, we are lined up on the side of the bridge and forced to salute the convoy with a stiff, raised right arm. Our hair is twisted into painful plaits and planted with daisies so we look innocent and pure. Sweet tidy little girls.

Despite my dirty ancestry, Frau Wippermann always places me first in line, as if I am some kind of figurehead at the prow of her flagship. When I ask her why she does this, she repeats the same thing every time: "orders, my dear, from above". I sometimes wonder what other undisclosed directives she may be harbouring.

Being the dark horse of the castle, I often feel at liberty to behave like an anomaly. My father used to clown and horse around a lot with us at home, always ready to prance around on all fours with us cavorting on his back, eager to play a practical joke or just act plain silly.

Or perhaps I got my antic disposition from reading Hamlet once too often. I suppose it wore off onto my character, making me something of a clown in my most excitable moments.

When the giddiness comes over me, I have difficulty taking most things seriously, even poetry at times, especially the romantic stuff. Even my fatherland, its turmoil, its gravitas and gung-ho patriotic sentiment sometimes grates on my nerves, despite the peril in which we find ourselves as a beleaguered nation.

In the current state of world affairs, having a clownish disposition is more than a bit of a liability. Before all this turmoil, it occasionally got me into trouble with teachers back home; a good deal more has come my way with Frau Wippermann. Everything is taken so seriously here! As if to laugh or even titter is to threaten the impregnability of the keep.

There's something so absurd about life since I was abducted that I cannot help but behave in the most foolhardy ways, often finding myself taken aback by my own intrepid comportment. It's as if I no longer care what happens to me. As if I am willing to expose myself to execution. And the more they put up with my loony behaviour, the more I feel like stretching the limit, to no doubt perilous lengths. I suppose I also do this in the irrational hope that they will send me back home.

Strange to say, though, I have so far been treated with near-impunity, if you discount Frau Wippermann's stern remonstrance and a few days sitting in the lap of the dark. The relative leniency I am treated with tends to make my behaviour rather reckless.

In the first few weeks of my stay here I experienced terrible difficulty towing the line, preferring to skip rashly over the tightrope of acceptable castle etiquette. I felt so lonely, so alienated and bereft I didn't give a fig what happened to my worthless frame. There were times when I felt so bleak I wanted to throw myself out of the mullioned windows.

I suppose I wanted to misbehave so they would shoot me or send me back to Poland as unwanted damaged goods, or at least to the same place Mila has gone to, a place that is in all probability far more bracingly nasty than this grim and grotty place.

Before I was taken from Cracow there were such terrible stories going round. It was

rumoured that people were being literally
executed in rows, lined up next to mass graves
for the sake of expediency. It was rumoured
that others were taken away to pen-like enclo-
sures and hemmed in there like animals to lie
in wait behind fences. It seemed so far-fetched,
so impossible to credit. I didn't give those wild
stories much thought, being generally wary of
such groundless gossip. It seemed like the stuff
of nasty fairy tales. And yet, her I am, Rapunzel
with a Bavarian braid.

No one will in all likelihood ever read what
has come to pass here, but it is such a pleasure
to indulge in a little scribbling. What unadulterated joy there is in turning sentences!

Writing all this is like composing an endless
letter to myself. Treat yourself to a little gratu-
itous lettering, I think. Record a few examples
of your misbehaviour to amuse yourself at their
expense.

The first time I was enjoined to raise my arm
in public to execute the salute at the castle gates,
I ended up not performing it. I hadn't actually
intended to renege. It was more like just a spur
of the moment recoil of reluctance.

Like all the other handmaids before me, I
spoke my obligatory vows on arriving. I pledged
to serve the castle and its cohort of upstanding
officers, but when the moment came to execute
the gesture my arm simply refused to rise

to the occasion. The whole situation felt so unspeakably ludicrous.

Not raising my arm made me stand out like a sore thumb of course, but I just couldn't bring myself to execute the salute, as if my body forbade it.

When it came to Frau Wippermann's attention that I had failed to salute the incoming vehicle, she was furious. It was the straw that broke the camel's back as it tiptoed across the red line. She actually had me thrown into a windowless room without food for two days.

I was admittedly less inclined to repeat the offense after that, but time slipped by pretty quickly during my punishment in the dark. I had a good long sleep and savoured being able to skip all my chores. So the next time again my arm refused to rise up.

Wippermann left me without food for five days that second time. All I got in the morning was a fresh pitcher of water for the day. It's a simple form of torture, but rather effective. I felt so weak and sick without nourishment I could hardly stand when they pulled me out. Being kept in the dark for that amount of time made me also slightly crazed. No amount of sleep was able to protect me from the boredom generated by prolonged pitch black darkness. When they finally brought me out into the brightness of day, it felt like the light was stabbing my eyes.

The next time round, Frau Wippermann

made sure she was standing right next to me in front of the gates, her cold, steady eyes keeping me in check in the minutes that preceded the arrival of the notable automobile. As the vehicle approached, she actually latched onto my wrist and yanked my arm up with main force, making it decidedly easier for me to perform the requisite salute.

Under Frau Wippermann's insistence, I raised my arm as high as I could, mostly so she would release her steely grip on my triceps. Not daring to engage in a disorderly scuffle at the gate in front of the incoming set of seated notables, Whippy reluctantly relinquished my arm.

But I didn't entirely get away with it. As you can imagine, my arm's newfound exuberance didn't go down too well with the castle's regimental brass. I think my gestures were construed as parodic (which they were not initially at least meant to be). In tones that suggested total loss of patience with a recalcitrant child, Frau Whip informed me that the approved form of salute involved the arm raised at an exact forty-five degree angle to the ground.

So I tried that for a while when I came across any officers on my daily rounds inside the castle, staring at my arm instead of the officer to make sure I secured the approved angle, lowering or raising it a little to adjust the inclination, as if I was some sort of well-oiled mechanical toy. I have to say the stares I got were rather interesting. I think the brass believe I've lost my marbles.

When my continued erratic behaviour came to Frau Whip's glacial attention, she rightly surmised that I was again making mock of the venerable salute. It made her fly into a fury like none I'd seen before. Imagine a mountain of ice suddenly spitting out lava and you'll have a good idea of what it was like to quake in front of her. Even the squawks and screeches emitted by the small brown-haired man with the tooth-brush moustache featured in the films they show us don't resonate quite as piercingly.

When she finished berating me, the household manager just stood there, bewildered and trembling with spent rage, not knowing what to make of me. Unlike some of the other officials in the castle, she knew that I wasn't soft in the head. She fixed her gaze on me for as long as she could hold it in silence (her mouth set at a venomous angle), considering me as if she couldn't quite fathom what was wrong with my brain.

"Fraulein Kaufmann, may I ask why you persist in refusing to take your position here with the required seriousness?"

"You are mistaken, Frau Wippermann, On the contrary, I take it very gravely indeed."

"Then why do you not properly perform the salute?!"

"Having difficulty executing the exact

approved forty-five degree angle you
prescribed, I raise my arm as high as it can go
to compensate for lack of accuracy."

"When I said a forty-five degree angle, did
you really think I meant you had to place a
bloody set square under your arm?!"

"Might I just point out that there are more
variations on the arm position than you care to
admit."

"There are no other possible variations,
Fraulein Kauffmann."

"In the film you showed us two weeks ago,
I saw the Führer himself trying out alternative
positions of the arm. I thought perhaps you
might instruct me on this point of etiquette."

"What on earth are you talking about?"

"I saw him tuck his hand back to his
shoulder with his elbow fully bent. At first I
have to say I was a little astounded that the
vigilance committee would let him get away
with such a free-handed gesture."

"Whatever the Führer chooses to do is the
Führer's prerogative. You, on the other hand,
are a lowly subordinate, a mere underling, a
cipher. A speck of dirt on his shoe."

This seemed to invite a show of humility
coupled to an extra bit of tongue-in-cheek.

"Thank you for reminding me of my place,
Frau Wippermann. Sometimes, though, I
wonder if the muscles in the Führer's arm don't
get a bit sore. I mean at the rallies. How long

does he have to hold out his arm? I've seen him swipe a whole motorcade with a quick elbow jerk of his arm at the end. There are times when I worry he is in pain."

"How dare you speak with such levity about the Führer! Does that demented brain of yours not allow you to experience fear and awe?! Do you not know what happens to mental defectives?"

Frau W's colour was now higher than ever. I realized of course at this juncture that the acid in her tone left me with scant room for manoeuvre.

Heaving and panting, she turned her studying gaze on my mouth, as if she was looking into my features to try to figure out an irresolvable enigma. I stood there, adrift, my curiosity piqued by this sudden disclosed secret which she seemed to be offering.

"What happens to them, Frau Wippermann?"

"People who are sent away are usually never seen again."

"Please allow me to remark that we were told in Proper Manners class that the Führer is exemplary in all matters and that he should be our guiding model in all things. If the Führer performs these gestures in public, then perhaps we should too."

"Mein Gott, Eva! Do you not realize that if you continue in this way you will get yourself into such trouble that I will no longer be able to protect you?"

"You protect me, Frau Wippermann?"

"Actually, I do, as a matter of fact. I have had to make excuses for your unseemly behaviour both inside the keep and at the castle gates. I have had to tell Herr Taubert that you were a little eccentric—if you only realized what happens to wayward souls."

"I am not aware of what happens to eccentrics, Frau Wippermann."

Frau W opened her mouth at me, unblinking and aghast. I had never seen her looking that sharp and wolfish. She stood there quivering, staring at me with undisguised disgust. This was not our best kindred moment.

"*Du lieber Gott*! Have you entirely taken leave of your senses?"

"Quite the contrary, Frau Wippermann."

"Oh, just shut up! You are brazen, unruly! If you persist in disporting yourself in this manner, I will simply give you up to face the music. The next time you disrespect the orderly functioning of this castle, I warn you I will no longer placate Herr Taubert's annoyance."

She had the high ground of course. I knew I would have to relent at some point before the conversation spiralled out of control.

"I understand, Frau Wippermann. I—will make an effort to integrate."

"Your presence here should be invisible. You

need to stop rocking the boat. Can you promise me you will do that and not just pretend to try?"

"I will do my best, Frau Wippermann. You have my word of honour."

"And stop saying *Frau Wippermann* all the time. You sound like a parrot."

"That is how you told us to address you, Frau Wip—"

"Oh, just—! Your backtalk exhausts me. Go to your room now and be ready to lay the tables at the appointed hour. We are to dress the rooms for one of the highest-ranking Schutzstaffel officers in the regime. Do not make the mistake of thinking that your beauty will protect you indefinitely."

3

It's been a long, tedious day. The SS officer who arrived this morning—can't remember his full name, some long double-barrelled German surname like Kleinhitlercamp[2] —insisted on inspecting the castle down to the very last nooks and crannies. He started by making us all line up in an orderly row for inspection.

His name means something like 'Hitler's Little Camp', which made me want to snicker a little as we toed the line under Frau W's stern regard and his own attentive gaze. He was so solemn, so stiff-lipped and priggish. His voice was molten tar—you could hear the gravel churning slowly in his throat.

K carried himself like a little regal cock forced to strut and survey a slovenly henhouse, as if at the slightest provocation he would

2 Editor's note: The reference here may conceivably be to SS *Obergruppenführer* Matthias Kleinheisterkamp, though there is no documented extant evidence that he ever visited or inspected the staff at Wewelsburg castle.

be much inclined to peck our pates. His name sounded to me like the German equivalent of Me Big Chief Little Camp. Strange to say, no one else seemed to find this hilarious. I sometimes think my satirical edge will be the death of me—this place seems to drive me to an immoderate but well deserved ferocity of judgment.

I've noticed these last few weeks in the instructional films we've been shown that a lot of these German dignitaries are not only called Klein, they are also rather small in stature. Even with his peaked cockscomb of a cap, Herr Kleinhitlercamp was still a good half head shorter than both me and Frau Whip (she and I happen to be almost the same size—a good deal taller than the other handmaids).

Anyway, having come to an agreement with Frau W, I had decided to behave myself. I promptly repressed the smirk rising up in my face in case I got an unseemly fit of the giggles in front of the lined-up assembly. I must admit that all that talk of punitive camps has left me with a shard of ice in my heart.

Frau Wippermann was all hot and bothered for the occasion and kept eyeing me nervously. Even Herr Taubert seemed slightly out of kilter. I could see why. Taubert's responsible for maintaining the whole castle and that Klein Camp fellow was a real stickler. Standing in for Himmler, he was apparently mostly here to oversee the refurbishing of the castle, but he clearly also wanted to take stock of every conceivable thing from how well we make the beds to how suitably hot we make the bed pans.

This is nominally in preparation for a major upcoming event: a generals' conference is to be held at the castle at some unspecified time in the future. Herr Kleinhitlercamp being there on Herr Himmler's own instructions, all the onus was on him and he clearly wanted everything to be spick and span and worthy of the great master.

Frau Whip was as jittery as a bug. She kept casting sidelong glances at me to make sure I didn't act up. I could see she was relieved that I'd finally resolved to behave in my own interests, in accordance with her wishes.

All day, we had to go about our chores with Kleinhitlercamp standing behind us in attendance. His uniform was so decorated with insignia it felt like being watched by a deadly-looking dark Christmas tree. He kept his peaked hat on all day both inside and out, as far as I could tell.

I couldn't help staring at the death's head in the centre of the peak. Perched on top of the skull image was an eagle that looked as if it was performing a precarious balancing act on top of an egg.

There were at least two more baubles hanging from Kleinhitlercamp's throat which tended to clink like a cow's bell whenever he moved. The girls have told me that these are actually known as Prussian iron crosses, a distinction you get if you do something foolishly brave in battle.

Kleinhitlercamp's collar was embroidered with a kind of oak-leaf lapel. His shoulder straps looked as if they'd been woven out of the finest golden Nazi hair.

Anyway, he's the highest-ranking German dignitary I've seen since they abducted me. The soldiers who took Mila and me away from our parents were a good deal more coarse-looking. Despite his laughable name and his guttural voice, this SS notable looked a little more civilized—but only just a little. You could feel the savage brute tensing for a pounce from deep inside.

When he caught me staring at his insignia, his cocksure expression softened a little, as if he was flattered by my attention. He even conde-scended to ask me where I was from.

The answer I gave triggered a moment of frozen silence in the room. All the handmaids lowered their heads or pretended not to have heard. I got a nervous glance of warning from Anna. Frau Whip was staring up at the ceiling as if she was praying to the whole pantheon of Nazi gods at the same time.

When he heard the word 'Poland', K's cock face did a kind of nose dive, as if the word had smacked him on the back of the crest. His beaky mouth twitched a little to the side and he visibly shuddered, as if I had said I had grown up in a pigsty, neck-deep in slurry.

Bethinking himself of his overseeing role, he collected his manners and refrained from blurting out the exclamation of disgust that seemed to have risen to his lips. With a strained look in his eye, Klein turned his head to fix Frau Wippermann's upturned head to inquire why I had been brought to the castle. He made it sound as if my presence here was an unjustifiable administrative blunder.

Frau Whip's mouth performed a kind of nervous contortion. Her eyes juggled a few balls in the air for a couple of seconds as if she couldn't think what to say with us listening.

After waiting a few seconds in case she was about to disclose, I put her out of her misery and answered that I myself did not know. Klein's gaze shifted from Frau Whip back to me with a mystery-imbued stare that made him look like an overfed pigeon trying to swallow down the whole unhulled shell of a walnut.

Preening his feathers as if I had ruffled them, he proceeded to ask me to give an account of my journey here from the beginning so I did. When I told him about the day I was pulled from my home in front of my parents, the silence in the room was as dense as a potful of dark coffee.

Frau Whip was still staring at the ceiling.

It looked like she'd stopped breathing and had turned into a pillar of salt.

I didn't make my account merely factual. I wanted him to hear the whole thing. His face being open and eager, I was keen for him to sample a little spoonful of the horror. So I told him as best I could how it felt with the relatively limited German vocabulary I possess.

All the other handmaids were staring down at the floorboards, but I stared him full in the eyes all the while. Taking care not to sound reproachful or indignant, I put him through the experience in as much detail as I could muster.

I wanted him to feel the enormity of what it felt like to be ripped out of your home, dragged away from you motherland, prodded like an animal and thrown into a cattle truck with a gaggle of squirming, screeching, weeping, terrified, heart-broken children. I wanted to see if there was any last drop of decency left in his shrivelled klein heart.

Though my German was too restricted to entertain exactitude, I think I managed to give him an earful of what it was like to have those vociferating human dobbermen enter our house, barking their orders and hefting their dark pointy gun claws straight at our faces. How they manhandled my lovely father, pinned him brutally down on the floor, pressing his face into the boards. How they grabbed my little sister by the throat and put a gun against the side of her head so that my parents would comply.

I told him that I have since learned that they came with the intention of removing only small children, but the officer in charge made an exception for me for some reason that escapes my understanding.

Like most men who see me for the first time, the officer who stormed our house couldn't take his eyes off me. He kept his gaze trained on me as if he was calculating something covertly, as if I was some kind of unusual specimen he wanted to showcase. When I said this to K, I saw him flicker-blink a few times.

I told him I had just turned eighteen and that like any aspiring young student in the vicinity, I was hoping to enter the University of Cracow to study Polish literature. I was on the cusp of signing up for enrolment when all the professors I looked forward to encountering were taken away in large, thick-wheeled trucks and never seen again.

When he heard I was keen on literature, Herr Klein's mouth smirked a little to the side, as if the words 'Polish' and 'literature' were oxymora you just couldn't politely juxtapose. I didn't tell him of course that when the soldiers came to take me away I had been studying it on the sly in underground Poland.[3]

---

[3] The expression Underground Poland refers to *Polska Podziemna*, the practice of providing clandestine tuition and theatrical performances in cellars after the Nazis closed down schools, universities and theatres in Poland.

The mention of the abducted professors failed to make him bat an eyelid. So I put him through as many unsavoury details as I could, holding his stare all the while, talking on relentlessly since he seemed rapt, bent on listening.

If the downturn of his mouth was anything to go by, he seemed not to favour what he was hearing, but something about the way I spoke made him listen. He stood there gazing into my eyes, half mesmerized by the intensity of what I had to say, or maybe just by my looks, I often find it hard to tell the difference. He reminded me of the little pipsqueaks who used to woo me in school. He wore that same open-mouthed, slightly glazed look.

I didn't care if he wanted to hear what I had to say or not, I just kept fording on. I decided to subject him to all of it, every last morsel of horror. I know how to keep a monologue going for as long as I want it to, having practised the art of rhetoric on my parents and my teachers and classmates for years. My parents thought I was so convincing they wanted me to study law, but I told them from the word go that it was going to be literature or nothing.

Anyway, I made Herr K swallow most of the story, hook, line and sinker. I fed it to him slowly, one little savoury bit after another. I told him how the officer in charge had barked some kind of order and how two of the soldiers had seized me by the arms and dragged me until they had me out of the house. I told him that being pulled from my home had felt like being a healthy tooth extracted from a mouth. Herr K's mouth seemed to flinch a little when I said that, but his gaze didn't waver.

I told him that I saw my little sister Mila being carried underarm out of the house, my parents screaming and crying and wailing behind her. I told him I would never forget my little sister's howling.

Herr K's mouth went thin-lipped and pale, as if I was eliciting in him some vaguely empathetic response that he wished to repress. Throughout my lengthy monologue, Frau Whip and the handmaids listened on. I noticed that some had bowed their heads in silence. They looked shifty and uncomfortable.

I shouldn't have done it, but it egged me on to more heated feelings. I tried to make them intuit what it was like to be thrown into a cattle truck next to about thirty other war-torn, devastated children.

Our hands and feet tethered with rope, we were ordered to keep quiet if we wanted to stay alive. From inside the house, I heard my father's horror-stricken outcries, the kind of screams that burst out of someone who has just had a bone broken or a shred of flesh torn off his body.

Herr Klein nodded a little and stared back at me blandly as if what had happened to our family was quite within the normal run of things. I could tell though that he was bottling up some kind of feeling deep inside that wall of flesh. I could tell he was stemming the trickle of compassion that had started to seep through the stone in his breast.

Mastering his voice, K muttered something that sounded like *"tragbarer Bevölkerungszuwachs"*.[4] I didn't understand what he meant by citing the expression and later had to ask Anna what it meant—though it still didn't make sense in the context once she'd explained it.

He mouthed those words with a look in his eye that suggested I didn't comfortably fit into the category he had just mentioned, as if I was a kind of elegant, but double-headed sausage-dog.

So then I told him about my fears that we would all be gassed in the truck. I had heard stories about people being gassed to death in trucks. I didn't know if they were true, but the moment I uttered my doubts I saw a tell-tale flicker of his lashes. Herr Klein blinked a little more when he perceived I had registered and interpreted the minute reaction, but then he just smiled a little condescendingly, as if gas trucks were something outdated, something in any case that I was ill-equipped to understand.

---

4 Translator's note: the expression, meaning "acceptable population growth", is misspelt in the original diary, either by mistake or design. I have taken the liberty of including the correct spelling for the sake of historical clarity.

Before I was able to continue, Herr K. put out his hand to stop the further outpouring of my words. He had heard more than he cared to hear and refused to indulge my account.

Only later that evening was I able to tell the rest, when Anna came to see me in my room. She said she wanted to hear about the rest of the journey, if I needed to tell it. There was a kind of hunger in her eyes that suggested she had come prompted by more than mere compassion. She was, I suppose, eager for a thrill and so I gave her what she seemed to crave.

I offered her a detailed account of the facility they took us to. The place where they measured us, me and the little children in the truck.

After a few hours of driving, the lorry came to a stop. They took the restraints off our wrists and our ankles. We were undone like carefully tied parcels so we could walk by ourselves.

We were then shepherded across a muddied cobblestone path to an exceptionally clean, brand new-looking, well-carpentered building. Although the outer walls were mostly wooden, it looked like a kind of hospital inside, with whitewashed walls. I noticed the little boys were sectioned off from the group, presumably to be taken to another part of the building.

Mila and I were lined up against a wall in a large laboratory with the other little girls and told to keep our hands by our sides. Like most of the girls, Mila was crying but I was unable to console her. I didn't know how to calm her down, so in the end I lied.

I told her this was just a field trip, an excursion, a kind of outing. I told her we would be back home in a few days. She didn't look as if she believed me but I could tell she wanted to. It quietened her down enough to make the whole experience slightly more bearable for me too, though quite a few of the other infants were weeping and whimpering in ways that were very close to unbearable. I felt like putting my hand on their little contorted mouths to stop them from shredding my nerves.

Two middle-aged men in white blouses told four of us to step forward and we complied. They pointed to me and Mila first so we stepped forward with the two little girls who had been selected. I had to pull Mila by the hand because she was too terrified to move away from the wall.

When they separated us, she began to howl again. But the white-clad operatives seemed to find howling perfectly normal I said pointedly to Anna giving her a meaningful stare. Although my nerves were wrung by all the screaming and crying I'd heard that day, it didn't even seem to penetrate the consciousness of the operatives we had to contend with. They didn't seem to think anything of it, reacting the way you would around lowing cattle and bleating sheep, as if crying and whimpering were no more remarkable than breathing.

The guards seemed to dislike it more though and they saw to it that we kept our mouths shut as the lab technicians made us stand next to a long desk that contained a number of files and papers and another one next to it containing several kinds of instruments, all sorts of measuring devices which they used on us. The man who was dealing with me took out an enormous pair of talon-like callipers and widened it to place it on my head with one tip on my brow and the other at the back of my skull. It felt like my head had been clasped by the giant talons of a metallic eagle about to pierce my skin to the bone in its lacerating clamp claws.

He started measuring my skull from every possible angle after that with all manner of technical equipment. He must have taken about twenty different measurements, I can't remember exactly. He even measured the exact length and width and breadth of my nose.

Having put down the first angular instrument, he picked up an even smaller set of callipers and started measuring the distance between my eyes and the girth of my nostrils. He calibrated the instrument to appraise the tender flesh of my lips, positioning the twin points of the callipers on the edges of my eyelids to measure their thickness as if pricking or gouging my eyes irrecoverably would be nothing more than an occupational hazard.

Once they had finished assessing and calibrating every part of my head, they took to examining the rather long hairs on my arms with inordinate interest. They even measured the down on my thighs and took out a magnifying glass to focus on what felt like the pores and presumably the non-existent hair on my back.

They made me sit down and measured and mapped every nook and cranny of my ears. They took up-close photographs of them from in front, above and from each side. Holding a long coloured chart covered in eye-colour samples, they made me stare straight out to compare my irises to the chart in the aim I supposed of capturing their exact colours.

I could see out of the corner of my eye when I was allowed to swivel them again that they were doing the same to Mila and the two other little girls. The howling and most of the crying had ceased as everyone was watching the strange spectacle of these stern-eyed men and women so intent and silent about their work.

I didn't say what I'm about to write here to Anna, wanting her to get an earful of only the most unpleasant aspects of the ordeal, but despite the chilling uncertainty about almost everything that day I have to admit that once I had got over the brunt of the strangeness in that laboratory there was something almost

appeasing about the experience of being
measured and mapped in such exhaustive
detail.

It was kind of odd all right, but something
about it made it feel a good deal more bearable
than being herded into the back of the truck in
the dark. Never have I had so much attention
lavished on my face and body, even by our local
physician back in Cracow. The most anyone
ever measured was the length of me from
head to toe. Even the short-term boyfriends I
have had tended to close their eyes when they
swooped in for a kiss. It's kind of horrible to
say, but there was something almost Petrarchan
in a cold sort of way about having my face
charted and detailed.

Although their stare was loveless and
entirely dispassionate, they looked at me so
closely and intently I felt like my face was some
sort of newfound territory they were trying
to decipher and understand. Had the circumstances been different, it would have felt as
relaxing as getting a manicure, a kind of delicate
fingertip examination of the body. Their touch
at least was delicate.

The man who registered my details wrote
down a few numbers in some boxes on a sheet
of lined paper. Then he scrutinized the numbers,
cross-checked them with another batch of
papers, carried out another dozen calculations
and stopped his jotting to stare at me as if

trying to capture the whole of me in one encompassing stare.

I gazed back at him, not understanding why he was staring so silently, unblinkingly. His head jerked back ever so slightly, the way the head of pigeons do. His brow crinkled a little in the middle and his eyes took on a slightly perplexed expression. He was considering me the way you might look at some kind of anomaly in the animal kingdom.

Still wearing that bemused look on his face, he carried his sheet of measurements off to two other measurers next to him to confer, putting his finger on the sheet to show the results he had just gleaned. The other men looked down at the sheet, then up at me with the same expression as the one who had taken my measurements. I was baffled by what was puzzling them so. I figured it must be the regularity of my features. I couldn't see any other explanation, but there seemed to be more than that at stake, if their expressions were anything to go by.

Anyway, after a little more conferring with the other two clinicians, the lab coat asked me in tones of hushed almost reverence to wait in a corner next to the two other girls they had also finished measuring. I asked if I could stay by my sister's side, but they said that I should not worry, she would be joining me shortly. They were decidedly less brutish than the soldiers we had had to deal with up to then, but again I left that out in the account I offered up to Anna. I must confess that in my reawakened wrath, I did not want her to feel that her kinsmen were anything other than monstrous.

When they had finished measuring and sorting out the line-ups of little girls into three corner groups,[5] each set was taken away in turn by two soldiers per group. They put us in a new truck and we drove for another few hours. We stopped three times on the way, but I heard only German spoken every time.

At our fourth stop, one of the soldiers sitting next to us in the van took hold of my arm and pulled me out of the truck.

I tried to seize Mila by the hand as I was getting down, but he had tugged me out so swiftly I was unable to do more than look back at her with outstretched hand, trying to look as panic-free and reassuring as I could.

I shouted her name to give her courage, but she screamed mine back in a voice that boded nothing but anguish and despair. The moment I was out of the lorry, it drove off and I was directed into a long black German limousine. We drove for another hour or so until we got to this castle.

[5] Children who were thought to possess undesirable traits were taken away to camps and sterilized so that so-called Slavic features would be eradicated.

A little later, after he had nipped my story in the bud, Herr Klein asked me if I had any siblings. He looked intrigued when I told him I did not know where Mila was. He said he would discuss it with *Burghauptmann* [6] Herr Taubert to find out why I had been taken here and inform me, if he saw fit to do so, in compliance with the Burghauptmann's wishes.

As to my sister's whereabouts, he could promise me nothing as this kind of classified information was never divulged to relatives or anyone outside the party. In fact, it was possible he would be unable to disclose anything at all if it was classified.

He then bragged to me in front of the sidelong-looking handmaids that he had himself taken part in the invasion of Poland as if it was some kind of prowess to be proud of. Seeing my disdain, he raised his eyebrows a little in mock compunction to suggest that it had been a regrettable necessity. When I asked why he thought that such a thing had been necessary, he answered that the Führer considered it paramount to fulfil the German folk's Lebensraum expansion. It's the German Dream, he said.

He pointed out that most of what I stubbornly called Poland had belonged to Germany in previous times, under the great Teutonic order.

---

[6] Means Head of the castle.

It was in the Führer's view only returning rightfully held land to its original masters. In the perspective of the Master Plan, Poland was going to be a New Germany, providing available land fit for homesteaders who wished to set up their families and farms in the new territories. Polish farmers had mismanaged these resources, he said. It was time to put this German land to proper use.

I was so gob-smacked by the glibness with which he trotted out such abysmal absurdities, I could hardly speak for the lump in my throat. I must have looked pretty shocked because Herr K started blinking almost uncontrollably again in response to the look in my eyes.

Looking a bit peeved and starchy the way he had when he arrived, Herr K instructed me to go about my tasks. He said I should join the other handmaids who had already been dismissed by Frau W.

With that, K. did an about-face and almost goose-stepped out the door like a mechanical toy. Frau Whip heaved a sigh of relief as if she had just been given back her breath.

4

Ulrike told me she saw a limousine leave the castle yesterday evening, so I suppose it means Herr K is gone. Not that I expected to get much out of him, but I suppose I did have a glimmer of hope he would be able to glean something about the whereabouts of my sister and the reason for my stay in this cold keep.

So it's back to humdrum work as usual, cleaning and dusting and polishing and tidying and washing and scrubbing and setting the tables. Frau Whip is exceedingly proud of the castle's tableware. She says its conception is unique as it has been manufactured exclusively for use in the Castle. I personally find the designs rather hideous. The plates all bear an over-ostentatious, stylized version of the Sig rune, the double lightning bolt symbol.

As far as I'm concerned, the silly sign is only bearable when the dollops of food cover it up. Unless I'm ravenous, I usually leave enough leftover slop in the middle of the plate over the symbol to keep it out of my sight, though it's hard to ignore the blasted thing most of the time. They have it pasted all over the place on the bunting lining the lintels, in large wrought iron letters at the entrance to the castle. You find Sigs on the tumblers, the cutlery, even the bedsheets are stitched with the bolts. You get almost used to them, thankfully. I've trained my eyes not to notice them.

The only moment I can't ignore the double Sig sign is when they teach us about the runes and when we have to engage in what they call spiritual-health sessions of rune worship along with the members of the *Reichsführerschule*. [7]

Once a week, the castle's staff crams into a small amphitheatre behind the freshly minted SS officers to listen to various different scholars harp on endlessly about what they see as the magical runes discovered by Karl Maria Wiligut (a cheerful chap who used to be known as Herr Himmler's Rasputin no less, according to Anna).

The other main discoverer goes by the name of Herman Wirth. He used to teach here occasionally around the mid-1930s, a few years before I got here. Wirth and Wiligut are referred to by our lecturers in hushed reverence, as if they are to be revered as semi-deities in a pantheon of national worthies no longer present on this Earth in physical, tangible form.

---

7 The SS training school housed at Wewelsburg.

Although I find the notions discussed in these sham lectures for the most part utterly laughable, listening to the speakers is still a welcome break from the tedium of servicing and dusting and pampering the already pristine interior of the castle.

There are times when it even gives me the pale illusion that I'm attending university. It's a pretty far cry from what I wanted to study, of course, but at least it gives me something to keep my mind from straying back to Poland and worrying myself sick about my sister and what fate may have befallen my parents.

Last week, a guest lecturer, a certain Karlernst Singer from Wiesbaden, tried to make us believe that runes were the world's very first alphabet. According to his blather, even Sanskrit is based on Nordic runes. He looked so serious-minded and stern that had I not known any better I might have believed him. In fact, I think he actually believed the guff himself.

In Earnest Karl's view, runes did not descend from the Etruscan, Greek and Phoenician alphabets, but the opposite way round. This kind of nonsense flies in the face of everything I was taught at school and I felt like saying as much, but decided to silence any objections that arose in my mind out of respect for Frau Whip's nerves and my own continued survival.

Earnest Karl told us that Herr Himmler is

keen to propagate these "firmly-grounded facts" because they prove that Germanic culture was there before any other form of ancient culture. If these state-sanctioned hypotheses are to be believed, everything ancient can be traced back to Germany.

I have trouble seeing how a theory can be held as proof without some form of substantiation, but when I raised my hand to ask where the evidence was to bolster such claims, our earnest lecturer look flummoxed.

Frau W gave me such a stare that I retreated into silence for the rest of the session. In his oh so reasonable voice, Earnest Karl adduced that German archaeologists of the highly prestigious Ahnenerbe were busy scouring Scandinavia and the Far and Middle East to find new groundbreaking hard evidence that will prove "this very factual theory" correct. In petulant tones, he proclaimed that the Ahnenerbe's scientific methods were of the highest possible standards.

Judging from the way they behaved during the barbaric conquest of my motherland, I initially assumed that the Nazis rejected Christianity entirely. But apparently that was a hasty assumption on my part. I was given to understand during our last lecture that the National Socialist Party is keen to foster its own Teutonic version of Christ.

I almost broke out laughing when I heard the theory according to which Christ was an

Aryan who was really at war with Judaism!

I have to say I had a lot of trouble restraining my mirth when the lecturer said that, but managed to hold myself in check despite the mounting pressure on my temples. I must have looked as red as an overripe tomato.

I could hardly believe my eyes when Earnest Karl wrote Christ's name up on the black board, spelling it Krist with a K, as if He was some sort of Bavarian divinity capped with Bismarck's spiky helmet. I couldn't help imagining the modified Last Supper, with a Teutonic Krist wearing a red and white apron, consecrating pumpernickel bread and a few pints of German glass beer to symbolize his Passion for beer-garden *kultur*. Drink this burp-inducing beverage in remembrance of me doesn't quite satisfy the ear.

We're treated to lots of etymology too. They even have a name for this new-fangled version of Christianity. They like to call it 'Irmin-Kristianity'. Irmin means 'strong' apparently, in old German. They seem to think of Krist as some kind of toughened, weight-lifting soldier wielding a jagged-edged sword with thick army boots instead of nails in his feet.

In their version of the Biblical story, Krist is actually a kind of pre-Christian pagan god—a kind of Nazi paradox all to himself. They're mad into paganism here. The whole castle is bent on reaffirming ties to Germany's supposedly glorious pre-Christian past. There's talk that Christmas is going to be replaced here with a Winter solstice festival next time round, and they're going to adopt a summer festival to match.

Despite its Christian connotations, they plan to maintain the Christmas tree, allegedly because trees go back to before the time of Christ.

Christ in his manger is to be replaced by a straw goat to remind celebrants of Thor whose chariot used to be led into battle by a berserker ram.

I've heard it said that last Christmas, the star at the top of the Christmas tree was replaced by a swastika. What a heart-warming thought …

They're so obsessed by ancient pagan lore in this absurd castle that even the rooms here have names like *King Arthur* and *Excalibur* and *Odin*.

The name on the room of my own cell is a rather stale *Gudrun*. When I made bold to ask one of the lecturers what Gudrun was (I thought perhaps it might be some kind of pagan rune), he looked shocked. He said Gudrun was one of the great heroines of the Nibelungen saga, that it was such an honour to sleep in a room presided over by such a great figure. After Siegfried's death, she is supposed to have married Attila and become queen of the Huns.

Apparently, the first version of Wewelsburg castle goes back as far as the Huns. They seem so proud of Hunish barbarity. It's strange, this paradox, the orderly, demure celebration of the barbarous. Everything here, the most risible, irrational custom, is treated with the utmost high seriousness. I find some of these things so unutterably laughable and have to restrain myself constantly so I don't blurt out something that will get me into trouble.

Rune worship sessions are an even more downbeat affair. I never much liked adoring the saints and relics back home, but this is far worse. To make it all mysterious and spooky in the stone-vaulted room, somebody dims the lights and a druid ancestor person dressed in a lowered hood comes in to add another bogus layer of thrill to the already gloomy atmosphere.

With a long stick of virginal white chalk, the druid scrawls a single rune on the blackboard after it has been wiped clean with a sponge. We're basically then asked to contemplate the timeless beauty of a few crooked scrawls. The one they put up today is called the *Ger* rune. It's supposed to symbolize the communal spirit of the SS.

They're always going on about teamwork and team spirit, and how you have to be a team player in the new Germany that is being forged. There's no room for individualism in the Stronger Than Ever New Germany. We are to leave individual thoughts and desires to our leaders.

We had to contemplate the damned thing for over an hour! I closed my eyes for a while to think of my own Polish Jesus, but was asked after the session by an SS officer who spotted me doing this why I had closed my eyes instead of contemplating the timeless beauty of Ger.

I said closing my eyes helped me to worship the communal spirit of the rune. I must have said it in a bit of an ambivalent way because he went a bit stiff and treated me to a bit of a scowl. My tone might have been off a shade.

One of the more bearable runes is the one they call the life rune. If it wasn't used by the SS, I would find it almost pretty. It reminds me of a tree and allows me to imagine Our Lord crucified upon it.

Since the start of the war, they've been putting it on gravestones to mark the dead person's date of birth. The death symbol is its exact opposite, an inverted version of the life symbol. It looks like a kind of primitive three-pronged rake:

Instead of the Christian cross on grave-stones, they've started using the Tyr symbol, also known as the battle rune. It's supposed to symbolise the Norse god Tyr (the one who gets his hand bitten off by Fenrir) but mostly just looks like an upward-turning arrow:

Our tutors say it stands for leadership in battle and has been used on the shoulder pads of some German uniforms. I imagine the arrow reminds shock troops to head in the right direction, straight into battle and no turning back.

Last week they invited a guest speaker who looked as old and worn out as Blake's Ancient of Days. A half-Finnish, half-German dotard.[8]

8   The most renowned Finn to have worked for the Nazis was Yrjö von Grönhagen, but he does not correspond to the description here as he is generally beardless in all extant photographs and only thirty years old at the time of Ewa's narrative. Grönhagen worked for the Ahnenerbe in the search for the original Aryan script, believed by the Nazis to be humanity's first language. It is possible that Grönhagen may have been instrumental in introducing the speaker Ewa mentions to Wewelsburg.

More like half-finished off, if you ask me.
He introduced himself to us in a low, stringy,
seaweed-like voice that sounded as if he was
dragging his slithering vocal cords out of a cave.
His beard reminded me of an uprooted, still
earth-caked tuber. It was so scraggly and filthy
white it looked like they had just excavated the
thing from the local cemetery. The skin on his
face sagged so much it gave the impression they
had caught him in mid-moult.

His accent in German was hideously uvular
and often incomprehensible at least to me.
All things considered, he was probably more
Finnish. His German seemed to have been
grafted on rather late in the day, judging from
the numerous grammar mistakes even I noticed
he made.

I find German already unnecessarily
guttural, but add another gargle of Finnish to it
and you're left with a gurgling gutter of Greek
and Dutch gobbledygook.

As the official, state-approved ancestral
druid, he was here to introduce us to the art of
rune meditation. Runes are sacred, he intoned,
they are the Nordic magic of our ancestors,
a kind of purified, more elevated *Kabbala* (he
pronounced the word *Kabbala* with emphatic
venom).

I was surprised, not to say a little shocked
by some of the words he used to incite us
to meditate. Sitting down tailor fashion, the

Ancient of Days invited us to position our bodies in a similar manner with our hands placed squarely on our knees. Looking at us with transparent dead eyes—the blue irises so pale they were really closer to light blue-tinted whitewash—he chanted some more of his gobbledygook and proceeded to tell us about the various genders of our body parts.

If I understood him properly, the ancient Finn declared that the shoulders were feminine. The elbows, he claimed on the other hand, were a decidedly masculine affair. Our navels and our breasts in his view were profoundly feminine; our knees and feet undoubtedly masculine.

When they did not match these determinants, the blue-eyed half-Finn argued, the genders of these nouns in the current German language proved untrustworthy. A mere debasement of the original gendered nouns of the gods.

I saw Herr Taubert flinch a little when the old Finnish druid referred to the German language as degraded, but he allowed the tuberous priest to ramble on unimpeded.

The druid's argumentation didn't deviate from the usual views propounded. The general belief held by the pseudo-scientific lecturers we are treated to here at Wewelsburg is that the original Aryans were gradually denatured by various lesser races and that returning to runes

was a way of regenerating the primeval purity
of the race, so diluted by time.

Once he had divided our bodies into male
and female zones, the druid encouraged us to
establish what he called the axis mundi within
us, by which I think he meant our spines. When
that much was established, he mouthed a few
more chanted words of exhortation:

"Now gonzentrate hall hov your henergy
in your sexxchual horgans. Once you haf done
dis, trace a line of light from your sexxxtchual
horgans to de left side of your vody. Extend a
hray of light to the hlimit of your haura. Don't
forget de axis mundi!!! Now ... balance de fire
henergy with de lunar henergy inside you."

I hadn't a clue what he wanted us to do
exactly so I raised my hand to ask what he
meant by fire and lunar energy. The muscles
in his features were so relaxed at this stage it
looked as if the skin was going to slip off his
face at any moment.

Working his facial muscles up into another
expression seemed beyond the force of the Finn.
He looked vaguely through me with his vapid
blue eyes, eyes that seemed to have contemplated the vast expanses of virginal Siberian
snows for so long that they had imitated the
colourless tint of them.

He said that if I had to ask it meant that I
had too much lunar energy inside me and not
enough fire. I needed to focus more on the solar

energies. When I asked him how to tap into these hidden powers, he muttered something that sounded like "shut up" in Finnish and closed his eyes.

"Now I vhill hinvoke de sick rune", he pursued in his drawling drone of a dead voice, "you must himagine de sick rune travelling up de nose. Let the henergy of de sick rune chirculate in de head. Focus on dis. And see vhat habbens. Now konzentrate on de vhonta- nelle. Gonnect your toes to dis. A ray of light is goming up from your sextchual horgans to de vhontanelle. Gonzentrate on dis, and see vhat habbence."

I imagine that the sick rune he was referring to was in fact the sig rune. As for the rest, although Anna kindly whispered the meaning of the word to me, I was having trouble locating my fontanelle, not having had one since I was a baby and not initially recognizing the word when he said it in Finnish German. Seeing that some of us were staring at him with a certain amount of bewilderment, the elderly Finn pointed to the top of his head and said "de vhontanelle is exactly here, put your vhinger on it so dat I gan see you haf de right blace."

In all his geriatric atrophy, the Ancient of Days got up slowly from his sitting position and moved around the room in slow motion to examine where our pointed fingertips were placed on our heads. Reaching out to grasp my hand in his own skeletal version of a hand, he pulled it a little to the left so that my finger was pointing at the very centre of my non-existent fontanelle.

"Now gonzentrate on your nafels and remain focussed on your sextsual horgans."

The druid seemed to think that we had at least two belly buttons, for some reason that escapes me. I wanted to put my hand up again to question his knowledge of anatomy, but refrained lest he lose patience with me entirely and send me back to my room.

I was quite enjoying the drollery of the situation and didn't want to be sent away at this point. I was a newcomer to the sessions so I imagine he had explained where the second navel was on a previous occasion, or else it was just a zlip of the tongue and he had not meant to add the 's' at the end of the word 'navel'.

"Do not vorget your sexxxstchewual horgans!!! Ahh!"

It was hard to forget them in the circumstances. I have never been told to think of my private parts in public before. No one in Poland had ever reminded me to consider and commit them to memory with such insistent frequency. In fact, my whole education up to then had been geared towards ignoring that we had any sexual horgans at all. The way he pronounced the most common words made one quite queasy. It made me feel as if I was some kind of bristly creature with hoary limbs covered in barbed thickets of hair.

"If you veel a disturbance, dis is just cosmic debris dat hass haccumulated in de vody. Gonnect your left foot to your right tshoulder. Gan you feel de polarity? Dare. Dare is fire in you now. Dare. Gan you veel it? Gan you veeeeel it???"

I mostly felt quite cold as the temperature was still low for early May and the castle was draughty at the best of times as soon as the mildest breeze was blowing. Being on top of a hill in the middle of a Westphalian plain means that we get the full blast of the wind whenever it blows.

"Iv you are mostly lunar," the Druid's voice dragged on, "you vill need to hactivate your solar bersonality. Always go back to your shpine. Ztrengten de henergy dare."

He got really excited then all of a sudden, as if he had plugged his finger in the mains.

"Hi am one wid de tunderbolt of Thor!! Tir-u, Tir-u, Tir-u!!! I am von wid de universal horder. Bless my sexxxxxstchewual horgans. Gonnect us all to Modder Hert. Bless... Hodin... Bless Loki.... Do not dink of tings as Good, hor Badtt. Dink of your deeeeeper self. Say tanks to de Nordic gods who live widin us. HEIL de gods!!!"

5

It's gotten a bit warmer in the castle since I last wrote. Spring has started to dazzle the eyes. The magnolias down in the grove have burgeoned completely. Tall white blossoms aligned on the branches like roosting doves with their heads tucked into the plumage.

I keep looking down at the coat of ivy furring the wall under my window. I wonder if it would take the weight of my body if I tried to climb down it. The stuff reaches up almost to the sill. I would just have to lower myself down to find a toehold in the sturdier branch-like parts under the leaves. It seems quite thick in places, though I wonder how it manages to cling to the smooth surface of the wall.

When I first came here the ivy felt like a skin disease oozing up the façade, a mouldering crust of gross German crud, crawling up towards me like a vegetal spider over the pink smoothness of the paintwork, giving me the shivers. But now I see it as a possible getaway, like Rapunzel's flow of knotted hair reaching down to the ground. I could just clamber down my own hair and flee this wretched prison forever. And probably break my neck tumbling down.

There's quite a flurry of activity in and around the castle. Last week they held a procession in the village. A few of the youngest officers drove a cart covered in Nazi bunting up the hill from the village to the castle. Behind them waddled a gaggle of little girls and boys dressed in folkish clothing, bringing bouquets and garlands.

Peering through the bars on my window, I watched them procession up the hill towards the keep. Flowers and swastikas, flowers and fun-sized Nazi flags bedecking the cart as if the two were ideally suited. As if the swastika was the most beautiful black flower they could dream of. More like deadly spiders lurking in the blooms. At the top of the cart, in that ghastly gothic lettering they cherish, it said "Genieße das Leben".[9]

Just after it came, another cart pushed by a group of blissfully jovial men. The lettering this time read "Freut Euch des Lebens", which as far as I know means the same thing in different wording.[10]

The handmaids have told me they are

---

[9]   In German in the text, it means 'Enjoy Life'.

[10]   This also happens to be the title of a waltz by Johann Strauss and the title of a 1934 German propaganda film.

celebrating because Hitler has just invaded what they call "the low countries". They added excitedly that all these lowly nations' wealth will now be ours to keep. [11]

There is a rumour circulating that a new, much larger prison camp is going to be established on the outskirts of the castle.[12] The makeshift huts on the Kuhkampsberg are still here. I cannot see the beginnings of the new camp from my window and can only rely on hearsay.

Anna says that despite the nationwide ban on all constructions that are not essential to the war effort, Himmler has been granted one hundred prisoners from Sachsenhausen[13] to build improvements on and in the castle.

[11] The events mentioned here occurred around May 1940, when Hitler invaded Belgium, Luxemburg and the Netherlands (then referred to as "the Low Countries"). The financial and artistic spoliation of these nations is well documented and requires no further comment.

[12] The camp referenced here was later to be named Niederhagen, after the nearby forest. Dozens of inmates were kept in various places in the castle compound and the camp was only fully established in September 1941, a little more than a year after the events mentioned in the text. The prison population rose from 480 prisoners to around 3,900 by 1943.

[13] Sachsenhausen concentration camp was a detention and extermination facility situated in Oranienburg, 35 km to the north of Berlin. It was active from 1936 to 1945 and later used as an internment camp by the Soviet army. It was the camp in which various mass killing methods were first experimented, before being applied to other larger camps like Auschwitz.

Only God knows how Anna gets hold of this kind of information. She says she hears it on the grapevine, mostly from the other handmaids. She's my only trustworthy connection to that kind of gossip—all the other handmaids treat me as if I'm some kind of foreign spy and never utter a word of this kind of thing in my presence.

The labour force employed on the compound is used to convey stones from the quarry down below to the castle to strengthen and build up the hub of the keep, the notorious North Tower. It's said that Herr Taubert is under strict orders to thicken the walls of the tower until they are entirely unassailable. According to Anna, some of the walls in the castle are now five metres thick.

None of the prisoners working on the castle are said to be Jewish. It is rumoured that Herr Himmler does not want Jewish hands to soil the stones of his sanctuary.

If only he knew. I laugh to think of it when lying in bed.

Hermann Bartels, Himmler's architect-in-command, is overseeing the construction of the North Tower. I have seen him strut around the compound, pointing, conferring, barking his orders. He's a stocky-looking swine with a grease-packed double chin and black-rimmed spectacles that look like they've been confected out of a straightened out band of twisted swastika.

He wears a decoration on his lapels that

looks like the Roman numeral II. I imagine it's
supposed to indicate his rank. Anna doesn't
know what it stands for either. Does it mean
he is second in command after Himmler at the
castle? Surely not outside the little world of the
castle. Not that it matters. We get our orders
directly from Frau Whip, Herr Taubert and his
warrant officer Gottlieb Bernhardt, when the
occasion arises.

The new prisoner facility they are supposed
to be building is called a *Schutzhaftlager* by
everyone at the castle—a camp for *protective*
custody. Protected from what or who, I ask
myself. The only thing they need protection
from are the Nazis who put them here. If there's
one thing they do not fear around these parts,
it is bucketfuls of irony: it seems nauseatingly
hypocritical to call it protective when you think
that the prisoners have been abducted and
coerced to endure nothing more than vilifying
forced labour. I sometimes wonder if they are
not using work as a weapon of destruction.

When I suggested a more moderate version
of the above paragraph to Anna in conversation,
she said they mean that it is German society that
needs to be protected from certain categories
of people. She utters these ineptitudes as if she
believes them. She says that the individuals
who will be put in the new *Schutzhaftlager* have
bad blood, blood that can infect and clog up the
purity of German bloodlines.

When I told Anna that I didn't see how blood could infect you when it stays harmlessly circulating through someone else's body, she looked at me. Still I tried to sway her to my point of view. Reluctantly, she conceded that the only time blood ever leaps out at you is if the body is cut. But when I pointed out that the Nazis have been cutting and wounding and killing people left, right and centre, her face grew all strained and congested. When I said that if anyone is being infected by bad blood it's because of the Nazis she looked horrified that I should proffer groundless, unethical ideas.

When I reason in this way Anna gets all hot and bothered. She's worried I will get us both into trouble with my over-rational arguments.

When the prisoners are working in the quarry and I am on duty in the North Tower, I can catch a glimpse of them labouring up the hill carrying or pulling a load. All of them are men. I haven't seen a single woman so far.

Although none of them look sturdy, the prisoners at work are treated like dray horses. The stronger-looking ones pull the cart up the hill. I sometimes see a weaker prisoner struggle up the hill, like a frail Sisyphus with a hewn-out square stone weighing down on his shoulder.

They all have a number printed onto the pants of their striped pyjama-like uniform. I wonder why they make them work in pyjamas—presumably so they feel comfortable.

Or is it to make them feel stupid?

They all have variously coloured triangles stitched onto their chests. And I haven't seen a single one of the yellow stars they used to put on Jews in Cracow which would tend to confirm the rumour that Himmler doesn't want Jewish people in contact with his castle.

The triangles I see the most frequently are purple. Others are black or blue, but there are also a few pink and red ones.

I initially tried to imagine what the various colours could stand for by the look of each prisoner, but they all more or less looked the same to me in their uniform. A few had slightly sallower skin, but they mostly all looked European, as far as I could tell.

The most frequent colour is purple. Anna has told me that it means they're Jehovah's Witnesses. The red triangle she has been told means they are communists or anarchists, or any kind of political dissident.

Brown, she says, is for Gypsies. Pink, for sexual deviants.[14] There are only four or five Pinks, as far as I can see. The green triangle is for criminals. Black is for anti-socials, which apparently just signifies that they preferred to

[14] The colour pink was attributed by the Nazis to homosexuals who were treated with terrible brutality in the camps. They were often tortured and even castrated in various inhumane ways. It's estimated that they had a higher death toll than any other category of person.

remain unemployed and are now being punished for their idleness. She's not sure what the blue triangles are for.[15]   Nobody seems to know.

I asked her why the triangles were all pointing downwards, and she said she thinks it's so they feel the weight of the hierarchy bearing down upon them—she added it was just a wild guess.

I fail to see the point of giving the camp workers all a different colour as their labour allocation is more or less the same. Only the weaker ones get a slightly lighter load to carry. I've noticed, though, that the pink triangles get treated the worst. The soldiers guarding the inmates tend to push and even kick them. I saw one soldier knock a pink triangle on the back of the head with the butt of his rifle. The poor man fell to the ground and wasn't able to rise again, until they yanked him up again.

I've seen the soldiers aim their rifles at pink triangles as if they're preparing for target practice. They laugh their heads off as if it's the best joke in the world when the men with the pink triangles look up in alarm and try to move out of their sights. I can't hear what they say from my vantage point, but I hear the hard bursts of laughter. I see the soldiers writhe and buckle over laughing. They twist and flail in the invisible fire of their mirth.

[15] Blue triangles were stitched onto the prison clothing of undesirable immigrants removed from German civil life.

6

Yesterday, in ideology class, behind the
SS officers eligible for Reichsführerschule, we
were allowed to sit in on a class that focused on
local legends. The lecturer told us the legend of
Schlacht am Birkenbaum.

It's apparently the myth that motivated
Heinrich Himmler to choose this particular
castle for his leadership school and make it into
a cult site for the SS. The Battle of the Birch Tree
happens to be an ancient Westphalian legend
that tells the story of a great battle between East
and West which is supposed to occur in the
nearby forest, the very same place that is said
to have been the site of the Battle of Teutoburg
Forest, where the Roman legions of Augustus
were finally defeated, putting a final stop to the
spread of the Holy Roman Empire.

Our lecturer that day called it a turning
point in world history, but I had never heard
of it before in my history classes in Cracow. He
said that having defeated Rome and the South,
the time had now come for a similar reckoning

with the East. He said that Herr Himmler had told him personally that conquering Poland was only the first step in the spread of the Germanic Empire all the way to the Far East. He eyed me suspiciously as he said this, obviously aware of my origins, as if I was attempting to offer resistance to what he was saying.

An expedition to Teutoburg Forest was organized this morning to allow SS officers and their ornamental handmaids to mingle in a natural setting while the forest's 'spirit of victory' enters their souls.

As usual, I've been excluded from the outing, debarred from participating in the jolly jaunt.

Instead, I had to spend the first few hours of the afternoon rubbing the already shiny swastika bronze lining the walls and the gate at the main entrance.

They keep me cooped up here like the Lady of Shallot. Although I am allowed to attend ideology lectures, I am excluded from other social gatherings between SS and handmaids. Even the castle compound is off limits. The only time I get a decent breath of fresh air is when we have to stand and salute an incoming vehicle. Like a figurehead, I am not allowed to reach beyond the prow of the castle.

I would have given much to walk out into the odorous wonders of a birch forest in mid-spring, touch the bark and the buds on those silvery white birch trees. Though the prospect of having to hobnob or flirt with those pretentious young men, so proud of their deadly black uniforms and their silly honorary symbols makes me queasy.

And sometimes, like right now, I am able to finish my chores early and put aside enough time to write.

I've been watching the prisoners toil in the copse, breathing in the fragrant scent of the freshly cut wood fibre as it wafts up to my window. A few of them have been sent up from the quarry to cut down some trees. I've watched them saw out a triangular piece of wood and then hack away at the kerf until the trees crack and fall. That awful rending sound has been shredding my nerves, though. A horrible sound, that grating, cracking, pounding noise as the tree smashes into the ground. Every time a tree is felled, it feels like they're tearing off a piece of nature's web.

I think the rest of the workers are still laying the masonry in the aim of thickening the walls of the North Tower.

The detachment unit of prisoners has been hacking at the youngest, the slenderest trees— apparently the younger the better. I've seen them lopping off branches and bark as if it has not been enough to cut the trees off at the root. They flay them and skin them like long ferrets. They strip the trunks down to a smooth finish.

Only late in the afternoon did I fathom why they were skinning them.

They started sawing some of the branches into shoulder-to-elbow-length sticks, and then they hammered and nailed the bits of branch to the longer staves to form the longest ladders I have ever seen. I wonder what they are going to use them for. Is it to climb up the tallest trees to fell them too? Is the entire copse going to be wiped away? If so, to what end?

The maids and Frau Wippermann haven't come back yet. They must be playing hide and seek or some kind of maying game in the forest.

Wouldn't it be wonderful if they could all get lost in there and never come back? I suppose I would miss Anna's cheering company. She isn't quite what you might call a good friend, but she's the next best thing to one in the frigid wastes of this desolate place. I have to keep steeling myself against sorrow when she's away. The sheer memory of my homeland is enough to lay me low for hours.

Writing on paper doesn't beat seeing trees up close, being able to finger the rough braille of the bark, but it does at least give me the illusion that I'm still in touch with Polish literature.

How pretentious of me to say that.

Oh, how I miss the poems of Adam Mickiewicz! What I wouldn't give to obtain a copy of his works. Of course there's no point in asking Anna to procure a copy of poems by a no doubt forbidden poet.

> *Niemen, my home river! Where are those*
>   *springs,*
> *And with them so much bliss and hopeful*
>   *prayers,*
> *Where is the peaceful joy of childhood*
>   *years?* [16]

My memory is a ruin. It sometimes feels as if the masonry of my mind is beginning to moulder. I used to have such a great memory for poems. Every day in this place a stone seems to crumble from the edifice of my memory. It's as if the castle is clogging up my thoughts, sealing up the doors and windows of my past, one by one. Let me be thankful for the fact that I can still invoke a few lines here and there from parts of *Pan Tadeusz*.[17]   But, oh, what I wouldn't give to have the slimmest collection of poems in my hands! Any poems at all, even a weakish, watery mawkish one, as long as they're in Polish.

Before sitting down to write, I took a little time to snoop about, making the most of everyone's departure from the keep.

The castle feels entirely empty. It sometimes feels as if the keep and my body are one and the same entity. It's as if I can sense what goes on

16 The third verse of "To the Niemen" by the Polish poet Adam Mickiewicz.

17 Master Tadeusz refers to the national epic poem by Adam Mickiewicz. It was first published in 1834.

behind each wall, just as I know what goes on inside my mind.

I can't hear a single noise from where I'm sitting and the door of my cell is wide open. Even Arnold the cook is silent as a mouse. I wonder if he too has left with the party.

I know that Herr Klamm is out and about in the town on some errands. I saw him leave about an hour ago.

I did not understand the nature of Klamm's function initially when I saw him lumbering in the wings. I mistook him for some sort of Nazi underling, but it appears he is much more than that. He is the official warden of the castle.

He is the *klamka* [18] of the castle, so to speak, a very useful part indeed.

A big thickset man in his late fifties, Herr Klamm looks like he has just walked out of a painting by Otto Dix. His rheumy, goggle eyes match the pendulous dewlap of flesh that hangs from his neck. He is graced with a pasty, bald pate fringed with wisps of smoky hair. Short arms are weighted with a pair of stubby-looking hands.

And yet there is more to him that disquiets the eye. The most startling aspect of his physiognomy is an incongruous set of eyebrows that resemble dark powdery smudges of soot, as if he has just put his fingers up a chimney flue and smeared off the black coke residue onto the ridge

[18] An obvious translinguistic pun on the warden's name, klamka means 'handle' in Polish.

above his eyes. The contrast between the colour of the ghostly grey hair above his ears and those smears of blackened eyebrow never fails to disconcert me.

Equipped with a pair of half-functional wheezy lungs, Klamm is possessed of a rasping sort of mouth. Although he is only into middle age as far as I can tell, there is a kind of geriatric slowness to his every move.

God, in his great sense of humour, has also granted Herr Klamm a sensationally large pair of ears—I think it's safe to say the lab technicians who measured me before I was delivered to the castle would be delighted to examine such wondrously capacious, flap-like appendages.

Would ears of that scale have passed muster and curried favour with the Führer? I can imagine him having them mercilessly lopped off and fed to his swine or else pinned up in a museum next to specimen butterflies. Where do I get such horrid thoughts? These stone-hearted walls are imprinting their hardness on my soul.

Klamm is servile and fawning every time I see him around Taubert, generally grovelling when I see him around Wippermann and generally libidinously leering around the handmaids, though he has kept his hands to himself for the time being—at least as far as I know.

He always sounds slightly winded, as if

walking round the castle is more than his heart
and lungs can manage. Following him up a
staircase is like walking in the wake of an ailing
vacuum cleaner with a torn dust bag. His asthma
gets so wheezy after a dozen steps he has to
pause in the stairwell to catch his breath.

I've been pretty curious about the West
Tower, the wing in which Himmler sets up his
headquarters when he sojourns at the castle. The
layout of the rooms is supposed to be a little
different to the East Tower where the maids'
rooms are.

Klamm told me that Himmler has a secret
vault within his lodgings, a kind of Bluebeard's
chamber that no-one is supposed to know about.
Klamm said it was strictly confidential and that
only Herr Taubert and he were in the know,
but my guess is that Klamm tells this to any
available handmaid to impress her, to give her
the illusion she is special and that he is confiding
and supplying top-shelf information. When I
mentioned the open secret to Anna, she knew
exactly what I was talking about.

And yet it's a little strange that Klamm should
entrust such confidential matters to me, of all
people. I suppose he sees me as a kind of nobody.
He probably thinks that telling me is the equivalent of telling no one. He also seems to want
to generate an aura of mystery around himself.
Perhaps he hopes that I will give him something
in exchange. What that is, I do not know yet,

though there are times when I fear to surmise.

I made my way over to the West Tower as quickly as I could, speeding down the corridor, my dress billowing behind me in the rush of displaced air. I was in a hurry to make it over and back as quickly as I could in case they decided on some whim or other to come back and fetch a forgotten item for the picnic or whatnot.

I dashed up the stairs to the top of the West Tower, but when I got up I found there was nothing much to explore, just a few ornamental swastika-marked chairs and one of those chunky, indestructible oak tables, so I made my way down the stairwell back into the belly of the tower.

As I wound my way down, I grew quite dizzy with the turning and the apprehension of what I might find, coupled to the fear that they would come back earlier than expected.

Three flights down, I came to a door that was locked.

My face fumbling at the keyhole, I managed to align my eye enough to see through a little. What I glimpsed looked like a sturdy chair riveted to the ground with metal bands. There were two clasps tied to the armrests, one on either side.

I couldn't see everything on the walls, but it looked like the objects hanging there were for the most part metal instruments, not callipers this time but pointed utensils, things that prod and gouge and sever.

Next to these were two short blackened chains equipped with wrist clamps. I looked away from the keyhole with a kind of shudder at what has surely gone on in that room in the past, perhaps even the present.

There is something I do not trust in Klamm. In fact there is no-one I trust here apart from Anna to a certain extent—I imagine she probably talks about me to the other girls behind my back, though. Not that I blame her. Time seems to stand still in this seven-teenth-century keep. Existence is so tedious here it's hard to begrudge her the petty group-bonding pleasures of gossip.

Anna confides to me the things she knows about the other girls; there's little doubt in my mind that she tells the other girls every-thing she has learned about me. I know the other handmaids like the back of my hand, their tastes, their families, the heart-sores, their aspirations.

In Teutonic order, their names:

Adelheide (large saucy eyes, loves flimflam and slashing her mouth with scarlet lipstick)

Adolfa (a gossip-monger, no moustache, despite the name, perceives me as a quisling)

Anna (always genial, though perhaps
somewhat gullible)
Bettina (peaked, emphatic bosom, given to
carelessly open blouse buttons)
Halag (sneaky, spattered with freckles,
rumoured to fart in her sleep)
Hildreth (tends to burble, much enamoured
of her forelocks)
Irmgard (an Argus-eyed quidnunc)
Klara (loves schmaltz, a certified nose picker)
Olga (hidebound, strait-laced, po-faced at all
times)
Rozmonda (frumpy, tow-haired)
Sigfrieda (biddable, though feckless)
Ulrike (loves to lockstep, keeps a tight watch
on others)

That's all the maids. The thirteen apostles,
with me included. Except when she places me
first in front of the gates, Frau Whip makes us
line up in alphabetical order for some reason
that escapes our comprehension. Placing me
near Anna, the order suits me just fine.

Large as it is, the castle doesn't need that
many hands. It means that a lot of our time is
spent needlessly ironing socks, bloomers and
handkerchiefs or just standing on hold awaiting
our orders.

It's clear to all and sundry that tending the
castle is not the principle function of the maids,
which brings me inexorably back to the enigma

of my presence. If I am not to be married off to the SS, if I am a lower order of human on the hierarchical scale of humanity, and potentially a quisling, then what is the point of retaining one such as me?

Although Adolfa's name makes her sound like she was called after the Führer, she was born and baptised before his rise to power. It's hard to make the allusion seem any more obvious, but she says her name is purely coincidental. I sometimes wonder if the name isn't assumed, though, as she's pretty fervent about Adolf. I think she actually fancies him. She's put a poster of his vile-looking face on her wall.

Being particularly plain, Adolfa looks at me in particular distaste. She's got the mouth of a wild boar, drooping eyes and a flesh-engorged nose that looks as if it was pasted on in too much of a hurry. Her smile is more like a barring of teeth.

Anna tells me that these days, lots of people give their children names that begin with an A or a H to honour the Führer. There are apparently parents who name all their children with names that begin with an H to canvas their loyalty to the party: a string of aspirate names like Heinrich, Herbert, Heinz, Henrietta, Hildegard, Hedwig, Helga, Hilda and Hulde.

7

The castle has been in a state of alarm since
this morning's announcement that the British
have bombarded Dortmund, Mönchengladbach
and even parts of Berlin.[19] Everyone is in a state
of dismay and disarray. I had to try to conceal
my dark delight at the idea of Berlin being
battered the way poor Poland was not so long
ago. The war and my abduction have made me
vindictive in a way I never thought possible (I
often hunger spiritually for the person I used to
be).

News of the attack sent Herr Taubert and
Frau Wippermann into a flurry of activity.
Taubert has ordered the prisoners to knock
down the rest of the remaining plaster from the
façades of the castle to make it look more like
a daunting fortress in preparation for the war,

---

[19] Launched by the Royal Airforce, these coordinated
attacks took place in May 1940, at which time Himmler's
mass child abduction programme was already in full operation.

as if a little bare ugly stone would dissuade an assailant.

The aim I am told is to wipe away all trace that the castle was once nothing more than a Prince Bishop's palatial residence. Herr Taubert is convinced that the stonework in itself will contribute to frightening off British bombers.

It all started with them hacking down the ivy draping the wall under my window, leaving an ugly ghostly beige shadow on the pink plaster. So that's that, there goes my escape plan. Operation Rapunzel nipped in the bud. Not that I seriously entertained any genuine hope of successfully fleeing. The lianas of ivy lie in a messy pile at the base of the wall, like thick cuttings of hair brushed into an uneven pile on the floor of a barber's shop.

When I first got here, the palace looked like a piece of pink pastry. With the crumbling of the pink icing from the facades, the torte is beginning to look like a grim, craggy cliff-face, which I suppose is the desired eyesore effect. Most of the walls are depressingly splintery now, all grey and desolate, like a crumbling, mouldering medieval castle in one of those gothic English novels.

I can't help thinking that this is what the National Socialist party must have looked like to the German people at the start: a brightly alluring façade with promised pink torte for the well behaved.

Perched all day atop their long tapering ladders, the prisoners have been hammering away at the walls like insistent woodpeckers, knocking the pretty, pleasing plaster off the edifice. Although the noise is muted a little when you shut the windows, the hacking and pounding has given me a thudding, throbbing headache. In the officer's room I was cleaning, it felt like they were hacking away at the inside of my skull.

The slicker officers have been engaged in combat training in the fields, getting their nicely groomed grotty uniforms all muddy again. I've watched them run around like headless black-coated chickens, pretend-diving for cover, shooting at targets and generally squawking and barking and howling at each other like enraged male animals. It's quite comical to watch, like a dress rehearsal for a battle with no one actually dying.

It's hard to imagine the castle being assailed in any way. The Westphalian countryside around here looks so peaceful and dormant, when it isn't being hacked at.

I've been so swept off my feet by the general panic that has overcome the castle that I haven't been able to write a word until just now before bed. I look down through the silent dusk and see the rubble piled up at the foot of the walls like the crumbs from a cake, or debris from a bombing.

It's strange how strongly I am beginning to identify with my own prison. Since they started the hacking, it has felt as if the protective layers I have wrapped around myself have started to crumble along with the plaster. I've felt exposed and raw and ill-at-ease all day, as if someone has chiselled off my clothes and left me bare and exposed.

The only interesting moment in the day occurred when one of the prisoners looked up from his work and saw me staring out the window.

Resting his bony chest against the ladder, his hammer and chisel lolling by his thighs, he gazed at me for what seemed like almost half a minute, panting all the while, with only the inclination of his body on the ladder to keep him from toppling off.

I suppose it must have been only a few seconds. Just enough time to notice he had one of those purple triangles stitched to his striped cotton shirt, and his serial number. Eight, I think it was, inscribed just above his triangular patch. The uniform he was wearing looked a good three sizes too small. From what I could see, the striped pyjamas bottom seemed to reach almost half way up his calves.

But mostly, I remember his eyes. Coal-black and smouldering inside a pair of gaunt sockets. Like the heads of all the other prisoners, his hair was shaved to a cropped bristle. I couldn't stop blinking as he gazed into me, and yet it was impossible for me to look away. A bottomless stare with an intensity of hammered bronze. Imbued with a degree of hostility, laced with a touch of searing interest. It quite unsettled me. I couldn't get it out of my mind all day.

I suppose he took me for one of those hopeful Nazi handmaids. We all look more or less the same in our drab, nondescript uniforms, as if we are all but near-identical versions of the one maid.

Does he not fear that I could report him for staring at me in that way? I know several handmaids who would have denounced him on the instant. A single untoward stare from a prisoner can be taken as an act of insolence, a punishable sign of insubordination.

A shout from one of the guards down below made the emaciated, pyjama-clad Romeo on his ladder pick up his work again. Still staring right at me, Prisoner 8 blinked a few times in reaction to either me or the yell. He glared right at me for another second or two, and slowly turned his head towards the wall.

A stare like a sting, but I really do not know if it expressed pure hatred, or a blend, a heady compound of hate and homage. It was more perhaps just an intensely searching gaze, as if he was trying to determine whether or not I would be the kind of pretty maiden to poison him with the venom in my tail.

He held his hammer and chisel as if they weighed at least a kilo each, the rest of his body pronated, clinging to the ladder for support. I noticed the workers are fastened at the waist by a length of rope in case they lose their balance, but it doesn't look quite enough to keep the ladders from slithering down to the side along the wall.

With weary swings, prisoner 8 continued to knock the pretty pink plaster off the façade, revealing the stony grey rubble masonry underneath. I watched him for another few minutes from the corner of my eye as I finished bedding and grooming the room.

There was something about prisoner 8, something whole and intense and unvanquished. Only my father ever looked at me that way, with that kind of full-hearted, unwavering stare.

In the melancholy reaches of the darkness, I take to wondering where my little sister has been taken. I imagine her as a small godforsaken squirrel sheltering in the hollow of an oak tree, deep in the forest, waiting for me to come and rescue.

That of course is nothing but a hopeless fantasy. I suppose she has been put in some camp or other, hopefully not in one of those horrible holes the rumours allude to.

I cannot help hoping at times that she has met a fate similar to mine. In my brighter moments, I picture her as a young maid in an elegant household, serving up dishes in a pretty white apron. It makes me so sad to think that in all likelihood I will never see her again.

What I fail to understand is why they need to abduct so many Polish children. Surely they have enough young helpmeets to serve them. There must be enough impoverished young German women willing to take up such jobs.

I have to come up with some way of finding Mila's whereabouts. I have to find a way to wheedle the information out of Klamm. He probably has no idea where she is, but perhaps I can make him ask Herr Taubert. If Taubert is unwilling to divulge, perhaps I can coax Klamm into ferreting papers out of Taubert's office. He does after all possess the keys to the castle.

The thought of escaping this draughty gaol is more than enticing, of course. I could probably tie a few sheets together and try to escape out the window in the thick of the night—the fall is not that high, perhaps three times my length. I might be able to make it out of the grounds.

But I've seen the German shepherds guarding the compound. Their snouts look as if they've been dipped in deep darkness, their whole heads immersed in and tainted by what looks like black blood but is only dark fur.

If I managed to escape the sharp knives of their fangs, how would I then find the means to locate my sister? Before planning any form of flight from here, I must first discover the name of the place she has been taken to. But then of course there is the problem of money, travel and food and, last but not least, being able to retrieve her from her captors. The whole thing is of course doomed to failure.

Carrying out any kind of escape will mean having to gain Klamm's complete confidence. He is the only worthwhile ally in the keep. I will not be able to secure anyone higher. Herr Siegfried Taubert is clearly not within my reach. He stares at me indifferently, as if he would like to send me back to the factory like a faulty lampshade.

Of Anna's ultimate loyalties I am unsure. I know that I cannot confide in her on this matter.

And thus I have to find a way to make Klamm indebted to me in some way. As a mere handmaid, I have of course no leverage, no power of any kind to wield. I have nothing to offer that may be of use to one such as Klamm. I have only my body to offer in exchange. The thought of giving myself to that bristly-browed toad as quid pro quo is far beyond repulsive.

It is not that I fear to lose my immortal soul in the transaction. The thought of Klamm's grubby, pudgy fingers pawing at my skin is enough to make me shiver with sheer loathing and disgust.

I noticed the headless dove blossoms have started to turn brown. How sad to think that even such sturdy, stately-looking flowers begin to wither on the bow before the spring is even half-finished. I inquired about the strangeness of this to Herr Rausländer, the chief gardener, but he says it's the same every year. It's always been that way, as far as he can remember. Within weeks the wilted petal-doves drop to the ground and the crows return to inhabit the trees. He says that magnolia blossoms never last for very long. Back home it was the same for cherry trees. The blossoms look like pink primed popcorn and then just as it looks like they're going to last far into the summer months in a matter of days the petals flutter down, making the ground look like the aftermath of a wedding. A few gusts of wind and there is not a single one of those pink petals left to behold.

When was popcorn first discovered? Did the Ancient Greeks make popcorn too? No one seems to know. Anna looked a little star-struck when I asked.

8

The general panic has subsided, life at the castle resuming its somnambulant pace. You can still hear the odd peck at the walls, but most of the prisoners have been reallocated to the rebuilding and refitting of the North Tower. I saw the guards shunt them over in that direction.

From my vantage point, it looks like most of the plaster has been scraped or knocked off the wall. The façade under my window looks all craggy and jagged now, the underlying rubble masonry left sharp and uneven like intersecting scars caked in icing. Hacked plaster still clogs and clings to the interstices between the stones, like food residue caught between the grey teeth of a golem.

Now that most of the hubbub has died down, the crows have alighted again and returned to their posts. I can see them waddling around on the cornices like fat-bellied black sentries, seemingly indifferent or oblivious to the change. I was woken by their cawing in the early morning. I couldn't get back to sleep and was forced to contend with their croaking—not exactly the soft pastoral trilling of tuneful song birds.

All classes have ceased at the castle. Even the Finished off Druid seems to have packed up and left. The handmaids are all annoyed because their eligible bachelors have been posted back to Berlin and various other fortifications around Germany. They fear they may lose their places in the hearts of their officers and be sent back to the different dullness of their homes in the spring, having forfeited their marriage prospects to Germany's purest and finest.

Anna too is out of sorts. Both melancholy and disgruntled in equal measure. I think she had high hopes of being propositioned off by an officer I saw her dallying with on more than one occasion, a reasonably handsome officer called Folker Meininger.

Having nothing better to talk about, I try my best to reassure her. I tell her that he will no doubt be back by the end of the summer, despite the fact that I think nothing of the sort. Adopting my most consolatory voice, I say he will propose to her as soon as he gets back.

I have of course no idea if they will come back. Chances are they won't, at least not the same ones. To my shame, I have to admit that I sometimes catch myself hoping that the lot of them will be blown to bit by British bombs. I know that is a very unChristian thought and I should not entertain it.

In my crueller moments, I take to wondering if the handmaids would still want their oh-so-pristine Officers if they came back maimed, defaced and fingerless. Would the handmaids still be interested if their precious idols came back without their Aryan sheen and shine, in tattered, torn black uniforms, smelling like stinky tortured trench rats, looking like shell-shocked tramps.

I think this place is doing something bad to me. I never used to rehearse such morbid, heartless fantasies. Being incarcerated here is making me morally insane. A footloose girl, I always felt the need to roam around. And yet here I find myself, penned in a stony fortress by invisible shackles.

I have not set eyes on prisoner 8 again. I imagine he has been given some other work assignment, probably down in the quarry breaking out bits of masonry or positioning the freshly hewn out stones on the battlements of the North Tower.

Perhaps they will be back in a day or two to cart off remaining debris. I should be able to catch sight of him again when they do.

I wonder what hides behind my prisoner's facade. I know next to nothing about the purple sign he bears. There were relatively few Jehovah's Witnesses in Cracow, but they were easy to identify. Always knocking on doors to convert others to the truth, but then as now, nobody wants to hear that the end is nigh. It made them unpopular as the bringers of bad news.

Even before the invasion of Poland, you sometimes saw them being chased in the streets. I myself once witnessed three grown women running after a child shouting "dirty Jehovah, dirty Jew!" For some reason, many people consider Jehovah's Witnesses to be Jews in different garb, despite the fact that they're Christians.

The fact that their bibles call the Lord by his Jewish name Jehovah is enough to create the link, despite the fact that the Jewish word is actually Yahweh, rather than Jehovah. Neither the Nazis nor the Witnesses seem to know that the J sound at the start of Jehovah is excluded from the Hebrew alphabet. My dear forsaken mother told me that when I was small.

It appears the Witnesses were right after all, though. The end of time has come, bringing with it not the Second Coming, but the advent of the Antichrist in Berlin. This isn't judgement day. It's more like the Second Coming of Satan.

Prisoner 8 doesn't look Polish. That much I can tell. He has a European sort of face, I suppose, for want of a better word. It's hard to think where he may be from. His hammered

bronze eyes in any case are all his own. Despite
the brutish haircut, his features are as finely
chiselled as those of an Italian Christ. I suppose
he might be Italian or Spanish, perhaps even
Greek. He has dark hair and a slightly sallow
complexion.

Although I do not myself have to wear
a coloured triangle, I have discovered that I
am circumscribed within a triangle without
realizing it. When they let me walk across the
inner courtyard of the castle the other day,
I dawned on me that the castle is triangular
in structure. The keep is constructed like an
arrowhead with the North Tower at the tip.
Thus I am bound within an isosceles prison.

I sometimes have to shuttle pails of water
to the Tower. I am to deposit the buckets at
the entrance so I never come into contact with
the prisoners. I enter through a wooden, trian-
gle-latticed portal at the tip of the yard.

Anna has told me it used to be the entrance
to a chapel. She says the prisoners have finished
making the second or third floor into what is
to be called the *Obergruppenführersaal* [20] which
sounds grand. She says it's been designed on
Himmler's orders. It is to be a special room in
which only the very highest ranking officials of
the Nazi regime are to assemble.

There has been more talk of an impending
meeting of the highest order, a conference of

---

[20] Generals' room.

grandees convened at Wewelsburg to discuss
a secret matter of the utmost importance. How
she got wind of this kind of classified information is beyond me. I have no direct access to
the juice or wine of Anna's grapevine.

You'd think they could have restored some
of the old masonry around the North Tower.
The carved figures on either column of the
former chapel in the yard are pretty ravaged.
Both of their faces have been rendered quite
anonymous by time.

I know next to nothing about Jehovah's
Witnesses, not any more than I know about
Mormons or the Amish. I have only heard talk
of them. As a girl, I was told by a neighbour
that they were little short of crazy, zealots who
believe they are the Chosen Ones. Back home
in Silesia they're generally considered fanatical,
a sect that clings to a quaint code of honour. A
thing out of the past.

Although there was great intensity in his
stare, prisoner 8 did not look like a fanatic when
I saw him. There was on the contrary an air of
great inner and outer calmness to him, almost
as if he was an ordinary stonemason looking
up casually from his labour to contemplate a
somewhat intriguing German maiden. There
was even a slight glimmer of a smile playing on
his features towards the end of the stare, once
the hostility had begun to drain out of his eyes.

All the other prisoners seem as grim and broken as the rubble. Most of them look as if they have lost the faculty of speech, along with the capacity to smile. At least that's what I thought until Anna told me the prisoners are not allowed to confer or interact in any way. The use of language is forbidden.

For some reason that escapes me, my diary entries seem to want to shrink. I don't feel the same urge to write in the evenings and have stopped for several days.

The buoyant flippancy that kept me going through those first few weeks has now forsaken me entirely. I suppose it is safer to feel despondent than full of inappropriate animal spirits in a place such as this. Flamboyant levity is hardly fitting for a foundling such as I.

Even my satirical bent has deserted me. I was already drained of joy; I am now emptied of my craziness and the drollery of casting aspersions.

I've stopped praying too. It avails me no longer. Increasingly, it feels as if I am talking to myself. Am I losing my faith? Writing this makes me feel so terribly guilty, as if I have forsaken my damaged God on his cross. But has He not forsaken me and my family and all the rest of us? Has He not left the whole world by the wayside?

I will continue to write as it comforts a little.

It offers a little balm, a tiny thing to bask in, a little soother for sleep.

I think from time to time about the period when I used to compose poems, little sonnets in praise of nature and God. Mere rhymes that seem trite and useless now that there is nothing left to praise or appraise.

I do not say there is no more beauty in the world, but it has been terribly tarnished, blackened into oblivion. I suppose it's all still there, hidden in the depths of the darkness.

The other day I felt a vague stirring, a yearning twitch to write one of those breezy sonnets I used to compose in my more soulful moments. I even came up with a few rhymes, but couldn't bring myself to set it down on paper. I couldn't finish it in my mind so I didn't bother to start writing. A poem about this beautiful but alien landscape felt somehow little more than hollow.

I think the time of poetry is over. The most I can hope to write now is leaden prose in tentative praise of what is left. The difficulty will be in finding the motivation to record all this futility.

I feel the castle bristling, like a stony hedgehog raising its shards.

9

I've made some headway with Klamm. It's made me want to put pen to paper again after all these weeks—no small feat in itself.

Like a chess player biding her time, I have lured him. I have coaxed him out about his family and ancestors. I've managed to create a little rapport, to get a little fake trust to grow between us.

Never have I had to source such deeply frozen depths of sympathy to pretend to warm to Klamm's soot-sodden eyebrows. A cold fish of a man if ever there was. And yet, despite his unprepossessing, dowdy presence, I have come to the realization that we have something in common. We are both dulled and dimmed, both ossified by having to keep solitary confinement in this godforsaken keep.

It appears that Klamm was born in Paderborn, the closest city to Wewelsburg. He told me that after the Prince Bishops of Pad ceased to reside at the castle, it was solitary priests until the 1930s. Klamm himself was appointed by Himmler when he first opted to lease the castle. It seems Klamm secured his position at the keep through family connections with the Lord Mayor of Paderborn.

He says that Himmler is not a bad fellow once you get to know him. When he's in a good mood, the castle leaser can even prove to be uncommonly generous. You just have to get into his good books and stay there as long as you can by mostly doing as he says. It's also safer to avoid being around him when he has his fits. Apparently, Himmler sometimes looks as if he's in a lot of pain. When this look grabs hold of his features, it's best to keep out of his sight.[21]

The very sound of Himmler's name I find off-putting, like the nasal humming noise produced by a nasty insect hovering into your face from the Himmel on high.[22]

A new, waspish creature: the Himmler.

Klamm says he has not set eyes on Herr Himmler in over a year, since the outbreak of the war. But he has got wind that Herr Himmler is preparing to pay the castle a visit as soon as he can get away from conducting the Führer's foreign affairs. The Schutzstaffel Reichsführer apparently likes to retreat here in order to get a

---

[21] It is attested that Himmler suffered from acute, stress-related intestinal pain that sometimes laid him low and bed-ridden for several days in a row.

[22] Translator's note: in German in the text, 'Himmel' means 'sky'.

break from the war, his wife and his mistress—a male sort of joke that sent our clammy warden into cackles of laughter. Having to peer into his mouth makes you feel you've seen the inside of an ogre.

When he managed to stop hee-hawing and lowing and wobbling his wattle, Klamm told me he himself was once married a long time ago—an unsurprisingly ill-fated union that did not turn out the way Klamm had hoped it would. His wife remained childless and she left him for another man only a year into the marriage. He confided this to me with his bulgy puppy eyes, pulling the bud lobe on one of his long flappy, grease-sheened jug-ears. I tried hard not to look as if I understood why she had left him.

Playing the role of confidant has allowed me to pluck a few heartstrings. I know it is calculating, but I have decided to try to play the role of the daughter Klamm never had, to see how that works. I prefer to keep things on a sexless basis. I do not wish to have to bestow any favours upon the clammy fish.

Yesterday, I asked K to let me into Herr T's office. I never dreamed he would even consider letting me, but figured it was worth a try. He looked a bit suspicious at first. It congealed his libidinous leer for an instant.

I had to allay his fears as best I could, saying that it was only to take a quick peek at my file. I said I wanted to know what Herr Taubert

thought of me. I alleged that he was stand-
offish with me, much more than with the other
handmaids.

I could see there wasn't much empathy
to draw on in Klamm's red-veined rheumy
eyeballs—his irises are the exact same dull-grey
colour as the stone walls of the castle. I could
see him calculating though. I saw him dither a
little reluctantly, but he finally gave in, putting
his misgivings to the side. I could hardly believe
my luck when he accepted.

Of course the downside is I imagine he
now expects me to do something for him in
exchange. It's hard to say at this stage. I'm not
always a good judge of character. I have learned
that the hard way more than once before.

Herr Taubert was out and about in
Paderborn on some matter at the Town Hall, so
I wasn't too worried he'd unexpectedly turn up,
but Klamm was pretty nervous, pulling at his
dewlap all the while as he kept watch. He stood
behind me by the door in the corridor while
I fished through the files in Taubert's cabinet.
They were all neatly filed away in alphabetical
order so it didn't take too long. I came across a
section marked "Burgmeiden",[23] so I plunged
into that.

I didn't find my name at first. In my haste,

[23] Translator's note: a compound noun which means 'castle
maidens'.

I'd forgotten I wouldn't be filed in the registry papers under my Polish surname. It slipped my mind on the spur of the moment that even my name was effaced when I got here.

Herr Taubert—or more plausibly his secretary—changed my patronym on arrival at Wewelsburg to a random, barely related, German-sounding patronym. God knows how they chose it, though I suppose they could have chosen worse. I found myself at last in the depths of the filing cabinet under 'Eva Kaufmann', my Germanized coat-of-tar alias. A real German *mädchen* with an ever-so-German-sounding surname.

My only comfort is that Kaufmann sounds vaguely like Hoffmann, one of the few German writers I ever appreciated, along with Goethe and Thomas Mann. I have such fond memories of studying some of Hoffmann's tales with my dearly beloved and probably now departed Pani Haperska.

Did they choose Kaufmann cynically because I was to be one of the main providers of coffee at the keep? Or is it that I have been bought for free from my native country to be brought here as an unpaid slave. I imagine they probably just chose it at random.

It was a small thing really, a fairly minor, almost comic twist but I must say it came as quite an unpleasant shock when Frau Wippermann first call me Kaufmann, as if my very soul had been reformed in her mouth, as if she had chewed me into shape like a malleable piece of caramel.

We give our names too much importance of course. They do not really define who or what we are. As Juliet once put it when despairing over Romeo's unfortunate surname, a rose by any other name would smell as sweet. And so Eva Kaufmann I am in name.

There was nothing on me in the file that I didn't already know. I had hoped absurdly that I could glean some information on Mila's whereabouts, as if they would have put that in the file. How naïve I sometimes am!

I suppose I hoped that they might have kept a register of siblings, but their aim is not to reconnect lost family members. It is quite the opposite. They wish to rip everything asunder, bury truth and throw away the key.

In fact I found rather less than I already know. The first document I came upon was the evaluation sheet I had seen them fill out when they were measuring Mila and me at the facility. It was now stamped with an inky eagle and a big black swastika to boot.

The only other file I found concerning me had "Geburtsurkunde"[24] written on it in thick gothic letters. The date of birth they put down

---

[24] 'Birth certificate'.

was entirely arbitrary, off by several months and several days. My place of birth read 'Krakow', the place where they found me, despite the fact that I was born in Katowice. They didn't even bother to ask me the correct details.

What hurt me the most in the file was that it made it look as if I had never had a father or a mother:

~~Vater:~~ ---

~~Muter:~~ ---

Just two crossed out blank lines for each. As if they were struck off the life list, as if it had taken that many slashes and stabs of the dash key on the typewriter to stamp them out of existence, all those little slits of ink to consign them to officialdom's oblivion. Oh, how I miss them all. I even worry about my dog.

10

Heinrich Himmler himself arrived at the castle today. At the very stroke of midday. The village belfry had just finished striking its twelve ominous gongs. I looked out the window to gaze at the crows doing their gargoyle imitations on the battlements and saw a black Mercedes Benz wend its long hearse-shaped body through a cloud of grey dust as it traversed the moat bridge and disappeared under the gatehouse.

I was pretty sure it was him when I spotted the registration. The number plate read SS1.[25] The girls had mentioned the glamour of this sign in their gossip. My tiny window is just above the gatehouse portal, a little to the right to be precise, below the bay window. When the black automobile breached the entrance, I got the distinct sensation it was entering my soul.

---

[25] Himmler had several armoured limousines and used the vanity plate SS1 to indicate his rank in the hierarchy of the *Schutsstafel*.

The vehicle's windows were darkened so I didn't catch sight of him, but I know it was the Beast.

We were caught unprepared and so missed such a splendid opportunity to greet him at the gate. He was supposed to arrive late afternoon. Oh how my heart aches with the pity of lost opportunities!

We were asked to plait our hair into Bavarian tresses to honour Himmler's region of birth and were at that for ages, having been made to get up for that sole purpose at six in the morning. Frau Wippermann showed us how to confect the braids using Adolfa's hair as an example. For some reason, she always choses Adolfa for that kind of exemplum. Adolfa's very name bestows on her an air of fitness to serve as a model for the rigours of the regime.

The tress is a convoluted tangle that I had trouble reproducing when the time came for me to perform it on Anna's frizzy airborne hair. Quite impossible to get all that foxy fuzz under control.

Frau Whip got impatient with my fumbling and ended up having to do Anna's hair herself. She knotted mine so tightly it feels like my head has been cemented into place. It feels like my scalp has been turned into a tightly-woven hat. It's now a tracery of iron coils, twisted, tweaked and braided into a rock-hard Bavarian bretzel. All I hope is that we won't be expected to keep

the damned thing in place for the duration of
Himmler's stay.

The Beast being scheduled to arrive later in
the day, all of our preparations for a smiling
bretzel-haired welcome at the entrance have all
been in vain. How wondrous to be spared the
indignity of that.

For the first few hours, Herr Houndfromhell
remained locked away in his treasure chamber
somewhere at the base of the castle. It is said
that he harbours all kinds of artwork down
there in the dungeons. There's even a rumour
that he hoards a stockpile of gold in there along
with a casket full to the brim of hideous SS skull
rings. Apparently, he's very fond of distributing the death rings to his officers the moment
they flower into full-blossomed wickedness.
The handmaids have told me in hushed tones
of reverence that the rings are the highest
decoration you can receive in the pecking order.
The skull rings being second only to the rings of
the Niebelungen.

I have seen these Totenkopfringe on a few of
the officers' fingers. Kleinhitlercamp wore one
on his ring finger as if he was betrothed to the
Reich. They're about the ugliest-looking jewels
you could possibly imagine. A celebration of
ugliness. Anna tells me they were designed
by Himmler's ideological advisor, Karl Maria
Wiligut. He's apparently very proud of how
dauntingly grim they are.

The castle porter took half an hour to unload the boot of Himmler's four-wheeled black sarcophagus. Himmler is said to do this every time he comes to the castle. He keeps bringing war booty back as decorations, keepsakes, like a magpie padding its nest. As it is, the halls are already covered in all manner of lavish faux medieval tapestries and paintings and hung ornaments of every shape and description. Any more and the place will start to look cluttered. It is said there is no end to the loot that the beastly Magpie desires to hoard and amass.

In a flurry of panic-stricken efficiency, Frau Wippermann assembled us in one of the state-rooms shortly after Himmler's arrival. She made us stand to rigid attention for several minutes before he entered the room, our chins lifted ever so slightly, chests poised at the ready for inspection, hands by our sides, making us look and feel like a row of statuesque geese.

Anna has told me that the Beast was originally a poultry farmer. Although it doesn't surprise me that the Beast was actually a bumpkin, it's hard to imagine the Reichsführer SS scrabbling amongst the hens and cocks in his currently spotless attire. When he finally appeared, he looked so cossetted and pampered, like an overfed baby fitted with thin silver-rimmed spectacles. He has that spoilt brat look about him, as if his mother indulged him too freely as a toddler. I can just picture her pinching the puffy fat of his greasy cheek and saying *ach! Du bist meine schöne Puppe!!!*[26]

The Beast has the manner of an articulated, talking automaton. Cocksure, a nasal voice. He paced in front of us after he stepped into the hall, lording it over us with his silly tonsured pate of hair shaved too far above the ears. The current hairstyle among men makes them look like proper louts. A good thing he couldn't hear my thoughts as I scrutinized him, deriding him secretly behind the mask of my composure.

Taking his time, he inspected every one of us, looking us up and down, complimenting Frau Whip on her choices. When he came to me, he stopped for longer, blinked an inordinate number of times and started gushing in a shrill, over-loud voice: "Aha! Aha! So, you! If I am not mistaken, you are the young Polish Fraulein!! Herr Taubert has told me that we are honoured to have within our midst the finest pearl of the East!"

I simply nodded and pretended to look vaguely chuffed by the backhanded compliment. But on he went, on and on, fingering my face and stroking my neck all the while as if I was some kind of prime quality, macaw-coloured bird that needed examining. I did my best not to flinch or look angry, but couldn't help shooting him a few testy stares when he started prodding

[26] In German in the text, it means "you are my beautiful doll."

my face. I didn't want to show him how much I reviled the touch of his pudgy fingers fiddling with my flesh. I didn't want to give him the impression that he had any effect on my feelings.

Anyway, he finally let up groping my features as if they were putty. Nodding his self-satisfied smirk, he called me Wewelsburg's Rheingold. Anna later explained to me that Rheingold was the highest compliment someone like Himmler could proffer. He's said to be obsessed by Germanic mythology.

Das Rheingold, Anna explained, is a hoard of gold that was guarded by the maidens of the Rhine in times of yore. Legend has it that this river gold was used in the forging of the Ring of the Nibelung, a treasure jealously guarded by a malicious being called Alberich, the king of the dwarfs.

Although he has the average height of a man, Himmler is certainly something of a moral dwarf, but saying that is no doubt being crassly unkind to meritorious, upstanding dwarfs.

When I said this to Anna, she seemed shocked that I would dare to openly entertain a thought of this nature and use such a word with regard to the one and only Reichsführer SS. She added that Alberich was also known as the king of the elves and that he was supposed to possess the strength of twelve men. Even Siegfried was only able to vanquish him because he was wearing the *Tarnkappe*, a cloak of absolute invisibility.

Anna knows all this stuff from school. She and the other handmaids seem to set great store by the story of the Nibelung. If you pronounce the word 'Nibelung' even casually in an off-hand sort of way, all the handmaids look kind of stricken, as if you've just uttered a sacred, magic word, as if they believe these stories are based on hard facts, not folklore.

When Frau Whip announced that Himmler was about to take time out to inspect us, the girls went into a flurry of excitement and wonder as if Mr. Nibelung himself had just deigned to grace us with his presence. I suppose they see the Beast as the ultimate bachelor, and themselves as the beauties that can bind him. He never comes to the castle with his wife and children. Even his mistress is kept out of the way. An oversight that is not lost on the handmaids.

11

Frau W summoned me this morning to tell me I have caught Herr H's eye. She looked at me as if I was supposed to be deeply honoured and delighted he had even bothered to mention someone as lowly as me. It seems he asked to see me alone shortly after the inspection when we had been dismissed and they were discussing the running of the castle. Frau W indicated I was to report directly to his office, the room the handmaids call the Treasure Chamber, a door labelled *König Artus*.

She gave me to understand that not even she has ever seen the inside of this chamber. She was eager to remind me that I was to be on my best behaviour in the presence of the Beast. Any levity on my part could cost me dearly she chided, upbraiding me all the while with a long, wagging finger: "Herr Himmler is not a man to be toyed with". He is much stricter than Herr Taubert and will not stand for any insolence or shilly-shallying on my part.

What she meant by 'shilly-shallying' I was

not sure exactly. She seemed to suggest that I
should be ready to give up soul and body at the
Reichsführer's slightest whim.

Not without some trepidation, I made my
way through the tenebrous maze of the castle.
The stairways in the West wing are unfamiliar
to me as I am never allowed to go there. I took a
wrong turning and found myself at the bottom
of a darkly engulfed stairwell that led into a
tiny hidey hole that looked like a kind of drain
pipe, but I could see only very indistinctly in
the dimness. I cannot imagine what else it could
be. Like Alice, I felt like stuffing myself down
the little tunnel to get away from it all.

But of course I did nothing of the sort and
just headed back up the stairwell to look for
another corridor.

I finally got to the room W had mentioned.
Vaguely gleaming in the penumbra, the words
König Artus figured on the door in golden gothic
lettering.

When I showed my hilarity at this name,
Frau Whip told me to watch my manners and
show some respect. She didn't seem to fathom
that it might be hard to take a man who thinks
he's King Arthur too seriously. When I hinted
as much, Whip again asked me in icy tones
if I wanted to end up down in Niederhagen.
She makes it sound like a journey to the
Netherworld.

Anyway, I knocked on the door and heard

a muffled *"Komm rein"* or something like that.
I pushed down the handle and saw the Beast,
his eyelids barely ajar, almost fully asleep in
his armchair. His signature Hitler-lookalike
moustache was sitting in its usual place, his
silvery circular glasses matching the roundness
of his tonsure. An inconspicuous, colourless,
harmless-looking sort of beastly bureaucrat. The
kind of man you wouldn't look at twice if you
passed him in the street.

His boots were crossed on the big slab of a
thick hardwood table. Rude as a hog, he didn't
bother budging to uncross them or take them
off the table top. Looking me straight in the eye,
he just stretched and yawned a loud cavernous
yawn showing me the back of his chubby throat,
beckoning all the while with his pudgy fingers
for me to step into the room. I have never seen
such gross manners. I suppose he thought he
was being convivial.

"Komm rein!" he gawped, seeing me
motionless at the door. "I was just taking a
little nap. The Führer expects me to take care of
so much. You know I haven't taken a break in
seven months. Remind me of your first name,"
he said, pointing his finger at my breast.

"Ewa."

"Ach, yes, of course! Eva... The mother of
mankind in Christian mythology. A perfect
ur-name for a perfect-looking *mädchen*. Please,
do sit down. I wanted to let you know how

delighted we are to have you with us at
the castle. I hope your stay so far has been
agreeable. They have not worked you off your
feet, I trust. You look ... well-fed, healthy as a
young deer. Tell me, how do you like the food
in these parts?"

"I cannot complain."

"Good, good. I wish you to lack for nothing.
These are hard times, but I see to it that my staff
is well cared for. My allowance has shrunk to
almost nothing since the start of the war, but
thankfully leasing this castle only costs me a
single *Reichsmark* a year! The district of Büren
has been most kind to the Reich. It allows me
to splurge a little in other areas. I see you're
impressed by my little collection. That skull
you're looking at is called Richard. I mean
Wagner of course. I have it on good faith that it
is his original cranium. A real genius, that man.
I adore being in his company. I've been remiss.
Can I offer you a drink? Liebfraumilch perhaps?
The lady's milk. Or perhaps you would prefer a
glass of gewürztraminer? I have some excellent
vintage wines in the cellar."

"Thank you, but I am not thirsty."

"Oh, you don't need to be thirsty to drink."

"I do not wish to drink."

"I take it you've made a confirmation vow
to touch nothing but blood of Christ. Heh heh.
I should not joke about these things. I know
you Polish people take religion very seriously.

I do too, as a matter of fact! You know I do not reject Christ entirely. It's just that I feel that what came before him was even better. Would you perhaps care to pop a Pervitin pep pill? It's a methamphetamine authorized by the Reich for its awareness-boosting virtues. Pervitin is absolutely energizing. It also acts as a fantastic confidence-booster that clears the mind and creates utter well-being. What more can one ask of a tiny pill? I myself am a bit shy. Thanks to Pervitin, I manage to overcome my reserve. A magic pill confected by our greatest scientists. It contains substances that make you feel entirely Nordic. Opium, by contrast, is for the dull, sleep-ridden Asian mind. Trust me, opium and heroin—for the weak."

"I do not dabble in drugs."

"I see you are a puritan! I suppose such a state of mind goes with your uncompromising character. I can assure you these little pills are utterly harmless. I've been taking them for years and look at me. They even put them in basic boxed chocolates. You know *Panzerschocolade*? A little perk that has given our tank operators and soldiers the advantage in battle. In fact it allowed us to blitzkrieg your country last year in a matter of days. There, I've let you in on a little secret of ours. It brings me back to what I was saying about your god. When you take a step back, you realize there's ultimately something a bit lame about Christ. Your Messiah could have done with a few of these German methamphetamines I can tell you. He would have lasted much longer on the cross. But seriously, this business of turning the other cheek is so limp-wristed, not to say downright masochistic. The Reich has no room for such self-harming weakness. And let's not forget that Christ was a Jew, and that is problematic, to say the least. All my men have vowed to renounce Christianity. The new Messiah is Adolf Hitler."

"Don't you think peace is better than war?"

"Oh, I couldn't agree more. It is simply that a little war has to be waged before we can achieve the *pax germanica*. But I have not summoned you to discuss religion or politics. I have something in mind that concerns you much more directly. Let us not beat about the bush. What would you say if I were to allow you to improve the human race?"

"The human race was made by God. It cannot be improved upon."

"I'm afraid, Fraulein, that I must disagree with you. Surely as a refined Christian you do not perceive a strict opposition between religion and science. You accept Darwin's findings?"

"I do."

"Then you must concede that even if God created man, he let him evolve over millennia."

"It may be so."

"Then if man evolved from monkeys, surely he can evolve a bit more."

"I suppose it's possible, but I fail to see how sequestering people can be considered an improvement of the human mind."

"I must say that although you are walking on a tightrope by voicing such statements I have a certain admiration for your frankness. Allow me to explain my train of thought. You may know—it is no secret—that I began my professional life as a most humble poultry farmer."

"I have heard it said."

"What you may not know is that I bred them with a most scientific method. That farm was in a sense my first laboratory. By selecting the sturdiest, most productive hens and breeding them with the strongest cocks in the pecking order I was able to achieve results you would hardly believe. You should have seen the size of the eggs I was able to bring forth."

He looked like such a proud, strutting golden hen in that moment, I felt like asking him if he himself had laid the best eggs. Something of this thought must have transpired in my demeanour, an unconscious smirk of derision perhaps. Had I bulged my cheeks and looked at his greasy jowls? I must have been betrayed by my own face. The Beast's geniality congealed as if a sudden ice age had descended on his features.

His face settled into a frozen, mask-like glare. Scouring my features as if in search of a trait to prey and feed on, he eyed me with a sort of vulture-like, carrion stillness. For a moment I wondered if I hadn't voiced my thought. Had he the power to read my mind? On a sound instinct no doubt, I lowered my gaze to the desk.

When I managed to raise my eyes again, his complexion hadn't changed. It was hard to feel anything but crippled and cramped under that withering stare. I couldn't move, as if he had crumpled me on the spot like a sheet of waste paper.

Gulping down despite my desire not to, I decided to attempt one of my most fetching smiles, to try to appeal to the Beast's sense of humour. There was after all no executioner, no attendees standing in judgment behind us. I have always found that power can be swayed at least a little when those who wield it know that they have not been humiliated publicly.

In the deafening silence that ensued, I was mildly tempted to follow up by imitating the crowing of a cockerel, but I didn't entertain the thought more than a fleeting second under the furnace of that gaze.

Inspired by my father's playfully irreverent example, I once tried out a little lowing in primary school, just after the teacher had let out what seemed to me at the time a rather unwarranted bellow because I had forgotten to do a spot of homework. Needless to say, my rendering of the bull didn't go down too well. I got a week of suspension for unseemly behaviour.

This was certainly one of those far graver fulcrums. Though I was hardly guilty of anything approaching gross moral turpitude, I could tell by the murderous look on Himmler's face that my very life hung in the balance. The impertinence of my expression had roused the slumbering beast in his breast. I could see it darting at me in each of his immoveable, death-dealing eyes.

But then, just as I was beginning to fear he was going to call in his guards, Himmler's features suddenly slipped into a rather ungainly, cracked sort of smile and he burst out into a menacing cackle.

"Ha! Herr Taubert told me you were a bit of a daredevil. I see you think you can trade on your beauty with utter impunity. Know that I will not tolerate abrasive behaviour within my own castle. Know that we tend to root out that kind of antisocial eccentricity. It creates too much disorder. Which brings me to my point. You see, I have decided to grant you the potential to generate even greater order within the Germanic empire. It is my enlightened belief that out of disorder, order can be formed. But let us not be too solemn either! There is in fact nothing I like better than to laugh at my own foibles. But let us also be serious. As I was saying, my little experiment on the farm showed me that genes can be improved within the space of but a single generation."

"You wish to groom me to lay eggs."

"I could make you queen hen of the castle. You could reign over Büren, Paderborn, the whole of North Rhine-Westphalia by my side."

"I have no wish to be here."

"I can secure the largest room for you, the plushest furnishings, the best food."

"I would still be cooped in a cell."

"I imagine that you would like freedom and safe passage back to your land."

"With my sister."

"You have a sister? *Meine Götter!* I am surprised that my men did not deposit her here. Where is this sister of yours? Why have I not been informed?"

"I was taken away from her and put in another truck before being driven here."

"That is a little irregular. I take it she looks like you?"

"Her hair is perhaps a shade or two darker."

"*Ach*, that could be the reason. I will make an inquiry. It shouldn't be too hard to find her whereabouts. Am I correct in surmising that she is younger?"

"She's five."

"*Ach, ja,* then she is either in a host family or in one of my Lebensborn institutions."

"Lebensborn?"

"It means Fountain of Life. A little hobby

of mine. I've started erecting a few maternity clinics, orphanages that provide placements for unwanted children with suitably Aryan traits."

"My sister was never unwanted."

"I'm sure she wasn't, but she was going to waste. In my Lebensborn institution she can have a much better life. Even in these hard times, she is no doubt receiving plentiful food and excellent care. But, ja, I understand, you wish to see your sister again. It can be arranged, I am sure."

"I need to know where she is."

"I will locate her precisely. In exchange, however, you will have to put your womb at the service of the Reich. A little trifle in exchange for your sister, I'm sure you'll agree. You should be honoured that nature has endowed you with such fabulously pure refined Germanic genes. Do you realize how high you scored on our scientific list of twenty-one criteria?"

"It is of little interest to me."

"You got full marks. *Nobody* ever does! It means you are the purest among pure Aryans. No one has eyes as blue as yours. Your irises are off the chart. Your hair is so blond it's almost white. You're as tall as a Nordic angel. You have the facial traits of a Madonna. Perhaps I should clarify a thing or two so that you can perceive how lucky you are. You see, there are three categories within the Aryan race. Pure Nordic, pure Phalian and Nordic-Phalian."

"I don't know what Phalian is."

"You happen to be housed in the Land of Westphalia. I am surprised that Frau Wippermann has not tutored you in these matters. Let me explain, then. According to Günther, [27] *Phalian* is a sub-type of the Aryan race, the lowest of the three most superior categories. You happen to be in the top one percent of Pure Nordic, the highest possible category. In this Westphalian stone castle, you are as it were the pearl encased in the uncouth grey shell of an oyster."

"But I'm a Slav."

"Pure deception! You don't even look a little bit Slavonic. Do you even realize what I am telling you?! I am saying that you are an Aryan changeling. You were placed in Polish lands like a genetic beacon by our ancestors, a beacon planted to guide us. You have glowed in the darkness, and now I have found you."

"This is nothing but mythology."

"What I'm saying is that you are the Holy Grail unto yourself. Do you even realize how beautiful you are?! Has your modesty made you entirely blind?!"

"I have no German ancestors. Not a shred of me is German."

---

[27] This is a reference to the Nazi race scientist F. K. Günther. His subdivision of the Caucasian population of Europe into three categories was widely adopted in Hitler's Nordicist ideology.

"*Ach*, that is what you think! The original
Aryan race spread as far as Asia, perhaps even
beyond! My Ahnenerbe scientists are at this very
moment measuring the features of Mongolian
warriors to chart the hidden map of the Aryan
diaspora. Of course the Aryan traits in those
far-flung areas are much diluted, tainted with
the blood of lesser races. My aim is to regen-
erate the Aryan blood pool, to cleanse it of its
filth and to reproduce the original Aryan bloodlines, before they were tainted and debased by
all this pointless interbreeding."

"You yourself do not have Aryan traits. Your
hair is brown."

Again, I saw his eyes bulge out, and yet this
time he seemed to find my impertinence a cause
for mirth.

"That is well observed, but what you do not
see is that I possess an Aryan brain!"

"An Aryan *brain?*"

"Like most Aryan people, some of my genes
have been degraded by mixing with inferior
races, but my brain. That is intact. The proof is
that I have been able to conceive of the master
plan. My organizational skills are most profi-
cient. Even in my sleep I am organizing mass
deportations. My dreams themselves possess
logic and realism. A precision and clarity you
wouldn't believe!"

"What is it that you would have me do?"

"I would not wish to force anything upon

you. As you have no doubt noticed, the names of the rooms in this castle are for the most part derived from Arthurian legend. I have also adopted a strict code of honour when it comes to interaction between the sexes. There is nothing I like more than courtly love."

"You will never get me to love anything here."

"Perhaps not, but perhaps in time you will come to appreciate what you are given. Perhaps in time you brain will become as Aryan as your body. That would be a feat indeed! So, to resume. I will never force you to mate with any lowly man. Your physical perfection is such that you deserve to be united with only the very best of my men. You know that to have the honour of joining the SS corps, my officers have to be able to prove Aryan ancestry back as far as 1750? SS officers are required to measure at least one metre and seventy centimetres. The political affiliation of their parents and even their grand-parents must be irreproachable! But above all, my officers must display human qualities and a strong sense of integrity and decency. I do not mean to pair you off with my rank and file officers, with those who just barely make the cut into the SS. I wish to have you bring forth a race of exceptional warriors, do you understand? Men of such fibre and mettle that they will be the exact replicas of the original race. Men with brainpower that is second to none. I mean you to bring forth a child sired by at least one of my highest ranking officers. One of the twelve most worthy that I have selected. One of my Twelve Knights."

"Do you really think that this castle is Camelot?"

"It is not the original Camelot of course. But when I have finished refurbishing this keep, it will be an improvement on the original. My eugenics plan involves greater improvements than you might think. As we speak, a trusted physician friend of mine is studying the genes of women who have borne twins.[28] He tells me he is on the cusp of discovering their secret. He just needs a little more time and opportunity, which is what I am to give him. When my wunderkind physician cracks the genetic code that allows women to bear twins, there will be no end to the number of Aryan children that the Reich will be able to bring forth. I have also made it clear to my officers that they need to disseminate their genes more widely. Marital monogamy no longer suffices at this stage. As a young man I thought it so important to remain a virgin before marriage. I used to avoid meeting women to maintain my virginity. But things have changed and time is now of the essence.

---

[28] This is probably a reference to physician Josef Mengele, who later went on in 1943 to become known as the Angel of Death at Auschwitz. He conducted a number of experiments on twins and the mothers of twins at that camp.

The Reich must be placed in front of your god's holy vows. My men must have countless mistresses. I have calculated that if the Reich is to last more than a thousand years, we need to increase the volume of the Germanic population to at least two hundred million."

"There will be no stopping the master race..."

"You've taken the words from my mouth. As I say, I wish to obtain your full consent. For courtly reasons, but also because it is well known that a woman must be in the best possible frame of mind to conceive the most outstanding offspring. Do you know that in the Renaissance it was believed that women should look at beautiful things to create handsome babies?"

"Then perhaps I should leave this room."

Thankfully, I said this looking straight at Wagner's skull rather than at Himmler's. He treated me to a lengthy scowl of a smile.

"You are such a funny creature. The beauty of an Aryan coupled to the sauciness of a Slav. But do remember what I have told you, Fraulein Kaufmann, I will only tolerate so much effrontery. Perhaps you would prefer me to have you sterilized instead and sent off to one of my camps? Consider what I have said, and I will look into the whereabouts of your sister. You may go back to your duties. I have no further need for you at this time."

12

I have seen him again. This morning, as I went to deliver water to the North Tower. When I entered the chamber behind the portal, there was no one to receive my buckets. There is usually at least one guard there to intercept me and bear the pails up.

I put the buckets down on the floorboards, thinking I would leave them there for the guard when he would reappear. But it occurred to me that carrying them up myself would provide an excellent excuse to find out what the prisoners were up to on the other two most mysterious upper floors.

I suppose I was also emboldened by my newly discovered function as an apparently indispensable breeder of Nazi progeny. I intend to make the most of my newfound status as the disempowered regal bee. Not that my position endows me with complete immunity, of course. Herr Himmler has made it abundantly clear that I am both essential and utterly dispensable material at the same time. I more than tested the elastic limit of what the Reichsführer is willing to hear from the likes of the potential queen consort. I saw my death loom large in his eyes when I taunted him. A stillness so intense I could visualize him having me melted to a blubbery mess on the floor of his mind.

Although we are under the strictest orders never to trespass in the upper floors of the Tower, I felt somehow emboldened by my potential new powers to attempt this breach of protocol.

And so I took to the stairs, my pails slopping water all over the first steps in a bout of almost uncontrollable trepidation.

The door on the first floor was locked.

The further I climbed, the more it felt like I was certain to be punished for this blatant infringement of this most stringent of rules.

When I got to the second floor, just under the battlements, the door was wide ajar. I was expecting to be stopped and shouted down at any moment by a posse of angry guards. Instead, the scene I came upon was one of utter calmness: three prisoners tranquilly trowelling a lather of cement onto a vast cylindrical block of light-green stone in the middle of the room, as if in preparation for the later insertion of a column.

All three drudges looked up when they heard me panting in the doorway. In response to their stares, I put down the pails as carefully

as I could and just stood there trying to catch
my breath, gazing into their eyes and then
around me at the room.

Before me stretched a vast round chamber
with a set of windows opening onto the outside
world in twelve different directions. In front
of each of the twelve windows in the room
were corresponding arched columns made of
what looked like pale green sandstone. A faint,
ethereal kind of pastel green hue. The floor was
still unfinished and there was one column that
still needed slotting in. A large, dust-covered, as
yet unfilled round crater gaped on the side of
the chamber.

I noticed the three prisoners were gawping
up at me with open mouths, as if they couldn't
believe what they were seeing, as if they hadn't
seen a woman in years. Two of them had black
triangles needled to their shirts. The third one
in the centre wore a purple one. I felt a flash of
recognition glimmer in his eyes. It was Prisoner
8!

"I have come to bring you water," I said in
even tones, not knowing what else to say.

They all looked at me as if they hadn't a clue
what I had just said.

Prisoner 8 rose slowly and somewhat
unsteadily to his feet. He took a few steps
towards me. Feeling a tad intimidated by the
silence that engulfed us, I picked up one of the
pails and handed it gingerly over to him. Our

hands touched briefly as our fingers fumbled with the metal handle of the pail. I could not help but notice there was a warm vitality to his hand. It sent a jolt of something pleasant through my flesh.

As soon as he had the bucket and I withdrew my hand, I felt a yearning to feel the touch of his skin again. Before I realized I was doing it, I had reached out to caress the back of his hand in a bid to renew the sensation it had given me.

Prisoner 8 stared at me uncomprehendingly, as if numbed and a little befuddled by the unwonted hardiness of my endeavour. He looked for all the world as if my tiny act of tenderness was something that he could hardly believe was still conceivable.

He managed to utter a tight-throated *"Vielen Danke"* in perfect German. Perhaps, I surmised, he was a native German after all.

I handed him the other pail and he took it with a slight quiver of his hand. No further words were spoken between us. He just stood there holding the pails, looking vaguely like a living statue, gazing into my eyes as if I were an allegory of Caritas and he had never beheld anything more startling. Not knowing what to say in the circumstance and feeling deeply embarrassed now by my forthrightness, I turned around and hurried down the stairwell without another word.

13

I am calling it my Faustian pact. Surely this is what Goethe himself would have called it—an agreement with the devil.

The choice is simply put: I can sell my sodden soul and body in exchange for my sister, or I can expend myself out here all alone in this dreary, drowsy castle, until my soul wears thin and disappears.

I suppose you could say that since my sister is my soul, I would be tricking the devil at his own game and thus exchanging my soul for my soul, and yet I cannot bring myself to concede such a thing without a struggle.

There must be some other way that does not involve horrendous self-defilement. The devil in the West wing made the pact sound light and airy, a thing of no real consequence, a mere trifle, and perhaps that is how I should envisage it. But the thought of bearing a Nazi child to foster the aims of the murderous, iniquitous Reich sends a chill to the very core of my being. It makes me shudder to think of Himmler or any of those officers' flesh inside my own and yet that is what is required of me if I am to save my sister.

The prospect of perpetuating the Reich through my own conscious doing is a thought more odious than any other I can conceive of. To carry their hateful, laughable ideology in innermost intimacy of my womb, to make it prosper and rankle in the midst of mankind like a mildew is a vision so loathsome and vile that I think I would prefer to end my life before the night is out.

But there seems no other way to save my sister from oblivion or a fate worse than death. The thought that she could forget who she is, that she might be assimilated and grow up to think she is one of them seems unspeakably wrong. Yet how am I to save her on my own? How would they let a lowly creature such as myself within a hundred yards of the gates of where she resides?

The devil has promised to locate my little Mila, to put his finger on her whereabouts. I must wait for him to give me at least that before I consent to render up my answer, before I forfeit my soul and seal the nasty pact. But I have at least one thing that the Beast does not know, one thing that he cannot control or undo.

It made me want to laugh with scorn when he described me as his Aryan pearl, as if I were the core, the cornerstone, the keystone in his great nonsense Nordic edifice. If the Beast only knew that part of me is Jewish, that he had slipped a little Jew into the seat of his empire, he would turn pale and quail.

If he knew that my mother was a Jewess, I imagine he would no doubt have me sent away and slaughtered. A Jew within their midst? A Jew in the heart of a Teutonic castle? A little Catholic Jew.

If I decide to give in to Himmler's wishes and do his base bidding, this little irremediable fact will stand as my only consolation. His perfect Nazi child will have at least one quart of Jewish blood. And, since Judaism is sternly matrilineal, passed on from mother to child according to the Talmudic laws of my ancestors, the infant will be strictly speaking entirely Jewish. A Jewish Nazi—the very thought would make the Beast rankle and rot from the inside.

My only regret is that he must never know it. If I keep this blossom of a secret to myself— and I have little choice in that if I wish to remain alive—I will never have the pleasure of seeing the colour curdle in Herr Heinrich Himmler's eyes.

If I am to give in to this moral madness then it will have to be on my own terms. As a supplemental perk, I will demand a free run of the castle compound and a pass to do as I see fit within the village. I have a plan that requires additional freedoms if it is to work at all.

The devil has given me until tomorrow to deliver up my decision. I wonder if he is not just giving me the illusion of choice so that he can indulge his courtly medieval fantasy of living in what he likes to call Montsalvat rather than Camelot—apparently Montsalvat is some kind of local German myth, an epic poem written by one of the Beast's Bavarian favourites, a writer I had never heard of called Wolfram von Eschenbach. His very name is enough to send gothic shivers down one's back. The book mostly sounds like a plagiarized version of Chrétien de Troyes's original *Perceval*. Anyway, Montsalvat is a sort of second sacred castle where the Holy Grail is supposed to be housed.

I do not know what will happen to me or my sister if I refuse the devil's offer. Perhaps I will just be left to stay on here indefinitely like my kindred spirit the Lady of Shalott, forever embroidering the emptiness, forever alone and bored to tears. Or else, I will be sent to Niederhagen the Netherworld or another larger work camp that makes you look like a walking skeleton. Some of those men are so thin you'd think a breeze would knock them over. More likely still, he will just force me to accomplish his aims and forget about the courtly niceties. I will be coerced into becoming a penned womb for the Reich and be given nothing at all in compensation.

14

I rendered up my decision to the devil this afternoon. He and Herr Taubert drove us all out in their Mercedes-Benz staff cars to a place called Externsteine. They managed to pack all the handmaids into two automobiles. Laughing his self-satisfied chuckle, the bespectacled devil referred to us as *stück*, as if we were just 'pieces' of something, not women.

I could hardly believe it when Frau Wippermann came to tell me that I would be allowed to tag along with the other handmaids for the first time. I have to say to do her justice, that she seemed almost pleased for me, though perhaps in writing this I am mistakenly granting her feelings of compassion which she is incapable of experiencing on my behalf. I imagine that by taking me out there, the devil was giving me a tempting foretaste of the freedoms I might enjoy if I submit to his eugenic programme.

Externsteine is a wonderful place, I'll grant them that. A real sight for sore eyes. And what a relief to leave the castle for the first time since I got here! Having been brought to this place in a windowless truck, I did not even know what the keep looked like from a distance.

There was a long printed white banner strung up between two poles at the entrance to the castle compound. I turned around in the vehicle to see what it said out of curiosity. I shouldn't have bothered, of course. I should have known it would be something inane, a disgusting political advertisement and a heart-breaking travesty of the truth: *Daß wir hier bauen erdanken wir dem Führer.* [29]

I turned around and looked at Anna. She didn't seem interested in discussing the banner, so I just closed my eyes and tried to savour the wafting summer breeze, the rush of wind into my face. I actually enjoyed every minute of the ride. Despite the circumstances, it was such a treat to get away, to be carted off like a piece of ballast into the hills.

The Extern Stones are a group of outcropping dolmen-like columns of rock that jut out of the hillocky terrain of Teutoberg forest. In his cheerfully nasal, unassuming voice, Herr Himmler explained that it was a sacred site frequented by the early Saxon inhabitants of the region who worshipped Irminsul, a pagan idol which Charlemagne later destroyed in the

---

[29] 'We are able to build here thanks to the Führer'.

course of the Saxon wars.

Irminsul, he expatiated, is by all accounts believed to have been a carved, pillar-like rock, now irrecoverable. It is thought by scholars that Irmin was in fact a by-word for Odin himself. Herr Himmler whispered the word Odin as if he was uttering the name of the Supreme Being.

As if this were not ludicrous enough, Himmler confided to us in hushed, drama-building tones that for the past three years he had been feeling in direct personal communion with the Norse All-Father. When I stared at him in amused disbelief, he felt prompted to add that he also believed himself to be the reincarnation of his namesake, the Saxon king Heinrich I, also known as 'the Fowler'. As the first king of the medieval German state, Heinrich the First was able to unite the Germanic tribes into a single kingdom. He has gone down in history as the monarch who went on to protect the unified Germanic nation from barbaric Eastern invaders.

Before a silent, wrapt assembly, Himmler solemnly stated that Arthur was in fact demonstrably a Teutonic knight. The drivel and dross that man is able to spout is enough to leave anyone dumbfounded in sheer disbelief. You get the feeling while listening to his palaver that anything is possible and that saying something is sufficient adduced evidence in itself. The worst part is that H is adamant he can prove his claims by dint of hard scientific proof!

He went on to talk about the sacredness of Wewelsburg castle, pointing out that the keep was historically used to house local witches as they awaited execution. Only the dungeon's three and a half metre thick walls were deemed sufficient to keep the witches from escaping. Of the hundred thousand witches eliminated in Germany, many of them saw their final hours at Wewelsburg—hearing that made me feel like one of them.

They were apparently executed in the triangular courtyard at the centre of the keep, after their confessions had been extracted in the castle courtroom.

We were walking around the outer circumference of the megaliths when Himmler beckoned me aside. The handmaids were skittish from all the witchcraft trials he had just been recounting and were prancing about. They kept looking back at us with muffled giggles and awe and sidelong envying glances until we turned into a megalithic passageway.

As soon as we were out of earshot, H encouraged me to offer up my resolution. Reluctantly, telling myself all the while I was making a grave mistake, I gave him my decision and in measured tones laid out my terms. He was delighted to hear my conditions, patting my shoulder and congratulating me for having proven myself to be amenable to reason. He granted all my requests unconditionally, as if they were but mere trifles easily lifted—he called them *eine Kleinigkeit* [30] which made me wonder if I should have asked for more.

I was relieved to hear that he was in no absolute hurry to begin the transaction and that he would of course see to it that Mila was located before our proceedings began. He told me he would telephone the head office of Lebensborn in Steinhöring, a village near his native Munich, to enquire. He just had a few other matters to attend to first in Paderborn before taking care of the matter.

It is difficult for me to believe that I am now to be authorized to come and go from the castle as I please. I have not yet even seen what the village of Wewelsburg looks like up close. I'm sure that discovering it will be as exciting as a journey to Paris. I am to be allowed to purchase victuals and prepare my own Polish food as I see fit.

I do hope they will have the ingredients I require. I cannot wait to cook up a good old pot of *gołąbki!!!* [31] I've been given leave to show Artus the cook how to prepare them for the whole castle including the prisoners working in the North Tower. I first suggested that it would

---

[30] A little thing, a bagatelle.
[31] A traditional Polish dish made of boiled cabbage leaves stuffed with a filling of minced pork or beef, chopped onions, rice or barley, served with an unctuous sauce.

be beneficial to prepare the dish for the entire prisoner community down in the tents at the foot of the hill, but Himmler demurred, telling me the one hundred workers had come from Sachsenhausen.

As members of a satellite camp, he claimed they should be fed in the same way as the inmates from the mother camp or this would otherwise lead to inequality and open a breach for unnecessary grousing. He even claimed that the prisoners' food was otherwise irreproachable. He did not want them to get used to easy living.

It was fascinating to watch him pour out more of the same kind of nonsense. He seemed to labour under the delusion that I had never seen the filthy, emaciated, bone-tired prisoners climbing up and down the hill on their way to the castle. He preached to me the wonders of the concentration camp lifestyle, as if the camps offered nothing but fitness enhancement and a life of spiritual contemplation.

Although the Beast concedes that the camps are hard, his view is that this severity is designed to foster a higher sense of values in the mind of the prisoners. It gives them a sense of purpose, he added, making them understand the true value of cleanliness. Prisoners also learn the meaning of things such as obedience, work, honesty, order, sobriety, sincerity, sacrifice and a strong sense of patriotism.

Again he called the prisoners *Schutzhäftlinge*[32] as if they were in need of some kind of protection from the German state.

I had so looked forward to bringing the food out to the tents and feeding the inmates a portion of wholesome Polish food—I've heard that some of the prisoners are Poles. It would have been such a treat for them especially. All I can hope is that prisoner 8 will be among those working in the castle when I go there.

In the late afternoon, a dozen black vehicles entered the portal mouth under my window, an endless succession of ominously dark automobiles. The castle seemed to be able to absorb them in endless quantities, as if the courtyard's belly could swallow any number of growling engines.

---

[32] In protective custody.

15

I woke up in the dead of night to the sound of what I initially thought was a gale moaning under the castle. I opened my eyes to realize it wasn't a rush of wind at all, but a kind of human groaning coming from inside the belly of the castle.

I got up and opened the window to my room, trying to locate the sound. I was able to ascertain with a degree of certainty that the deep rumbling, wailing chant seemed to be resonating from somewhere inside the North Tower, probably from somewhere inside its crypt. It was a cavernous, eerie sort of sound that seemed to emanate from deep inside the keep, or from the ground itself, as if the Earth itself were groaning. It was perhaps a dozen voices monotonously chanting low, undulating bass notes, more or less in unison. It put me in mind of the poor downcast women who had been incarcerated in the castle, lying in wait for their false trials and their very real immolations. Were these the after-sounds of their groans as they waited for death?

Chilled to the bone despite the summer heat of the night, I closed fast the window and snuck back into bed. I considered creeping out of my room in my nightgown to see if Anna was also awake. I was so stricken by what I had heard I felt like climbing into her bed for a little comfort and warmth, but I didn't know how she would take it. I used to love sleeping next to my Mila, her little body like a teddy bear to snuggle next to.

I stayed lying in bed for perhaps another hour until the ominous chanting finally ceased. It must have been around two o'clock in the morning.

When I asked the other handmaids at breakfast in the refectory if they had heard any strange chanting sounds in the middle of the night, they all looked at me blankly as if they hadn't the faintest clue what I was talking about. I could tell that some of them were also a bit peeved that I seemed to have been taken into Herr Heinrich Himmler's horrid confidence.

With eager, open eyes, Adolfa and Rozmonda inquired what the devil had told me. They were all dying to know what he had said and why he had taken me aside during the excursion to the Extern Stones.

I told them semi-truthfully that we had been discussing my sister's release from a Lebensborn facility, without mentioning the Faustian pact. Himmler has sworn me to secrecy and I do not in any case wish anything to be known about the contract I have sealed with the beastly leaser of the castle.

Availing of my new liberties after having changed the bed clothes in all the rooms of the West wing, I took myself off to converse with Artus the cook in the kitchens. Being in my daredevil risk mode, I told him that Herr Himmler himself had given me the right to prepare the day's menu.

Being an amenable sort of fellow, Artus voiced no objections. I said I would go into the village to acquire enough meat and cabbage to make the dish. Artus said he had enough rice for the filling, but I decided to buy a few extra kilos of the staple, just in case. The devil gave me enough Reichsmark bills to purchase quite a lot of foodstuff.

Artus told me where I could find the gardeners so I could ask them for a barrow to carry the groceries comfortably back to the castle.

In exalted spirits, I wheeled my swasti-ka-marked wheelbarrow through the town, getting a few stares along the way. The symbol on the barrow gave it the impact of an official staff vehicle, gaining me instant respect from both grocer and butcher alike. I bought up all the cabbage heads they had in the grocery along with half a dozen kilos of rice. With the rest, I acquired all the minced meat in the butcher's shop and had him mince another eight kilos of his best beef.

Back at the castle, I showed Artus how to cook the meat and the cabbage and prepare the gravy that went with it. He said that my *gołąbki* were similar to a German dish he knew, but that the sauce was quite different.

By one o'clock the *gołąbki* were ready to be served up. I asked Artus if I could get some help to carry a large potful of the dish up to the prisoners in the North Tower. Ever the gentleman, he kindly instructed one of his assistant cooks to do the heavy lifting so I didn't have to lug it up myself.

When the assistant and I entered the doorway on the second floor of the Tower, there were half a dozen striped prisoners sandpapering the green sandstone slabs, but prisoner 8 was nowhere to be seen.

I asked the two guards on duty where he was, but they looked at me blankly as if to say how should we know? Then one of them said he was probably down in *die Knippe*,[33] by which I think he meant the quarry.

I had asked Himmler for the same rights as the other handmaids, but the maids were not permitted to roam anywhere near the quarry or the prisoners' tents at the foot of the hill on which the castle is perched.

---

[33] From the low German verb *Knippen*, meaning to cut. The Wewelsburg quarry was locally known as 'the cut'.

I was so disappointed that prisoner 8 was not there to taste my *gołąbki* that I decided on the spot to go down and serve him in the quarry, or by the tents if he was there. Full of wiles and will, I told the cook's assistant that Herr Himmler had given the order to bring the canteen down to the quarry.

I said it with such authority in my voice that he didn't think to contradict me. I felt empowered by the pact I had sealed with the hound of hell. I very much doubted that the devil would bring me to task for such a trifle.

And so we headed straight down to the quarry, but found no sign of prisoner 8. A wave of angst washed over me when I found that he wasn't in or around the tents either. I was beginning to wonder if he hadn't unexpectedly died and been carted off to his grave before his time. He looked so thin and drawn that time I saw him in the Tower.

I asked one of the guards if he knew where prisoner 8 was and he said he was probably with a group of ten prisoners who had been tasked with wheelbarrowing off the last remains of the rubble at the foot of the castle.

So off we went back to the castle.

We came across the group of rubble removers busily piling on bits of scattered plaster onto three swastika-marked wooden wheelbarrows. I spotted prisoner 8's figure trying to push an over-heavy barrow up the incline. He was moving so slowly it looked like one of those slow motion Musger films everyone gets so excited by.

We waved him over. He put the barrow down and walked stonily towards us and I announced to the guards as he approached that lunch was going to be served on the spot. When I said the word gołąbki, I noticed two of the prisoners repeat the word to each other as if they knew it. I guessed from their famished eyes that they were Polish, but I didn't want to lessen my authority over the guards by speaking to them directly in our tongue.

The guards were already casting sceptical sidelong glances at the steaming pot I had just revealed in front of them. By the look in their eyes, the last time they'd received an order from a woman was when their mother last told them to give themselves a lick and a promise in front of the mirror.

I asked Hans, the assistant cook, to pull the lid off the pot. Opening the bag I had been carrying with the authorized spoons, the ladle and the aluminium plates, I started dishing out generous helpings of *gołąbki* bathed in lavish portions of sauce.

Having more or less ignored him up to then, I was eager to hand the first plateful to prisoner 8. He seemed astounded by what I was doing, almost aghast, as if I had just walked out of some enchanted dream. He kept staring at the

food as if meatball manna had just fallen from
heaven into his plate. The dumbfounded look
in his eyes gave way as soon as he tasted the
first morsel and his blistered lips cracked into a
smile.

16

I was however mistaken in my estimation
that the wretched *Reichsführer* wouldn't mind
a little bending of the rules. I discovered to
my detriment that the Beast was a real stickler
when it came to orders. I should have known he
would have no breaking or bending of anything
that pertained to the prisoners. I should have
known as much after his palaver concerning the
prisoners' well-being.

I was summoned to Himmler's dungeon-like
office that very evening, just before dinner.

To say he looked disgruntled is an understatement, though I suspect there was some
other problem that was fuelling his wintry
discontent. The moment I set foot inside the
office, he ordered me to stand to still, as if I was
some kind of biddable soldier.

"It has come to my attention through Herr
Taubert that you have been creating havoc in
the castle."

"I take it you are referring to my distribution
of *gołąbki*."

"Go-womb-key? What is this go-womb-key you speak of? Please have recourse to a civilized language that everyone can fathom."

"*Gołąbki* is the dish I mentioned. It was agreed at our last meeting when I gave you my conditions that I would be allowed to prepare it."

"Forgive me if I am mistaken but I don't think anything was said about distributing such a dish to all and sundry! It has been reported to me that you availed of my name to suggest that this dish of yours should be freely shared amongst the prisoners. I thought I had made it clear that the inmates at the bottom of the hill are not to be treated to such things as tea and sympathy. They are being kept here to teach them the value of hard work and honest living. They are part of a *Schutzhaftlager*, not a holiday resort!"

"Although the food you give them may be irreproachable as you put it, they are obviously getting far too little of it."

"And you are the judge of this?"

In the silence that ensued, I decided to quarry the Beast for further information.

"One doesn't need to be a physician to see they are severely undernourished. Can I be so bold as to ask how much meat they receive?"

"Not being the lowly cook or the Burghauptmann of this place, I have left such matters to the discretion of Herr Taubert. As far as I can tell, he is doing an excellent job. The North Tower is almost completed and I'm pretty sure we will have the third floor in operation by the middle of next year."

"Are you not worried that your labour force will collapse and die before the job is done?"

"What happens to the *lumpenproletariat* and foreigners is of no concern to me at this point. If the enemy dies, then that is good for Germany."

"Some of these prisoners are German."

"Those that are German are reprobates, criminals, the scum and dregs of society. They have forfeited their right to be German. By their misconduct they have weakened the master race. It is my belief that those who deserve to live will survive. My camps are designed as a Darwinian test, you see. A form of natural selection. A way of separating the chaff from the wheat. Humanity will thank me for this one day. I will make mankind a tougher, far more resistant breed."

"Tougher and less human."

"Oh, human! Why be human when we can be gods?"

"Inhuman gods with no sense of decency."

"Utter nonsense! You do not know! With my own eyes, I have seen hundreds of men shot in the head. I have had foreign brain matter spattered onto my clothes. As I am a sensitive man, it made me vomit on the spot. But do you know what? To have seen corpses piled up and to have remained decent in our own eyes, that has made us tough. That has ennobled us."

"Do you not even see that what you are saying is a complete contradiction."

"I am no barbarian, believe me. I am not bloodthirsty. I would prefer not to have to dispose of anyone at all. I just have a very high sense of duty and purpose. I owe this to the Führer. I owe it to mankind! Do you know that Germany is the only nation that is humane towards animals? We are also humane towards human animals. If they are strong enough to survive, then we will let them. If they deserve to die, they will be killed humanely, using the most modern scientific methods. I can assure you I act altruistically, in the name of a great cause. History can be triggered you see, and that is what we are doing."

"I fail to understand what you are saying."

"That is because you do not have an Aryan mind! But I know your thoughts can be improved so that your mind will be in tune with your looks. I am a strong believer in the virtues of education. Come, come, I do not wish us to fall out. We have come to such a satisfactory arrangement. Here, have a Pervitin. I think we need to clear our minds."

Popping a pill into his open mouth as if it was no more than a peanut, he handed me the small metallic box. I hesitated but then put my fingers in the box. Raking out a small handful of the little white pills, I slipped them into my pocket before he, or even I, could see how many I had withdrawn.

"By Odin, you're changing already! Make sure you don't take too many at the same time. Not more than two or three in the same day. They are not quite as harmless as bonbons."

"I promise to use them judiciously."

"Can I ask what triggered this sudden change of attitude?"

"I want the child that I am to conceive to be strong."

"Why how fantastic! Your mind is improving already. The pills will see to it that the infant is born healthy and hale. It had never occurred to me that Pervitin could be a useful additive to infant milk. Why, you have given me a wonderful idea! I will put it to my scientists, to see what they think. I'm delighted you have got used to the idea of carrying an utterly pure Nordic child. The German tragedy is that so many modern women these days no longer wish to be mothers. Young women are so strong-willed, so ... naughty. Especially in Berlin. All they want to do is go out to parties and drink and have fun, without a thought for the morrow. No sense of moral purpose. You know the birth rate right now is lower than it has been in hundreds of years. It makes me worry a lot."

"Perhaps I will conceive of twins. My mother was a twin. These kinds of things often hop a generation."

"*Ach*... how utterly splendid! You will be as a goddess of bounty within our midst. People will refer to you as the Venus of Wewelsburg."

"I meant to ask you about my sister."

"Ah, yes, your sister. I'm afraid I have not yet had the time to attend this matter. Remind me the next time we meet, in case I forget. I will be back in about a month or two, if everything goes well. The Führer wishes me to put a little order in the Netherlands. The Dutch are proving most wily and recalcitrant—I suppose it proves the Aryan blood is abundant in their veins. I will have to threaten them with deportation if they persist."

17

The idea of Himmler's departure, coupled to my newfound freedoms, has left me elated — which of course is most irrational, as he will eventually return to claim his pound of baby flesh.

And yet I feel relieved, as if a lid has been lifted off the sky above me. For an extortionist, the Beast has proved most courteous and tactful so far. Although he was at liberty to do so under the terms of our contract, he has not groped or fondled me like booty. In fact, he has not made the slightest pass at me.

I suppose he senses the extent of my reluctance — nay, my revulsion — at the thought of any contact whatsoever between us. Although he has mentioned my being impregnated by one of his highest officers, it is abundantly clear that he is himself the ugly, brilliant officer he has in mind for the first helping. Perhaps his goal is to have me passed around from officer to officer like a jug of wine until everyone is served.

The most I have had to endure so far is my fingers held a little longer than I cared for when he made me shake hands at the end of our last conversation. The Beast stretched forth his hand in such a ceremonious way I felt it best to comply to make up for what he sees as my terrible misconduct.

I wish to stay in the Beast's good books so that I may extend my rights when the time comes. Given my apparent capitulation to Pervitin, he probably thinks that my body can be won over too, given a little Nazi tenderness and time. The Beast possesses an almost endearing degree of naivety. Though he is at least twice my age, it sometimes feels as if I am the more experienced person.

The limousines departed today, a few hours before the devil took off in his roaring black Benz. I suspect the visitors were at the source of the nocturnal chanting the other night. I cannot see what else it could have been. I do not believe in witchcraft or revenants and I doubt I ever will.

The castle is quiet now, coloured faintly by the moon in gentle streaks of cloudy yellow. A nightingale is singing its heart out amongst the trees, as if all is well with the world. And yet, I have to say I am at peace once more, at least for the time being. My plan is safe, for now. Given a little luck, who knows, it might even come to fruition.

I am still untouched, still undefiled. And

that is something for which to be thankful.

If I am to foil my captor's designs, I must at
all costs find a way to encounter prisoner 8. I
wish I knew his name. It seems so demeaning
to refer to him as a serial number. I should have
asked him the last time I saw him, but it would
have seemed too forward in front of the guards.
They already looked so suspicious. Besides, I
keep forgetting that he is not allowed to speak. I
can no longer just walk up to the inmates again
for all to see without causing another local
storm in a teacup.

The smallest things have acquired such
momentous consequences. I suppose that is a
good definition of absurdity: when the inconse-
quential trifles of everyday life carry so much
more weight than they should.

I have to find a way to isolate 8, to meet him
unaccompanied, alone in some room where we
cannot be found. But where can this happen?
Where can it take place? The prisoners are never
alone, never secluded, even in their beds. I am
not even sure if they have any privacy at the
privy, or if they even have a proper latrine at all
come to think of it.

Perhaps Herr Klamm can assist me in this
matter. He will at least be able to have me
take a discreet peek at the prison register,
if it happens to be kept in Taubert's office.
If he is willing to help a little more without
also demanding something in exchange for

services rendered. I will go and see him directly tomorrow morning the moment my drudgery is done.

18

I should have foreseen that Klamm would be unresponsive, even sulky, when I went to see him, as if I hadn't paid my dues, as if he felt somehow neglected. His sooty eyebrows were all clenched, his wattle wobbled to and fro as he muttered, busying himself about his office.

When I asked him if there was anything the matter, he got hot and bothered and didn't want to speak his mind.

Pressured by my insistence, he turned his head, waddled the wattles a little and looked straight at my breast, giving a little nod in its direction as if he expected to be suckled or something of that nature.

I feigned wide-eyed surprise and hostility until he lowered his eyes. It is abundantly clear that I cannot hope to be granted any kindness in this heathen place without paying for it directly in the flesh.

The thought of Klamm's stubby hands or even his caterpillar-black eyebrows anywhere near my bare bosom is more than I can take without feeling queasy.

Ignoring his overture, I decided to ford ahead and ask him for any information he might possess concerning the prisoners, but he just raised his eyes to my breasts again like a brow-beaten spaniel, as if I had just granted him almost limitless authorization to ogle.

Eventually, having lingered long enough on the protuberances of my chest, he raised a hopeful stare to my face. He must have read the revulsion and outrage inscribed there as he just turned his head away and muttered something about being busy. Perhaps I could come back another day and he might be more inclined to offer his *services*. He stated this in a clipped, matter-of-fact tone, emphasizing the word services, meaning that every favour should come at a fixed fleshy price.

I turned swiftly away, uttering a mild mutter of displeasure to indicate how displeased I was with that kind of situation. I heard him jiggle his keys behind me, as if he was baiting me with his powers, but I kept my course, forcing myself not to turn around. He obviously thinks that I might barter my breasts for a trifle like a key. I wondered for a moment if the Beast had let him know about our arrangement, giving him ideas of his own. Thankfully, I don't need Klamm enough to stoop to his level. I determined to get hold of the information on my own terms.

Just a moment ago, I was on the point of
tucking my diary under the mattress for the
night when I heard a knock on the door of my
bedroom. No one ever does that at this late
hour. I stood there, frozen, like a rabbit caught
in the headlights of an oncoming Benz. Fearing
Klamm's importunate intrusion, I figured it
might more probably be Anna or one of the
handmaids, perhaps Olga or Klara, but no.

In a quick panic, I slipped the diary under
the mattress and made a dash for the door.
There, to my relief, was Hans, the cook's
assistant, grinning as broadly as ever. His hands
were loaded with a tray that held a cup of what
looked like steaming hot chocolate and a plate
with a few slices of cake.

I thought for an instant that he might be
trying to seduce me. Hans is pretty handsome
and he's my age, but for some unaccountable
reason that eludes me entirely I find myself
drawn so much more strongly to prisoner 8,
a captive slave, both older and careworn and
bedraggled by labour.

Hans put the tray down on my table and
explained that he was under strict orders to
bring me the same fare every evening. Would
this hour be convenient? When I questioned
him further, he said that Herr Himmler had
instructed Artus to arrange this.

Thus am I to be fatted, to be stuffed like a
Christmas goose, for the eminence of the Reich.

As soon as Hans was out the door, toting the empty tray under his arm, I slipped the hot chocolate and fruitcake away under the bed so that I would not be tempted to taste them.

19

I have not come across him in four days. An eternity it seems. I think about him all the time, of course, which is rather odd, all things considered, especially considering that I don't know the faintest thing about him. And yet constantly I try to imagine what he is doing, what he is thinking, what he is undergoing at the hands of swinish guards and other human devils.

He has such an aura... And the look in his eyes—I have never seen anything like it.

I suppose he is working inside the North Tower again as I have not seen him in the team of prisoners working to rake and tidy up what remains of the plaster rubble at the foot of the castle. I have not dared to go down to the quarry to risk being deprived of my dearly-won freedoms.

I imagine they take it in shifts, so the workers are able to labour more efficiently without succumbing to exhaustion. Presumably, those in charge are savvy enough to have them get the job done before they expire. I sometimes worry that prisoner 8 may die of accumulated fatigue, worn out by his exacting tasks.

Why I have taken such a shine to him is still beyond my comprehension. He looks so careworn and frail. Only a few seem to have any solid flesh left on their frames.

All this waiting around and criss-crossing the compound in the hope of encountering prisoner 8 has made me resourceful. I came upon a way of making our paths intersect again early this morning as I was hanging out the washing with the blathering handmaids.

As soon as my morning chores were completed, I went for a discreet walk in the grove and managed to dig up an egg-shaped stone to hide it in one of the deep pockets of my dress. I'm pretty certain no one saw me stoop to prize it out behind the thick cover of foliage.

Back in my room, I made sure the other handmaids were well out of earshot. A few of them were still preparing the tables for lunch. I figured the others were no doubt either idling in their rooms, polishing the banisters or embarked on various other futile errands.

Hefting the egg stone, I was suddenly put in mind of Robert Campin's *Triptych of the Annunciation* with its miniaturized Christ child flying through the window without shattering the pane, a symbol of the incarnation achieved while leaving Mary's virginity intact. How strange the kind of thoughts you have at the oddest of moments! I suppose the image was triggered in my mind by what was to follow next.

Aiming the stone carefully at the window, I fired it clean through the pane. I was so terribly afraid I might miss and send the projectile against the stone façade, making it rebound and clatter onto the bridge, but it struck home exactly with just the faintest sound of cracking glass.

I had hoped the window wouldn't shatter completely. You could see the exact shape of the oval stone where it had struck cleanly through the glass. The rest of the pane splintered, but remained tightly fixed to the frame.

As soon as I was able to bring my heartbeat down to an acceptable degree of pounding, I set my features as seriously as I could in the circumstances and took myself out to Herr Taubert's office.

A short-statured, small-featured bourgeois of a man in his early sixties, Taubert is generally genial. He's the kind of individual who was granted his cushy job thanks to the cordiality of his manner and a distinct willingness to please. The kind of debonair gentleman who smiles at the prisoners and even shakes their hands on occasion—at least the German ones—as if they're just casual farm-labourers come to put in a day of jolly labour at the fairy palace.

I see him as the smiling face of Nazism, though I have overheard the handmaids saying that Hermann Goring is supposed to be a real barrel of laughs and that even Adolf Hitler loves to entertain his guests with jovial imitations. Hamlet would have been astounded, had he lived in these troubled times. That one may smile and smile and be a villain has never been so perfectly illustrated.

With his copycat toothbrush moustache crouching under his nose like a growth of underbrush, Taubert is a cross between Hitler and a good-humoured dwarf. Being in his company feels like enacting *Snow White and the Seven Nazis.* He's so tiny and ludicrous-looking, I have trouble keeping the condescension out of my voice when I address him.

I was pretty sure he wouldn't kick up a fuss when I said I needed help fixing a window. When he asked what had happened, I said perhaps one of the crows had pitted itself against the window by mistake. He gave me a questioning squiggle of his eyebrow, so I said I initially thought it might have been Adolfa who was a bit jealous of my recent interaction with the Reichsführer, but that I did not want to incriminate her unjustly.

Although Adolfa has been spiteful towards me since the first day I got here, I instantly regretted having framed her inadvertently for something she didn't do. I should have thought about the consequences of that more before blurting it out.

To my dismay, Herr Taubert said he would have a word with Adolfa. I quickly dissuaded him from doing that, stating that Adolfa would dislike me even more if she thought I had complained about her. I assured him I would speak with her in confidence and smooth over our differences. Ever the cheerful leprechaun, Herr Taubert seemed satisfied with that conclusion and I thought nothing more of it.

When I asked if I could borrow one of the prisoners to fix the window, though, the idea seemed to trouble him. He pointed out that Herr Klamm being the warden, it was Herr Klamm's decision to make.

And so I agreed to take up the issue with Herr Klamm. T seemed content I had bowed so swiftly to his wishes. If there is one thing I have learned about Nazis, it's that they like things to be clear-cut—they have no time for the Polish virtues of *combinovać*. [34]

Though reluctant to have anything to do with Klamka after our little fall-out, I nevertheless repaired to his office to get the matter

---

[34] Translator's note: the Polish verb '*combinovać*' has a number of varying significations, though it generally implies that things are done in an expedient, pragmatic manner, regardless of convention and/or legal considerations. This kind of behaviour emerged in Poland in response to Nazi and later Soviet occupation.

sorted. I felt pretty certain I could count on Klamka's inherent laziness and reluctance to withdraw his sooty poundage from his comfy armchair.

Having honey-packaged the idea of borrowing a prisoner for the repairing of my window, I had no trouble convincing him that it was the best way to proceed.

As I intuited, sulky, sullen Klamm didn't even bother to come and see the broken window. When I asked if I could be given a signed document to show the guards, he just waved me off, saying that there were some old window panes left in one of the gardener's sheds and that I could just ask them for one of those. It appears the old window frames were replaced just a year before I came.

20

Feeling leaden at the prospect of having to face off the guards again, I steeled myself for confrontation. They were their usual brash, disgruntled selves, but it went rather well in the event.

Having safely achieved my retrieval, I let prisoner 8 follow in tow to suggest to those who might be watching that I considered him a mere tool, nothing more.

As soon as we reached my chamber, I closed the door, put a finger to my lips, and turned the key in the lock. I had made sure the coast was clear to avoid being spied on by other hand-maids. As soon as prisoner 8 was safely stowed inside my cache, I made him sit down on the mattress. The poor man looked a little bewildered, half afraid of what I might do or say.

Crouching down, I slid out the now lukewarm chocolate-flavoured drink and the plate of fruitcake from under the bed, and settled them both on his knees between his hands.

It's hard to describe the look that came over prisoner 8's face. He stared down at the plate of sweetmeats as if the crown jewels had just been deposited onto his lap. He sat there looking listless in his striped pyjamas, as if he couldn't come to grips with the festive abundance now residing in state on his knees.

I had been expecting him to wolf it all down in great slurps and gulps, but he didn't even look ravenous, just numb and exhausted and mostly in shock in front of the feast. He looked like someone whose muscles and appetite have forsaken him, as if he no longer had the strength or even the will to convey the food into his mouth.

"Take it," I said, "you can have it. It's yours."

I thought he might be embarrassed, but I think he was just thunderstruck by the unexpected refinement, the lavish display of the food so unexpectedly at his disposal. He raised his soulful eyes towards me then, as if asking for permission although I had just granted it.

I placed my fingers on the trembling hand grasping the cup. I tried my best to soothe him, but I couldn't calm his tremors. Moving in towards him, the stale smell of his unwashed skin and clothes floated about him like the thick tang of too much human perfume.

Gently, taking it slowly, I helped him to raise the lip of the cup to his mouth. Not anticipating anything, he unstuck his chapped whitened mouth only at the last second, once the cup had already reached him. Even parting his lips seemed like an effort. He took a short, breathless sip of the summer-warmed liquid. The cup only stayed in place beneath his lips because I was there to firmly support it.

With my help, he swallowed a lengthier mouthful and paused for an instant to savour the taste. A little of his strength restored, he pulled my hand towards his mouth so that he could pour the whole cup down his gullet in long steady gulps, his stubble-peppered Adam's apple bobbing like a buoy under the surface of his skin.

Even after he finished drinking, he kept the cup raised above his lip, letting the last droplets trickle down the china into his half-open mouth.

Finally, he lowered the cup and I took it from his quaking hands. Despite the awkwardness of the interaction, the touch of his fingers was somehow delectable. He had long, bony, veined fingers, but they possessed such delicate quivering elegance.

I felt a sudden impulse to caress them once again as I had done that time in the North Tower. Again, he gazed at me as if I were the kindest person on Earth. Just staring into his pain-shot eyes was enough to make me want to cry. I could feel the crying liquid stinging my eyes.

I repressed the impetus to weep though and instead placed his hand on the fruitcake. Time was of the essence, if my plan was to succeed:

"I will go and fetch the window pane we are to mend", I said. "As soon as you've finished, lie down on my bed and take a rest. I promise I'll be up as quickly as I can. If anyone comes in here, let them know I ordered you to lie because you had a moment of weakness."

He just nodded slightly and watched me leave the room.

Having wrested a pane of glass from a stack of them piled in the tool shed, I asked the handymen if I could avail of any putty they might have in store. It was half-expecting a negative answer, but one of them said *ein Moment* and walked away. He came back with a small aluminium box and said *kitt*.[35] I thanked him profusely and dashed away with as much grace as I could.

When I got back to my room, prisoner 8 was still there lying on my bed. He still stank to high heaven, but strange to say it didn't bother me. In fact, I felt vaguely stirred by the strong human smell exuded by his flesh. It hung about him like a kind of aura, the essence of his being.

Only then, as I contemplated his feeble body lying there did I think to ask his name.

---

[35] Putty.

He seemed to recall it, as if it were some long forgotten word.

"Ernst", he said finally, "... Meier."

I told him my original Polish name and then holding his gaze all the while, with steely determination and a pounding heart, I started to divest.

Ernst Meier's mahogany eyes widened perceptibly and took on a hue of sombre alarm, as if I had just taken the lid off a hive of furiously buzzing bees. Perhaps it was my imagination getting the better of me, but it seemed to me in that moment that his irises had suddenly started to pool and deepen into fathomless wells of darkness.

I undid the last few buttons of my attire and unclasped my girdle. Hesitating for an instant in the grip of some embarrassment, I let my smock slip off my shoulders to a moulted pile on the floor.

Ernst Meier seemed to have stopped breathing, his body as stock still as the furniture. The awe-smitten look on his face made me fear his heart would fail him. I removed my slip and pulled down the somewhat drab yarn crepe bloomer that comes with each handmaid's uniform. When I undid the hooks on my cone-cupped brassiere, I heard a sharp intake of breath, as if he had suddenly resumed the act of inhaling after a deep dive under water.

Holding his stare all the while, I removed my stockings as becomingly as I could, despite the deep embarrassment of revealing myself in so forthright and immodest a fashion to an almost complete stranger.

I had decided to doff every inch of clothing so that I would appear in all my nudity, a vista of warmly inviting carnation. At least I hoped it would appear that way. I needed him to be as alert as he could be in his condition. His body seemed so ravished and enfeebled I figured he would have trouble making it function correctly.

He just lay there supine on the bed, looking crushed and breathless, as if a stampede of battle horses had just ridden rough-shod right over his chest. Trampled and lifeless, his breathing started to come in short, laboured spurts. I worried for a moment that he might be unable to enact his part in my plan.

But when I began to pull off his pants, I saw that everything would go well. His rod of flesh leaped out like a fresh pale rigid eel. Pulling it towards me, I parted my legs and straddled him, gently inserting the long lever of flesh as smoothly as I could between my legs.

When I lowered my body onto his stake, pushing it into me as far as it would go, I expected it to hurt much more than it did in the event. I imagine my riding sessions in Cracow served to take the edge off the pain—a secret which all teenage horse riding girls know.

It was sweeter than I thought it would be, though a little strange, somewhat invasive and uncomfortable, at least to begin with. If I am to be frank, it was a more like inserting a 300 gram suppository in the wrong orifice than anything else, but there was something pleasant about it too that seemed to get better as I rode onwards. Rising and falling upon him, my body seemed to know instinctively what to do and what not to do—not that it was very complicated, but I sort of knew how to go about it and quickly got the hang of riding him. It helped infinitely that his eyes were so wondrous and lustrous to gaze into.

I felt mesmerized, utterly absorbed by his face, as if it were an infinitely more intriguing, denser, more fathomless version of my own. Peering into the deep darkened water standing in his eyes was very much like letting myself sink into a pool of unctuous lapping liquid.

But then came a few awkward moments.

The cylinder of flesh bucking inside my loins somehow slipped out of a sudden like an importunate salmon leaping out into the air.

In the awkwardness that ensued I couldn't help feeling that I was stuffing an ungainly Liverwurst sausage back into its casing, and then when I thought the discomfiting moment was past us it just slithered out again of its own accord for no apparent reason, slippery and frisky as a oblong bar of soap and impossible to come to grips with or reinsert.

It was actually quite hilarious and I very much wanted to laugh, but Ernst Meier looked stricken and utterly in earnest about it, as if he was long past experiencing mirth. So I pressed the bubbling merriment back into my chest until it popped and vanished.

It all worked out pretty well in the end— though I imagine I have God to thank for that.

His bucking flesh disgorged a kind of white frogspawn-like substance that trickled down my leg a little way as I got to my feet. I gathered the clinging baby seed in my hand and pushed it back up inside me with my fingertips, up as far as it would go. I have heard it said that that is what one must do to enhance one's chances of conception.

Despite a throbbing pain in my belly for hours after this occurred, I think I will certainly try it all again if given the chance. Blended in with the ache and the discomfort, there was a sort of yearning in my loins that seemed to throb indefinitely with a new pulse. If possible, I will attempt this over and over. In fact, I will do it a hundred times over if I can. I know for a fact that it can take several attempts to conceive of a child. I need to make our encounter happen again before I am passed on as a chattel to be fertilised by Himmler's and his henchmen's hateful seed.

When he shouted his hoarse groan, I had to put my hand over Ernst Meier's mouth lest anyone hear us.

The most pleasant part came after, really, when his moaning subsided and I lay down under his shoulder next to the swell and fall of his chest.

We must have lain there for several minutes, just panting and sweating and I suppose you might say almost happy. A sort of carnal glow came over me, but there was more to it than aimless bliss. It was perfectly irrational, but I suddenly felt almost free, almost as if I had broken out of the castle and shucked its stony, straight-laced tegument. It was kind of strange and droll and an absurd, heart-warmingly sweet sensation.

I took hold of Ernst Meier's steadily shrinking seed dispenser. I had rather always thought that it would be fun to see what it felt like to hold one, to take a look at one up close. All I can say was that it made me feel somewhat like Alice in her Wonderland: the large, firmly-packed, family-size Liverwurst of only a few seconds earlier shrivelled to the size of a mere cocktail sausage in my hand. The blood seemed to have rushed out of it, as if it was much needed elsewhere in the other parts of his poor ravaged body.

21

As soon as we found the strength to pull ourselves off the bed, we rose to our unsteady legs and vested, wrapping ourselves in our own thoughts. Having pulled up his pyjama-like britches, Ernst Meier watched me don each item of clothing out of the corner of his eye, as if I was putting on gorgeous vestments for some kind of ceremony. It looked like he had trouble taking his eyes off me.

When he was finally clothed, he sat on the side of the bed, bemused and bewildered, his lips slightly ajar as if he was in awe of me and what I had just accomplished like a kind of mesmeric trick.

I flashed a bashful smile and looked at him in inanely proud amusement. His weathered face broke into an almost painful, fatigued and weary sort of grin. I made him close those unbearably deep murky eyes and kissed each of his lids when they were lowered. He stood there passively, blind and expectant. I whispered in his ear that we had to make haste or we would surely come to a bad end.

Fully dressed and looking more or less presentable again, we set to fixing the broken window pane. Removing the splintered shards one by one around the hole, we lay them down carefully in a jutting-cutting pile on the table.

I took it upon myself to hold the new panel of glass against the frame without a stir—out of the three I had carried up, the one I had selected proved to be a perfect fit. I had not thought that the pane would need to be held in place with nails. It seemed surprising to think of nails in conjunction with glass.

Mercifully, Ernst Meier said it did not matter that I had not thought to obtain a new set of nails, that we could use the old nails still embedded in the woodwork of the frame.

Ernst plied the old nails into place around the pane of glass. Easing out the dollop of putty the factotum had given me, he slacked it a little with the tip of the trowel I had found in the tool shed and started smearing it onto the edges of the pane to cement it smoothly into place.

Within a matter of minutes, almost magically, the window was reinstalled. I ran my finger over the putty a little to see if it was firm yet. It had a moist, dough-like feel to it that much resembled the texture of sweat-sticky flesh.

Ushering Ernst Meier through the safest backstairs passageways out of the keep, I accompanied him to the foot of the castle and let him hurry as best he could in his enfeebled state down the rest of the way to the quarry where he was expected.

Having no tasks to accomplish, I decided to walk out into the grove of mismatched trees—the only part of this place that had some unarranged spontaneity to it. Everything about the castle was so spick and span, so unrelentingly ordered and regulated. The haphazardly planted copse felt like the only place I wanted to be after the bewildering unreality of what had taken place in my bedroom.

Did I feel more of a woman? In all frankness, I did not feel any more womanly, not any more than when I chewed our daily share of oatmeal and honey for breakfast. And yet, it felt somewhat supernatural, as if something beyond the realm of the possible had transpired. I could not stop myself from thinking that something even more magical might be preparing to unfold in the nether darkness of my womb. A tiny human being the size of an ant's feelers perhaps or even more diminutive still, growing imperceptibly as the hours flicked by.

Weaving my way through the ash and the elm trees, the anarchically juxtaposed larches and the birches felt so natural, so fluid and unimpeded. I was saturated with a kind of drunkenness after what had happened between this unknown yet fondly held man and me. I let myself wobble unsteadily from tree to tree, swinging from my hand on each trunk. I was so carefree that I did not care how disorderly my gait looked now that I was out of view.

I came to rest my back against an oak tree towards the bottom of the slope within a stone's throw of the wall. I stood there gasping, barely holding myself up. I put my arms around my chest and cradled my breasts for a while.

There was still a sort of gentle throbbing in the silky silver sliver of my loins, as if my nether region had developed a pulse of its own. Sensing that something lay unfinished, I chafed and rubbed at the ache between my legs until the same sort of groan that I had heard in Ernst's throat leapt out of mine. After the intense surge of that, my body simply dissolved into a sort of limpness. There was nothing I could do but collapse with well-being in a near fainting fit at the foot of the tree.

Unable to move an inch to save myself had there been danger, I lay there for quite a while looking up at the leaf-dappled sky. The breeze was playing the tree harps and when I closed my eyes it sounded like I was far out at sea.

Releasing myself from my surroundings, I imagined myself afloat on a raft, drifting at random on the open ocean's ceaseless toss and flow. How strange, I thought, that only a stone's throw from this moment of utter freedom lies nothing but bondage and human evil. In the

Grimm brothers' fairy tales I was read as a child, wickedness tended to lurk in the depths of the forest; it is quite the opposite here.

And yet of course, I was experiencing only the illusion of freedom. I was no more at liberty to wander away than the trees were. All they could aspire to was to have their hair mussed by the much freer fingers of the wind.

The extent of my captivity was about to be brought home to me. I opened my eyes and took myself off to roam the outer reaches of the wood, heading in the direction of the perimeter wall. In my lofty elation I had got it into my head that I could scale the piled stones of the rampart and make a run for my life.

But no sooner had I caught full unimpeded sight of the stony façade than I came up face to face with two growling wolf dogs a few dozen metres to my left along the wall.

Somehow, they must have sensed my approach, despite the blowing of the wind, despite the stormy rustling of the leaves. I was already anticipating the bite of their slavering teeth on my calves, the sinking burn of their black-spattered snouts insinuating their breath into the wounds of my body.

With this horrific thought in mind, I backed away and started running erratically back towards the castle as fast as I could through the thicket.

The two slavering mastiffs were almost upon

me when I heard a slightly more human Nazi bark to my right. Two guards were warding the animals off. They had no doubt recognized my handmaid's uniform and figured me for one of their own.

Eying me suspiciously, they nevertheless reigned in their dogs. Out of breath and danger, I thanked them briefly, lowered my head in a show of submission and took myself off to the East Wing without uttering another word.

22

As I was hanging out the sheets to dry this morning, vaguely looking up at a waste of clouds, a squadron of airplanes crossed my line of vision. They were arranged in the sky in a swastika pattern, one behind the other in perfect alignment, as if pilots these days had nothing better to do than decorate the heavens with that unholy horror.

I hate that sign so much it makes my flesh crawl, and yet outlined against the sky, it caught my attention. For the space of an instant, I found the airborne ugliness almost compelling. In the crushing boredom of the castle rigmarole, it came as an almost pleasant diversion. I caught myself enjoying it for a split second only to feel utter disgust at myself in the next.

The other handmaids were in ecstasy when they spotted the planes. I heard their gasps of pleasure and surprise from behind various bits of laundry, as if they had never seen any bird more wondrous than that patterned battalion of flying morons.

The handmaids have been in good spirits all

week because a squadron of young SS officers have returned, apparently not the same ones they knew. A new batch, the others must have died in the war but nobody mentions that kind of negative detail. It's deemed contrary to the spirit of the war effort.

The new recruits have been practicing their moves out on the streets. You can hear them marching to and fro through the town to the mechanical sound of the commanding officer shouting *Links! froh, links! froh, links! froh* in a horsey-looking pants pinched out to a ludicrous extent at the thighs.

Unless I'm mistaken, that means "left! happy, left! happy"... What a staggeringly ridiculous thing to say in any language. Spectacularly stupid.

And then they started singing their awful songs again to the sound of a beating drum. *Hitlerleute* and *Panzerlied* and *Deutschland Erwache*: basically my three pet hates.[36] Although these songs probably contain the most soul-sapping lyrics ever composed, I caught several of the handmaids humming or singing along as we went about our tasks. I suppose I can't blame them for gleaning a little fake happiness where they can find it. To them it is just Deutschland doing what it ought to, given

---

[36] *Hitler's People*, *Tank Song* and *Germany Awake*.

its military strength—what a throwback to the nineteenth century.

The air is getting chillier again. It's sad to think that the summer is already over with September already upon us. I suppose I have had my summer fling and should not complain, but it was so brief and unrepeated that I cannot help but feel more than a little frustrated that we have not been able to secure another secret assignation.

I have not been able to catch sight of Ernst since our bedroom tryst. I have not seen my gentle prisoner for weeks and am so soul-sick because of this that even writing has seemed pointless.

I have tried to espy him in various places around the castle, but he is nowhere to be seen. I have gone several times to the North Tower in search of him. The prisoners are still assembling in various parts of it, still rubbing away at the pale powdery green sandstone as if they are polishing their own graves. But Ernst is never with them and no one seems to know what has become of him. He is never in the quarry either and the workers have deserted the foot of the castle now that the rubble has been cleared away.

I've been half sick with worry. I fear that somebody (but who?) witnessed something of our exchange and that he has been transferred to some other unholy place. I keep wondering if they have beaten him to death or punished him in some awful way. Could someone possibly have heard or spied on us? Surely, if that had been the case, I too no doubt would have been punished by now—unless my new status protects me.

I dare not go down to the tents to inquire after prisoner 8 so directly and yet I will have to if I am to find out sooner or later what has become of my man. I am so worried that he has been chastised in retribution for my wily plan.

I fret that something terrible has happened to his health, some sharp and sudden decline. I imagine him sick, with a fever, or worse. I have had to drink the hot chocolate delivered to my room every night now for many days. I have no way of keeping the victuals fresh enough to hold for days, but some of the cakes I have been able to store at the top of the wardrobe wrapped up in a sheet.

The other day I caught a rat nibbling away at one of the pieces I had left under the bed, unprotected on the plate. It did not see me, so I had the privilege of watching it eat in the privacy of its hideout. I saw it eat the whole slice. It was actually endearing to observe the tiny jaws chew with such gusto and speed. It kept looking at me furtively, almost trust-ingly, with its beady brown eyes. I felt more kinship with the rat than with any of the other handmaids, Anna included.

23

I keep examining my belly, deluding myself into thinking I can detect a bulge, but ultimately it seems flat as ever. In fact, my midriff is more than strictly flat. It actually curves slightly inwards, especially when I stretch. But it may still be that I am pregnant. I have not bled as usual. These things have a way of showing up late in the day. My mother used to tell me that you could hardly tell at all that she was with child even six months into her first pregnancy.

At other times I worry that if I am carrying Ernst's child, it will be visible too soon. Himmler would no doubt smell a rat. It is not that I relish the thought of being pimped out to his high-ranking SS death's heads, but if Himmler realizes I have foiled or marred his plans he will in all likelihood make sure I am snuffed out like a candle.

Waiting for Himmler is like waiting for Bluebeard to return, and yet I need him to come back rather sooner than later. I find myself stuck in the position of almost hoping he will come back so that I can use him as a smokescreen to cover up the betrayal lying in my belly.

It crosses my mind more and more often now that I may never see Ernst again. If his seed is infertile or if he has been executed or transferred elsewhere, my heart will be broken and my operation will have been a failure.

This morning I decided I would need a little extra help from God. It being Sunday, I thought it might be an idea to let the Supreme Being weigh in a little on behalf of prisoner 8. After all, He has let so much misfortune come my way, I thought perhaps He might listen to my entreaties, especially if I pray for Mila and Ernst and give myself up as a sacrifice.

But then it occurred to me how sacrilegious it was to think such heathen thoughts. All this talk of human sacrifices in pagan times has started to rub off on me. I am becoming like these heathens.

I went to see Herr Taubert again to ask if he would allow me to venture out as far as Paderborn cathedral. I added I also needed a long overdue haircut. He looked at my hair as if it was no more than the tail of a horse that required no trimming if it was to be operational as a fly swatting appendage.

I did not want to go to mass in Wewelsburg for fear of having to stand beside Frau Wippermann and the other handmaids in a pew. The SS officers are no longer allowed to attend mass as Himmler has asked them to renounce

Christianity, but there is some tolerance for the lesser orders of my rank. Himmler gave me to understand that he was a devout church-goer in his youth. In concession to his youthful ideals, he allows some of the staff to indulge in the weakness of traditional mass.

It occurred to me that it would be a pleasant change to experience the lofty elevation of architecture, in a place where prayers can be granted some ascension. I had heard Paderborn mentioned so many times I was a little bit eager to see it for myself.

I had been ready to walk the twenty kilometres from here to the city had that been necessary, but Herr Taubert—always the affable Nazi gentleman—actually offered to drive me to Paderborn in his blood-red Mercedes-Benz 770. He referred to the car as Der Großer Mercedes as if it was some kind of penile Big Bertha with wheels.

Out on the roads, he kept trying to impress me, speeding inconsiderately on the narrowest of dusty country paths, showing me how close he could get to 170 kilometres an hour on the gauge. I have never experienced such horrendous speed in all my life and felt quite giddy, not to say queasy, after he dropped me off.

As we slowed down at the entrance to Paderborn, Herr Taubert even confided in hushed tones that he missed going to mass,

but that it was his duty as an SS officer to lead
by example. He added that Hitler claimed
that Christianity as a religion was only fit for
slaves, the limp-wristed and weak at heart,
and that it was in his view the systematic culti-
vation of human failure. According to Taubert,
Hitler believes that one is either a German or a
Christian. One cannot be both.

Herr T was keen to impress me with his
savviness in all matters. In teacher-like tones,
he informed me that 'Mercedes' is actually
a Spanish name that means 'Mercy'. When I
pointed out that that was a strange brand name
for an anti-Christian party to use, he said it
was named after the car constructor's daughter,
Mercedes Jellinek. When I pointed out that
Jellinek sounded like an Eastern European
name, he chuckled smugly and rectified my
ignorance, claiming with a self-satisfied smirk
that Jellinek was authentically Austrian.[37]

The Cathedral was elegant enough I
suppose, though hardly awe-inspiring.
Taubert told me the entrance was nicknamed
Paradiesportal.[38] I was also advised to keep an

---

[37] Jellinek is in fact a slight Germanization of the Czech
name Jelinek. Ironically, Emil Jellinek, the industrialist who
patented the Mercedes-Benz brand, was the son of a rabbi
called Adolf Jellinek. To compound this irony, let it be noted
that Adolf Hitler himself was thus driven in a car manufactured by a namesake of Jewish ancestry.
[38] Means Paradise Portal.

eye open for what he called the *Doppelmadonna* hanging from the ceiling of the nave. When I asked what a double Madonna was, he just closed his eyes into two Cheshire cat pleats and smiled enigmatically.

I was crestfallen when I crossed into the edifice to find that the inside of the cathedral was decked out in the nastiest of Nazi bunting. The supporting columns were all hung with giant gaudy black, red and white swastika-laden banners and a golden idol of a sculpted eagle balancing atop the shaft. I was horrified to discover that there was even a dismal swastika flag attached to Christ's loincloth on the cross.

I had to close my eyes to concentrate on the Lord's message, but my prayers felt more or less hollow. As soon as the proceedings of the mass came to a close, I wandered around the town in search of a hairdresser. There was only one in the whole city as far as I could tell, and it seemed to be more of a barber's shop than anything else.

I should have been wary when I saw the look of bored disdain in the bald barber's eye. It should have alerted me to his character. As soon as he heard my foreign accent, he closed up even further.

His brisk, wiry manner seemed harmless enough to begin with. He threw a white linen towel over my chest and tied it firmly around my neck as if tying a noose. In a curt, clipped, gruff voice, he asked me how I wanted my hair cut, so I said short, but not too short. Around shoulder-length would be good.

He took out his scissors then and started snipping away at my head as if I was a female version of Samson and he had to be quick before I woke up to what he was doing. A steady whirr of insect wings it seemed to me at first until he started going at like some crazed, uncontrollable machine. He kept wetting my hair with what looked like a wall-painting brush (as if he was daubing the inside of a church with Lutheran whitewash) and then stab-combing my scalp as if he was tilling a clunky, cloddy plot of land.

And then it was back to clack-clack-clacking with the scissors again. It felt like my head had turned into a typewriter and he was typing out one document after another. It put me in mind of the documents I had perused in Herr Taubert's office. Each clacking assault on my head seemed to finish off one of those death-dealing documents.

~~Father~~ ------------ ~~Mother~~ ---------- ~~Sister~~ ------- ---- ~~Grandmoth~~er ----------- ~~Grandfather~~.

Each clack, click, cluck and chitter of the scissors seemed in the process of finishing something or someone off.

When he had finished painfully raking my scalp with the comb one last time, he took out a drier brush and started flinging the hair clippings off my shoulders and my chest with brisk nervy flicks of the wrist, as if I were some kind of cruddy interior ornament to be roughly dusted off.

When Herr Taubert picked me up three hours later in the city square in front of the cathedral, I felt utterly downcast. I cannot fathom that the Vatican has not yet found the courage to excommunicate Hitler, Himmler, Heydrich and all the rest of them. How many more kidnappings and killings will it take before my church chooses to do what needs to be done?

24

The eager beaver *Burgmeiden*[39] were all excited this morning at the inauguration of the castle museum. A rather tiny, insignificant affair on the whole, but I was keen enough to examine the local dinosaur bones on display.

There were a few daunting human skull items too. One of the skulls under a square glass box was labelled 'Jew'. Although the skulls looked similar to me, the curator who guided us through the exhibits was adamant that the shape of the bone revealed the inferiority of that particular boxed and labelled skull. He made us notice tiny variations on the surface of the bone that seemed either laughably minute or virtually imperceptible to me. I'm no scientist of course, but the idea that miniscule declivities and protuberances in the skull might have an impact on the quality of the brain matter beneath the bone seems utterly risible.

The *Burgmeiden*, however, were completely

---

39 'The castle maidens'.

enthralled by what the curator was saying and kept simpering flirtatiously. The poor things could hardly keep their hands off him, they're so frustrated by the fact that the new batch of officers spend all their time training and marching and ambushing each other around the town.

In fairness, I understand their frustration, being myself unusually edgy at the thought that my man may be in grave danger or already deceased. I was so worked up this morning I had to leave the museum to calm myself down in the castle wood — I call it a wood, but it is more of a mere coppice. Yet the crunch and crackle of the brushwood under my feet never fails to take the edge off my fears. And the cool breath of the copse is always a relief, even now that the sometimes hellish summer temperatures have abated.

But after seeing all those bones and skulls at the museum, the usually reassuring snapping of the twigs under my feet served to conjure up macabre images of a giant in a peaked cap stalking over the bones of the dead on a battlefield. It reminded me of the battle that is supposed to have taken place not far from here in the ninth century in Teutoburg Forest.

Himmler and Taubert visibly stiffen with pride whenever the forest is mentioned, just because the Romans are thought to have been defeated there. Himmler has told us that he chose Wewelsburg castle as his headquarters in honour of this very battle. It is his firm belief that another war will be enacted here, an armed struggle that will once again prove Germany's heroic might. Grandiloquently, he calls it the 'Battle between East and West'.

For one so infatuated by the wonders of the West, he's bizarrely obsessed by the East and has told me more than once that Germany's destiny lies there. He seems to love the idea that I come from a country that happens to be situated eastwards, as if my captivity is living proof of Germany's geographical future.

Crunching through the coppice under-growth, it came to me. The resolution that I have to seek out my prisoner and deliver him from bondage—that is, if he is still alive and has not been removed to some other place of detention.

I will seek him out no matter what happens. I will find some pretext. I cannot stand this waiting any longer. I'll ask Taubert to grant me permission to go down to the encampments and I'll fish my man out if he's there. I must come upon some half-truth that will allow me to make this venture seem natural. If Taubert does not permit it, I will go down there and do it anyway. I have nothing to lose.

25

Pulling and pressing in opposite ways, pushing hard with my feet and tugging as much as I could with my hands, I managed to dislocate the cross stretcher of my Nazified art deco chair. It took me over half an hour of crazed tugging and stamping, but I finally prevailed over the piece of massively recalcitrant furniture. The damn thing was built to last as long as the Reich, but I finally managed to pull one end of the stretcher out, though my whole body was dog-tired and in a sticky sweat from the exertion. But the chair was nicely rickety after that.

I was afraid Herr Taubert would get suspicious about a fresh complaint coming from me, but it was my only hope in the circumstances.

I reached T's office door to find it locked. He was apparently out, so I had to make do with Klamm's lackadaisical signature.

K is happy to get anything bothersome out of his way without having to lift as much as a finger. The man is so unutterably lazy he's reluctant to draw out enough energy from his flab to sign a dispensation. He didn't even lift a single sooty eyebrow (presumably for fear it might tire the muscles of his forehead) when I claimed that one of the castle's virtually indestructible oaken chairs had come undone. I tried to look as solemn as I could, but a smirk of satisfaction kept wanting to steal up the side of my lips as I lodged the complaint.

With K's flaccid initials monogrammed onto the document, I made my way out of the castle and down the grassy hill to the tents in the valley. My mouth was as parched as the bottom of a sandpit in summer with sheer apprehension. I was terrified lest they inform me that prisoner 8 had died or been transferred to some faraway camp. I was in any case convinced that trouble had befallen him on my account.

I couldn't help imagining the worst. Something bad had occurred, that much was sure. The most likely scenario that kept uncoiling its horror was that one of the guards had caught a glimmer of happiness creep over Ernst's face and had punished him for exhibiting joy, breaking his foot or his jaw with the butt of a rifle for indulging a few seconds of mirth.

Or else they had shot him and he was already dead and buried in an unmarked declivity at the foot of the castle.

I was all out of breath by the time I reached

the encampment. There wasn't a single prisoner or guard to be seen. They were all presumably up in various parts of the castle, eternally sandpapering the soft powdery sandstone, or else down in the quarry hewing out more slabs for bedraggled Sisyphean labourers to shoulder up the hill to the Tower.

In a spasm of apprehension, I lifted the flaps of each tent. Every single one was empty. There wasn't a trace of Ernst to be found.

Then at the back, slightly set aside from the others, I caught sight of a tent that had a weather-beaten red cross painted on the canvas.

I rushed over and stuck my head in the opening and there, to my utter joy and relief, lying asleep on a stretcher, was Ernst Meier, love of my life.

I write it so because it appeared to me on the spur of the moment. I felt such a surge of emotion at the sight of his limp body lying there in the penumbra of the tent that it occurred to me suddenly that what I was experiencing could only be called love.

I have never felt anything more intensely and still I cannot understand why I feel it. I suppose I am stuck in a place and time that fosters such inexplicably urgent, instant, intense attachments. In other circumstances, I would probably not have felt so much so soon and promptly. But perhaps I am needlessly rationalizing again—another of my flaws.

Having been inundated by such relief, I felt a short pang of fear when I saw him not moving. I figured that if he was dead though they would surely have disposed of him quickly and not left him to convalesce in the infirmary.

Sitting on the side of the stretcher as delicately as possible, I put my hand on his chest. He didn't wake, despite the physical pressure I exerted, so I placed my hand on his cheek and wiped the sweat from his brow with my sleeve. His face twitched and he was instantly awake, looking up into my eyes, jolting and then juddering in alarm.

I hushed him instantly, putting a finger to my lips and my other hand on his chest to ease the shuddering. The look of gratitude that stole over his features as he calmed was one of the most moving things I have seen. His face was furrowed with a kind of underlying pain. You could sense something was wrong with his body.

When I asked him what the matter was, he gestured down to his left foot.

In my rush, I had not noticed the tip of a thickly bandaged limb sticking out from under the blanket.

"What have they *done* to you?" I shriek-whispered in an angry rush of syllables, almost forgetting where I was. I was certain they had shattered his foot with the butt of a rifle.

"Nothing", he answered faintly. "They

have done nothing. It is an infection. The camp physician called it a phlegmon."

"A phlegmon?"

"It's ... an acute inflammation of the flesh. It has deteriorated into an abscess."

"But when did this happen?"

"The swelling had already started the last time I saw you. I don't know if you noticed. It was already quite red. The day after you invited me to your room, it started to flare up uncontrollably."

"Does the physician know what caused it?"

"He says that I should have come to him earlier about it, that I should not have left it unexamined, untreated. It came from a sore I had in my sole. The old, over-cramped shoes I was given when I came here. They were at least two sizes too small. My only relief now is that I don't have to wear those damned shoes."

"And you say that it isn't their fault?"

"I suppose it is ... indirectly."

"Of course it damn well is! All of this is their fault. Can I take a look at your foot?"

"Well ... If you like ... I must warn you, though. It isn't pretty."

"I have a few small skills in nursing. I did a training course in first aid back in Cracow, before I left school."

"How nice to have you as a nurse."

His face cracked into that lovely smile of his and I felt like weeping, but I gulped it all down.

I undid a few layers of what I though was a heavily bandaged foot only to discover that his foot was so swollen up it looked monstrous. My stomach almost heaved when I saw that the sore in his sole was alive with what turned out to be tiny maggots. I almost vomited on the spot, but somehow managed not to.

"My God, do you know that the wound is unclean?"

"I haven't seen it, but I know it's got maggots. The physician takes them out every day."

"Has he given you medicine?"

"He says there's a new treatment in the making. It's called penicillin."

"What does it do?"

"It's a miracle drug that can apparently fight off bacterial infections like mine. The physician says he is sorry, but there is none of the treatment available for prisoners because that kind of medicine is in very short supply. The little they possess of it is reserved for wounded German soldiers on the fronts."

"How can they say that?"

"I've heard them utter worse things."

"You could die if you don't get proper medication."

"The physician says he'll amputate before there's any danger to my life."

"So you're willing to lose a leg as part of the war effort?"

"Don't take it that way. The physician is a good person. He's doing what he can. He's limited by rules and regulations."

"Perhaps then I will have a say in the matter."

"Please, Ewa, I don't want you to get into trouble."

"I won't get into trouble. I've signed a kind of pact with them. They'll give me what we need. I'll make sure they do."

26

Once I had alleviated Ernst's pain a little, he managed to pour forth his seed again into my womb. I had to ride him with the utmost care so as not to budge his leg. As soon as I was able to slip my bloomer back on, I stole out of the tent and slinked back to the castle, unheeded, as far as I could see.

I headed straight for Klamm's office, but of course the lazy lecher gave me to understand that the wellbeing of prisoners was not in his remit, and no concern of his in any case.

Frau Wippermann gave me more or less the same answer (minus the leer). She didn't look pleased at all that I was consorting with what she called "criminals and the dregs of society". It was not becoming in a decent girl of my age. When I told her about the phlegmon and the maggots in prisoner 8's leg, she looked at me as if I were some kind of slimy monster dredged out of the bowels of the earth.

So I bided my time, waiting for Herr Taubert to return. With my evening duties accomplished, I betook myself off to the window to watch over the bridge in the hope of accosting the *Bürgermeister* as soon as he entered the yard.

To my dismay, he didn't return until late in the night. I was so befuddled by lack of sleep that by the time I blundered down the staircase to intercept him, he had already retired to his chambers for the night. When I knocked on his door, no one answered.

I went to see him first thing the next day as soon as I had laid breakfast with the other handmaids. With his usual lofty, debonair condescension, the Burgomaster seemed not entirely unsympathetic. Positioning his head to the side at a falsely compassionate angle, he contemplated me with a sort of distant, dreamy, slightly amused expression, as if he couldn't quite figure me out, as if I was a child trying to save an ailing frog, a wounded hedgehog on the road.

When I insisted that prisoner 8 needed urgent attention and penicillin, he looked at me as if he had never heard of the word. I told him it was a new experimental drug invented by the British. The word 'British' seemed to displease him. His mouth twisted into an expression of distaste, as though I had just used improper language, a kind of crass curse word that did not behove an employee of my standing.

Taubert told me that my best hope was to wait until Herr Himmler's return. As Reichsführer-SS, he would be in a position to

know if there was any wonder medicine in
the works, but Taubert looked dubious about
the idea of any drug working miracles of any
sort. As a proud rationalist, he said he couldn't
accredit such hearsay.

Although I managed to secure continued
visiting rights to the encampment, I left his
study feeling thoroughly crestfallen. Taubert
had no idea when Himmler would be back and
the antibacterial medicine seemed so far out of
reach. Taubert doubted very much if it was to be
come by in the Wewelsburg village pharmacy. If
the drug was still in the experimental phase as
the physician had suggested, it might not even
be used in the dispensary in Paderborn. Taubert
had suggested that perhaps one of the dispen-
saries in Dortmund and Hanover might have it
in stock, but he had urgent matters to attend to
and was not available to bring me out that far
afield. It all seemed so hopeless, and I had no
idea when Himmler would return to these parts.

The next day, I insisted on meeting with
the camp physician, Herr Doktor Kolb, a
soft-spoken kindly man with gentle green eyes.
I warmed to him immediately. You can tell from
the way he looks at you that he has a good soul,
despite being German. He has the same round
wiry spectacles as Himmler, but on his sensitive
face they don't look sinister in the least.

I can tell Dr Kolb is quite worried about
the state of Ernst's foot. He showed me how to

clean the wound and remove the new maggots
and larvae with tweezers without increasing the
pain caused by foraging inside the open, suppu-
rating flesh.

I pulled out another three miniscule maggots
like soft writhing bullets and put them down
to squirm and squiggle in a dish. They increase
and fatten so quickly it seems quite impossible,
almost by spontaneous generation. Within a few
hours, they grow fat on Ernst's tender flesh.

Kolb is a steadfast believer in the germ
theory of disease and infection. After every
cleaning of the wound, he douses the infected
swollen parts of Ernst's foot with a chemical he
calls carbolic acid. He says that unfortunately
the acid works best to offset infection before it
gets a chance to set in. He's worried that Ernst's
inflammation is too far gone for the ointment
to function effectively. Ernst's resistance is
low because he hasn't been receiving sufficient
nourishment.

I know that Herr Kolb is a good man,
because he has given Ernst extra food he has
brought with him from home. As in zoos where
it is forbidden to feed the animals, it is strictly
forbidden to lend the prisoners extra sustenance. He has thus taken a risk that may not be
that slight. He added that my fruitcake would
certainly help to keep Ernst alive.

Last night, oh irony of ironies, I found
myself praying again for Herr Bluebeard to

return with news of Mila and rapid access to the
drug.

27

I have been tending Ernst's wound for several weeks now. Herr Doktor Kolb claims that his state has stabilized a little, but I fail to see any perceptible improvement in his condition. He lies there inertly on the camp stretcher all day, enfeebled and sweating. His temperature has now dropped to around 38°3 Celsius, which I suppose is something. Doctor Kolb finds it very encouraging. I sometimes think he is just trying to give me hope where there is little. He says that the oncoming cold weather of early winter will help us in the fight against germs—though unfortunately not against Germans.

My belly is still as flat as a pancake. Perhaps I'm infertile, in which case King Heinrich's Aryan fantasies will go unfulfilled in his queen bee. But of course it could well be that Ernst's baby seed has grown inoperative due to ill health. He is no longer able to regain consciousness sufficiently to pour forth any more of that jelly. I hope the fruitcake will give him back a little vim in time.

Still no sign of Horrid Himmler. Taubert has confided in me that Hitler expects Himmler to run all the occupied territories virtually single-handedly. He has him constantly rushed off his feet, leaving him no time at all to visit his beloved Arthurian court.

The latest news is that Himmler is still busy in the Low Countries organizing deportations left, right and centre to my fatherland. He is apparently constantly on the move, having the reputation of being everywhere at the same time.

Taubert says that King Heinrich (which is what he affectionately calls Himmler)[40] is in the process of transferring the entire Dutch population to southern Poland where newly vacated land is being redistributed to farmers manifesting approved Aryan traits. I was horrified to hear that my homeland was once again being torn apart and land-grabbed, but I kept my indignation to myself in the interests of advancing my urgent request for the miracle medicine.

According to Doctor Kolb, the drug Ernst requires is based on a lowly piece of mould that

---

[40] As indicated earlier in the text, Himmler was so convinced that he was the reincarnation of the Saxon king Henry the Fowler that many of his closest collaborators, including his mistress Hedwig Potthast, called him König Heinrich.

occurs naturally in certain conditions. When I suggested that we grow a piece of this fungus in the wound, Kolb laughed off the idea. He says that penicillin has to be chemically synthetized in a laboratory if it is to be effective. A purified compound of the bacterial mould has to be cultivated in optimal conditions and he has neither the wherewithal nor the equipment to conduct such delicate experiments. He says you cannot just grow penicillin in a wound and hope for the best.

I have been thinking much about my parents of late. I keep wondering if Himmler might allow me to receive their letters, if they are still of this world of course. I have already put several letters to them in the village letterbox, but have received no replies. I do not even know if my house as it was still stands at this time.

I also harbour fears that letters destined for Poland and elsewhere may be censored or destroyed at the post office after they have been collected by the postman. I have no way of knowing what happens to my missives once they are deposited in the box. Perhaps with enough wheedling, ratty Reichsheini might be induced to allow my correspondence safe passage to Poland.

I sometimes also fear that the letters reach their destination but that there is no one left at home to receive them. Generally, I imagine my

home not only childless and emptied of joy,
but entirely empty of people. At other times,
I imagine our house burnt to the ground or
occupied by Dutch or German settlers or by a
few Polish squatters. I cannot get my father's
last screams out of my head. My greatest fear
is that my parents have been deported to some
detention camp or shot dead in the street like
pestilent vermin.

28

Yesterday was pleasant. Having dispatched my duties in the morning stint of scouring the canteen's hollowware before lunch, I was able to spend most of the afternoon by Ernst's side. He was feeling a little better and managed to find the strength to tell me a few stories about his life before the arrival of what he secretly calls 'the black plague'.

He sees the Nazi calamity as a test of mankind's mettle, a kind of scourge which God has allowed—Ernst is very *Old Testament*. When in a jocular state of mind, he even refers to himself as Job and Jonah. When I get a little over-concerned about his well-being, he calls me his ministering whale.

I asked him why he is a Jehovah's Witness rather than just Christian. He said that his parents were both Witnesses and that as a result he grew up in their faith.

It's a religion that puzzles me. I cannot for the life of me fathom some of its tenets. The oddest of their beliefs I find is that they are adamant Christ wasn't crucified, but tied to a stake, as if it really matters either way.

In Ernst's eyes, the cross shouldn't be used as a symbol as it is fundamentally an instrument of torture and thus ultimately more horrific than the swastika itself. He glances at the little wooden cross necklace I bought in Paderborn with visible distaste.

Ernst doesn't believe in hell either: he says that the notion was invented by Satan to frighten people into submission. He believes that our soul dies along with our body and that only a few of us are finally to be resurrected. Those who are chosen by God for resurrection on Judgement Day will only be brought back as God's memory of us, and thus not in our current shape.

I questioned him about why he calls God 'Jehovah' and he said that it is simply their way of pronouncing Yahve, which apparently is the Hebrew for 'I am'.

Witnesses are also against blood transfusions. Ernst says that receiving someone else's blood would be like modifying one's essence. When I said that that sounded a bit like the land and blood ideology that we were taught at the castle in the early weeks of my stay, he went all quiet and thoughtful and I had the greatest difficulty in making him smile again. I suppose it wasn't very kind of me to make the comparison, but I'm so utterly sick and tired of all this Nazi palaver of good and bad blood.

When I asked Ernst if he felt German, he said not any longer. He claimed that in any case, he and his family had always placed their religious beliefs above the notion of nationhood and that that was ultimately why Hitler had such a tooth to pick with Witnesses.

Shortly after the Nazi party rose to power, Jehovah's Witnesses right across Europe were ordered by Hitler to renounce their religion or face retribution and incarceration from the state. Before that injunction, there was a little persecution here and there, but nothing too severe. Although their houses and shops weren't pillaged and defaced with exactly the same amount of venom, Jehovah's Witnesses were generally considered by most German people as Jews in disguise. Ernst told me that as a young man he was often called Jew in the street.

The Nazi party considered that printing the word 'Jehovah' in the Witness Bible meant that Witnesses were referring to the Torah. If you were caught carrying the Witness Bible in the street in the late thirties you could be chased out of the area or reported to the police.

He told me that another thing that still gets a lot of Witnesses into trouble here is their refusal to execute the Nazi salute. According to Ernst, only God should be hailed because He alone is hallowed. Hailing someone like Hitler is doubly blasphemous in his view because it involves reverently saluting a deeply flawed human being who happens to be the closest thing to Lucifer on Earth. I must say I agree with him wholeheartedly on that count and others.

Ernst himself was incarcerated because he refused to renounce his religion and declined to serve in the armed forces when he was called upon to do so. His religion forbids any involvement in armed conflict as it contravenes Christ's fundamental message of peace. It made me think that Ernst and his kind are the only real Christians left. It occurred to me on the spur of the moment that Ernst's religion was the only Christian branch that didn't bow down before Hitler and grew ashamed of my own limp-wristed denomination.

But when he gave me to understand that all he had to do was sign a paper renouncing his religion to be released from bondage, I pushed him to make a show of renouncement so that he could be taken to a hospital facility and receive the necessary penicillin as the fully-entitled German citizen he still is.

I argued that it was only a piece of paper and that what he wrote on it wasn't truly binding. He could continue praying to Jehovah and keep Christ in his heart. But he said that would be lying and that to lie is to sin against God.

I said that God probably sees lying to Hitler and his ilk as an act of defiance against Satan, but he only looked at me in silent rebuttal with his deep, soft smiling eyes. He raised his hand to my cheek then and asked me to kiss him, but no amount of pleading could convince him to write a single line or tell a single lie even to the devil himself.

Finally, seeing that I was not going to be able to persuade him to relent, I got up in a huff and stormed out of the tent. I waited for a while outside the tent within earshot, but he did not call me back.

29

Frau Wippermann showed us a film today.
The reel arrived in the post early this morning.
I settled down with the other handmaids,
expecting the usual fresh stream of nonsense
from the rotten heart of the Reich.

I suppose the damned thing was interesting enough in its own foolish way, at least
something to keep my thoughts engaged,
though I felt like laughing more than once at
how self-importantly the figures flickered and
flitted and pompously trotted and strutted by
on the screen.

One sequence remained with me after
the projector had finished casting up its
fake-smiling manicured images and its overloud
triumphal sounds. A scene in which the Führer
was seen to embrace and interact with little
blond-haired children. What disturbed me the
most was not the propaganda or seeing the
moving images of these horrid humans in their
pretty, well-tidied, lavish abodes. It was viewing
Adolf Hitler in good spirits and a friendly

mood. It shocked me to see what looked like genuine happiness in his eyes.

The most unbearable moment of all occurred when he dandled a little blonde, curly-haired girl on his knee. The look of actual tenderness that stole into his eyes was something I just had not expected. I did not think that someone as hollow and callous as he, someone capable of cawing like a wrathful bird of carrion into a megaphone, someone capable of having little children torn away from the arms of their parents and having innocent people shot like rabbits in the street, might be capable of anything remotely close to tenderness.

I observed the look in his eyes as his lids narrowed and pleated under the seemingly genuine grace of his smile. They carried the unmistakable stamp of deep-seated, authentic affection. I saw his face glow for a second or two with what looked like genuine goodness. I saw the little boy he had been a few decades earlier swim up suddenly to the surface of his face, as if that little boy were coming up for air.

It wasn't acted. Perhaps I am mistaken, but I don't even think it was a piece of calculated propaganda. It is of course possible that I am deluded and merely tricked by the ploys of cinematography in thinking this, but he seemed oblivious to the camera, as if he had forgotten its presence, even before that moment, as if he didn't even know he was being filmed. It

shocked me so deeply that something like this
could be possible. That a Beast of his calibre
should be human after all. It occurred to me as I
watched in stunned, dismayed amazement that
if he could perceive or feel even a tiny fraction
of the misery and mayhem he has caused,
perhaps he would relent. I am convinced
since this morning that it is the disconnection
between his words and seeing what they
produce that has made him into a monster
capable of tenderness.

And then a more chilling thought occurred
to me and I understood how he could do it.
We, the normal human beings, we do the same
to animals. We capture them, we put them into
tiny, stuffy cages before breeding them by force,
fatting them and killing them. It even makes us
happy when we sink our teeth inside them.

30

The Himmler Beast has finally returned,
but too late. Ernst's health has declined since
our tiff and I cannot help feeling that it is all
my fault for having over-reacted to his refusal
to renounce his religion, albeit only on paper.
Although it was hard and I kept berating myself
for unpardonable neglect, I managed to stay
away from his tent for a full two days as a way
of signalling my opposition to what I see as a
form of passive suicide.

When I went to see him late in the afternoon
on the third day after our wrangle, his fever
had shot up and he was shaking with the
chills. I have chided myself over and over
for the stupidity of punishing one who is
already undergoing such enfeebling amounts
of suffering and pain. I took the stability of his
condition for granted and now he is worse than
ever. I cannot help feeling I am much to blame.

The swelling that had stabilized and even
started to decrease has started to move up his
calf and his foot is swollen once again beyond

recognition. Doctor Kolb told me in no uncertain terms outside the tent that I had been remiss. He is counting on me to be at Ernst's side as soon as I have finished my duties. As the village physician, he is only available for visits at set hours. He is not free to be at the encampment whenever he pleases.

He says that he will have to amputate Ernst at the knee in a few days if the swelling continues to increase, unless he is given the penicillin. But apparently, even the potent antibiotic may not be enough to halt this unexpected steep rise in the infection, even if it is administered forthwith.

I do not feel like writing anymore. Circumstances have left me dry, devoid of will. I have tried to keep a steady eye out for Himmler since he arrived, but he is nowhere to be spotted. I have even gone as far as to knock on the door of König Heinrich as well as on the other door, the one labelled König Artus.

Herr Taubert too is nowhere to be found in the premises. When I made bold to enquire about their whereabouts, Frau Whip upbraided me quite severely, saying that they were not to be importuned.

It may be that Himmler possesses another secret chamber that I have been unable to locate. I will try to ferret him out of his hiding place tomorrow morning before breakfast.

Unforgivably also, I drank all the hot

chocolate instead of bringing it to Ernst in his hour of need. I fail to understand what possessed me. The craving just rises up in me uncontrollably at certain hours. At first, I thought I would just take a sip, just a dip of the lips in the rich, brown, lukewarm liquid, but it tasted so good that before I knew it I just gulped more than half of the cup down, and then it seemed too embarrassing to bring Ernst a mere half cup of cocoa, so I just swallowed the rest down my gullet in one guilty swig.

I have a strange, irresistible urge to eat in large quantities and especially to guzzle milk. Could this mean that I am pregnant, at last? Is this the sign I have been waiting for?

My belly's as flat as ever. Though perhaps I should not try to evade the possibility that I am merely becoming infected by the black plague that abides here all around me.

31

Went to seek out Himmler this morning, as planned.

I came across him almost by chance in the second floor corridor of the West Wing. He was nattering away, exchanging civilities and oh-so-pleasant niceties with Taubert in front of one of his dust-coated faux-medieval tapestries of Heinrich the Fowler on horseback. They were both gazing thoughtfully at the scene depicted in the woven hanging, cooing nostalgically about what they called "the good old middle ages" as if the era of the Black Death had been the golden age.

As soon as he saw me, Himmler straightened up a little, as though I were a lofty queen and he my vassal. With a loud commanding voice that contradicted this reversal of power, he bowed deeply in a gesture of mock court-liness, removing his hat and pressing it against his chest in a kind of exaggerated parody of mock submission. Herr Taubert chuckled at his antics and both of them beamed as if I were their godchild or the local wunderkind of Wewelsburg.

When I asked to speak with Himmler about a private matter of some concern, he became all solemn of a sudden and said that he would be able to hear me out forthwith. Taking leave of an amused, nodding Herr Taubert, I followed Himmler down to the basement of the West Wing to King Heinrich's private quarters.

Behind the desk inside this other room crouched a massive bronze cast of Adolf Hitler's dark, daunting head. You could feel the sheer weight and density of the leaden load of metal radiating meteoric blackness throughout the room. The thing must easily have weighed forty or fifty kilos.

To the right of the bronze head was an almost equally resistant-looking man-length safe recessed slightly into the wall. It looked as if it would take a few sticks of dynamite to open the likes of that.

A portrait of a man with a falcon on his leather-gloved arm adorned the wall to my left. I noticed the bird looked a good deal more expressive and soulful than the man.

The wall behind us as we entered was hung with a tapestry depiction of thirteen men seated around a round hardwood table.

"Please, do sit down," said Himmler, sitting down himself between me and the Hitler head so that it framed his own like a tenebrous metallic halo, "I see you appreciate art."

"I do, when I see it." I replied. I don't think he even noticed that my rejoinder came laced with a touch of irony. Perhaps becoming used to my style, he proceeded as if none had been offered.

"I love to surround myself with beautiful things, which is why you have my attention at this very moment, Fraulein Kaufmann. So, tell me. What ... can I do for you?"

"I have two requests. The first pertains to the whereabouts of my sister. You said you would look into it and give me news of her as soon as you could."

"*Ach*, yes ... I'm ... I'm afraid the news is not good."

"What do you mean?" I was terrified he was going to say that she was dead.

"It is not that I have taken the matter lightly. I know and can understand that your sibling means a great deal to you. The problem is that I'm afraid I have not been able to locate her. Admittedly, a most embarrassing admission from one who prides himself on keeping order in the Reich. I have wired Karl Wolff. Apart from being my liaison officer with the Führer, Wolff is also the officer I have put in charge of the Lebensborn programme. He phoned me back the next day having found no trace of your sister. I even called the officer in charge of pacifying Poland, Friedrich-Wilhelm Krüger—a

delightful man and most faithful—he too was
unable to find any record of your sister. Now, it
may be that this piece of classified information
lies with Krüger's arch-rival Hans Frank, a
high-ranking officer over which I have unfortunately no authority whatsoever as he was
appointed directly by the Führer and answers to
him alone."

"Can you not incite officer Krüger to ask
Herr Frank to cede the information?"

"Yes, well ... I'm afraid you do not realize
the full extent of our dilemma. The two men are
not just rivals. A mild way of putting it would
be to say that they are constantly at logger-
heads. There can be no exchange of anything
between them, no concessions whatsoever."

"Could you not ask him yourself?"

I gave Himmler an incredulous stare. For the
second most powerful man in the country he
seemed suddenly powerless.

"I am not on speaking terms with Herr
Frank either."

"Can I ask why this is so?"

"He is aware that I have asked the Führer
to replace him and so refuses to have anything
to do with me. Your sister's whereabouts is
a complete mystery. I'm afraid that in the
current state of affairs, with this internal power
struggle, your sister simply cannot be traced.
She has fallen off the map."

"I assure you my sister is very real. I would

not joke with such a matter."

"Please do not use that tone of voice with me. I do not appreciate the current suffragette attitude that some of your gender adopt towards the stronger sex. I have done what I can. You must be satisfied. I realize this puts me at a disadvantage when it comes to our little arrangement. Perhaps I may be of service in some other way. I do wish to remain on courteous terms with you. It is essential to the happy outcome of our accord."

"The second matter I wished to ask you about concerns one of your prisoners."

"You speak of prisoner 8 ... Herr Taubert has informed me of your charitable enterprise. It displays your human qualities. I like to see that you have retained your virtues, but do be careful not to waste your energies on the infirm."

"If Ernst Meier does not receive proper treatment, he will die. If you can spare just a few doses of this new drug called penicillin, he will grow strong and hale again. Prisoner 8 can work on rebuilding your castle. He is a very able craftsman."

"If he has grown ill, it means that he is meant to die. He is one of the weak in a world that requires robustness."

"I beseech you, Herr Himmler. Have you never yourself been taken ill?"

"Ha! I must say you have your wits about

you. I was in fact somewhat sickly as a child, but I grew out of it. My Aryan genes were strong enough to fight off the genetic dross that was weighing down my body."

"If you provide me with enough doses of penicillin, you may begin to enjoy the terms of our contract—regardless of whether or not you can locate my sister."

"You're an able negotiator. Fine, let it be so. I will bring you this medicine. It is in short supply, but I should be able to procure enough of it to bring Prisoner 8 to his feet."

"Thank you, Herr Himmler. I will uphold my side of the contract."

"I very much look forward to it. May I ... call you Eva?"

"This transaction of ours must remain nothing more than a contract. I do not wish to talk of love. I hope you understand."

"Spoken like a true Aryan! I have myself little time for lovey-dovey matters. I have come to the understanding that love is mostly a need to spread one's seed. I see that now that I have gained the higher ranks of the Reich."

32

The Beast invited me to bathe in a swimming pool today. I never thought I would ever write a sentence like that, and yet there it is. It is not the local pool in Wewelsburg. There is none as far as I know. I'm not even sure there is a public pool in Paderborn, or even Hanover come to think of it. The pool he brought me to was of a peculiar kind and I still shudder to think I accepted to bathe there.

Herr Himmler is set to inaugurate a new facility, a stone's throw away from the castle. He drove me down there in his *Große* Mercedes, as if we needed the automobile for such a short jaunt. The trip took about a minute or so and he held his hand in front of my eyes all the way down the road until we passed the guarded gates and found ourselves at the edge of the pool. Despite the shortness of the drive, though, I had no idea where we were and it didn't occur to me until it was too late where we were parked.

From out of the trunk of the Mercedes,

Himmler took a rectangular box wrapped in gaudy paper and handed it to me, his smile beaming up to his jug-ears, his little moustache pushing up into his nose. I opened it to find a red and white polka-dotted swimsuit with a decorative ribbon bow to knot at the waist.

He laughed and said he knew I'd like the Polish colours. He obviously thinks I'm as naïve as a child, that I can be baited by a garish piece of cloth tinted with the bicolour pattern of the Polish flag.

Himmler is convinced the polka is a Polish dance, despite the fact that I have told him it is Czech.

Ever the faux-gentleman and sensing my deep reticence to be anywhere near him, the Beast keeps trying to soften me up. He knows of course that he could have his way with me straight away, especially since the vows I voiced in the course of our last discussion. There is little I could do to hinder him now that I have surrendered for a little quid pro quo. But I think it amuses him to simulate the slowness of the courtship process. Perhaps he even needs it. I suppose that he wishes to produce the illusion that he is somehow seducing me, that regardless of the soulless contract he has made me enter, I can be won over despite myself, despite the fact that he and his smoothly-dressed savages have ravaged my country, lost my sister, possibly executed my parents and had me imprisoned in a pseudo-medieval castle to occupy myself with endless, mindless drudgery in a country I have always considered with both fear and loathing.

There was an outhouse next to the pool that he told me to enter so that I might don the swimsuit. I should have realized something was amiss when he told me to enter that little construction. There were no changing rooms or cubicles around, no diving platforms, no demarcated swimming lanes on the tiles at the bottom of the pool, no chrome-coloured ladders the way there are in other public swim halls. The fact that it was outdoors too should have given me pause. I had never seen an outdoor swimming pool so I just figured that was what they looked like.

When I emerged from the outhouse, Himmler was already splashing about in the water, sputtering and flailing and laughing like a stripling. He shouted modestly that he had never been much adept at swimming and that fencing had always been his strong suit. To prove his point, he splashed over in a messy crawl to the side of the pool. Sputtering and panting, he made me witness a small fencing wound he had sustained as a student at the University of Munich. He even wanted me to touch the scar with the tip of my finger.

I must have looked a bit foolish, standing there, bending over to look at the scar in that gaudy polka-dotted swimsuit. I felt like a giant dotted present with that pointlessly long bow tied at the waist. I suppose that was the point of it, to make the woman who wore it feel like a gift to be unwrapped.

Pressed insistently by the Beast's shrill injunctions to jump in, I put a ginger foot into the water to see how warm it was.

It turned out to be rather chilly, but I decided to do the Beast's bidding and go in any way, to spare myself having to hear his entreaties and also because I must admit it was a welcome change from being such a sullen drudge at the keep.

As soon as Himmler doggy-paddled into the middle of the pool no doubt sensing that I was waiting for him to move away, I sat down on the edge of the pool and lowered myself in.

The pool was rather shallow and didn't seem to have a deep end, another detail that increased my suspicion that it wasn't designed to be a swimming pool at all.

After about an hour of swimming to and fro—Himmler keeping thankfully to himself and respectfully distant—another man around Himmler's age came to join us at the pool. He was civil enough, though a bit haughty with me. Himmler presented him as *Hauptsturmführer* Adolf Haas.[41]   I though the name was written

---

[41] Hass means 'hate' in German.

Hass and only realized it was spelt Haas until much later.

It was only once we emerged from the pool and had changed back into our clothes that I realized where the Beast had taken me.

Adolf Haas was to be appointed *Kz-Kommandant* in the coming year and I had just taken a swim in what was to be the drink water reservoir of Niederhagen concentration camp.

The Beast was delighted to show me around the facility, so inanely proud to display how well the prisoners were being treated. He was providing them with all the new amenities, with such hygienic new latrines and a dining hall fit for pauper kings.

33

It was with a guilty heart that I went to visit my dear draft-dodger that afternoon. Although nothing has happened between the Beast and me, I couldn't help feeling I had betrayed him by spending an almost pleasant moment with another man, especially the one responsible for his captivity.

I also feel terribly deceitful about keeping Ernst in the dark concerning the pact I have signed with the arch-deceiver. Ernst deserves to know that I have sold my soul. He ought to know that I have also attempted to buy my spirit back with more deceit, by using him as a substitute progenitor. I do feel for him greatly, but cannot keep myself from thinking that I would not have seduced him so expediently had I not urgently needed to carry his child. Would he forgive me for this act of manipulative treachery if he knew? Seeing how much he loathes lies, I somehow rather doubt it.

I do not know how or when or if I will tell him, nor how he will react to the understanding that I am to enter into carnal relations with such heinous men as Himmler. I fear he would turn from me in sheer disgust.

But what choice do I have? I could run away of course. That would not be too difficult now that I can venture outside the castle unattended and unheeded as far as I can tell when I look back at the castle to see if I am being watched, but what would that avail me? My sister could be anywhere and I would lose my bond to Ernst. With my Slavonic accent, I would be soon caught and put in gaol, unless somebody lost in the back of beyond agreed to hide a fugitive Polish girl.

It saddens me when I realize that given the choice between kissing Ernst's infected wound and Himmler's moustache-fringed mouth, I would experience less disgust in choosing the latter. I suppose my body is designed to be repelled by any cut in the fabric of the flesh. My ethical, religious revulsion against the Beast thus counts for less than my disgust for maggots. I suppose I should not blame myself— to entertain such moral conundrums is no doubt ludicrous—but it's hard to have to come to terms with the blatant limitations on one's moral fibre.

Ernst is always so glad to find himself in my company. He was so happy and relieved to see that I had got over my sulking. He looks at me with such tenderness I feel a pang in my heart when I think of what I'm withholding. It's as if he draws his real sustenance through his eyes as he looks at me, and not from the fruitcake and other morsels which I have started filching from the kitchens.

He has trouble keeping down the prisoner rations allotted to him since his sickness. The rotten sloppy cabbage soup they serve is so glutinous it would make a slug retch—I tried it myself to see what it was like. Well, unappetizing is a potent understatement. Ernst tells me that some newcomers are unable to swallow the gloop and tend to let themselves fall into what he calls starvation sickness.

Last night, when I stole into the castle larder to gather any remains I could find, I felt that sudden craving for milk. Not even the bottle of apple juice I came upon could hold my interest for a second. It was milk I had to have and nothing else. I would have sucked it directly out of a cow's teat had I found myself in a dairy farm. It held me like a fever for a few interminable minutes until I thankfully came upon two churns full of the magical liquid.

Once I had pulled off the lid, I seized the heavy cylinder by the handles and lifted the whole container to my mouth with such grim determination and drive, my strength startled me. I was in such a hurry I drenched my chest in slopping milk. I drank down half the churn and would have continued had it not occurred to me that there might be consequences if Artus complained about anyone filching substantial amounts of dairy and victuals.

The only way I can make sense of this craving is that I must be with child. What other explanation can there be? I have never loved milk to this degree before. If it transpires that I am with child, then the timing is near-perfect. Himmler will not be able to complain that I have gone behind his back and nullified our contract. My belly will start to swell in perhaps a few weeks from now and no one will be the wiser. They will not be able to detect that I will have planted a changeling in their midst.

34

Himmler has been going on again about what he calls the Reich's pragmatic parallel marriages. He seems to imply that he wishes me to take part in this alternative ritual. He plans to co-opt me as one of these hidden brides, women secretly wedded off to SS officers who are already officially married elsewhere. The fact that this practice contravenes German law is irrelevant, according to Himmler. He says he is now the law.

He told me that he would like to divorce his wife (as if I could give a hoot about her being his wife), but he has decided not to divorce her on principle, in consideration for their youthful alliance and his former beliefs. He also says he cannot be seen to divorce when he has forbidden the practice within the order.

No SS officer is allowed to file for divorce unless he is granted special permission from the Führer, a dispensation which makes Himmler testy beyond all measure. He feels there should be no exceptions to the rule and is incensed by

Karl Wolff's desire to leave his wife. He refuses to allow Wolff to do so.[42]

He says he wishes me to be married to the SS, the way he and all the other officers are wedded to the order, bound by pernicious pagan rituals. When I asked what the point would be, he said he wished our union to be sacred and blessed by the new Aryan Krist—I think he mentioned the Nazi Christ only to cajole and coax me into the fold. He doesn't give a fig for Christ or even Krist, as far as I can see. There isn't a single cross in the whole castle, not to mention a single portrait of the Virgin. When I pointed this out to the Beast, he simply scoffed and said "what need do we have of the Virgin or her son when we have you to grace our thoughts?!"

I do not contradict him too confrontationally and tend to humour these flights of misplaced enthusiasm. He has procured a dose of penicillin and that is all that counts. I need him to keep supplying Herr Doktor Kolb with as many doses as it will take to get Ernst back on his feet. I suspect that Himmler deliberately offered this insufficient amount. Handing the single dose to me, he muttered something about medicines needing to be rationed.

---

[42] Himmler and Karl Wolff parted ways two years later, in 1943, when the latter divorced his wife, having obtained the right to do so from Hitler.

My dearest draft-dodger remains weak and resigned and has not responded adequately to the penicillin so far, but the physician says it will take a few days at least before he shows signs of recovery, if any at all. He still does not know if Ernst will make it. I have to say the smell from the bandages on his leg is deeply disturbing. I cannot bear to look any longer at the open wound when it is undressed and rely on Doctor Kolb to cleanse it.

35

I am pretty sure that there is a little swell on my midriff. Of course this may just come from all the milk I've been guzzling these last few weeks. Because I save the cup of cold chocolate for Ernst, my longing and frustration are so intense in the evenings that I am forced to assuage the full thrust of my thirst in the pantry. Surprisingly, no one has complained of theft so far, despite the fact that I typically swallow half a churn every night before bed. I also find the milk helps me to sleep. Either someone is covering for me or they think that the milk is being served up to Taubert, Klamm or Whip, the three-headed divinity of this God-forsaken castle.

My appetite has also increased tenfold it seems. I wolf my meals down with the frenzy of a savage and find myself looking at the other handmaids' plates, yearning desperately to lift the food off their forks even after I have hogged down my plateful and the dessert. I try my best not to draw attention to the unmanageable hunger stirring inside me, but that is no easy task.

So I stuff myself with bread from the basket, as inconspicuously as I can. It allows me to leave the cake and chocolate nightcap I am brought each evening safely stowed under the bed so I can convey them untouched to my beloved patient.

Resisting the temptation to hog that down too is a real test of my mettle. I've had to stop taking even tiny sips and morsels from the tray because once my appetite is whetted I find it next to impossible to desist. I never thought I would have to face such a petty moral dilemma.

Although I realize I'm being utterly immoral by even entertaining such unquenchable cravings, saving anything for Ernst is a real challenge. Just holding the plate of moist fruity cake makes saliva pool in my mouth.

Ernst needs every ounce of energy he can get to fight off the infection. He's so weak he scarcely chews what my ravenous hand puts in his mouth before swallowing. Mostly, he just lets the food sort of dissolve in his mouth. It takes him a whole hour to finish the plate— having to watch him eat is a gruelling ordeal.

His temperature is still far too high and yet the glint in his eye when he gazes at me is enough to shoehorn a good measure of his charm into my soul. I love the gap between his two front teeth. Such riveting sweetness! I don't know how to explain why it leaves such an endearing impression.

I hope the fact that early winter is upon us will not weaken him further. I find myself beginning to shiver slightly under the blanket during the night since I gave my second blanket to Ernst. The bedcover he was granted at the camp is as cruddy and crusty as a dirty doormat and has probably never been washed. I must ask Klamm if there are any clean blankets to spare. I'll have to pretend to be extra-sensitive to the cold.

The Beast is still trying to win me over with his counterfeit courtliness. The other day, he took me to a fancy dress ball in Hanover, making me dress up as Frieda, the Norse goddess of fertility. He even ordered Frau Wippermann to tie my hair up into a tight knot of interconnecting runic-looking plaits. A long flowing golden dress was made to fit—I had to go and get myself measured again at a tailor's in Paderborn for the occasion.

Himmler went dressed as Odin with a laughable black patch over his eye. It made him look quite ridiculous and I had trouble refraining from scoffing. With his horrible German fashion haircut and his would-be Hitler moustache, he's about as far as you can imagine from a Norse god.

He informed me of what I already knew,

that Odin the Wise gave away one of his eyes in exchange for absolute knowledge. I felt like saying that his Beastliness wouldn't be any the wiser if he gave both eyes away, but refrained from aggravating him pointlessly.

He's still bent on putting me through one of his parallel wedding ceremonies. The very thought of getting even parallel married to Himmler or any SS official makes me shudder, but I play along, forcing my repulsion into a neutral sort of lip shape. Oddly conventional for a self-proclaimed pagan, the Beast claims he does not wish to dishonour me by making me pregnant outside of wedlock. He added that his Aryan child should be no bastard offspring. He needs his progeny to be blessed by the gods.

The thought of being married to Himmler, even in a ridiculous pagan ritual, is unutterably revolting, but I will have to do my best to endure it if it comes to that. Surely it cannot be worse than having to be pawed by him in the unwanted intimacy of a bed.

The Beast wishes the celebration to take place in early spring. I find myself having to urge him to hasten the ceremony so that my belly does not swell too visibly. My sudden eagerness surprised and chuffed him, but he is obsessed by the summer and winter solstices, the high points of pagan festivity, and wishes to abide by these at all costs.

And so I have to egg him on to let us be

wed in time for Winter solstice. My apparent keenness has not failed to flatter him—I'm sure the beastly dullard thinks I've fallen for his dashingly manly demeanour, despite the fact that I rarely manage to bring forth anything vaguely resembling a genuinely soulful smile in his presence. I force a grim grin out only when it is absolutely necessary, like today when I asked him for another two doses of penicillin. To give my smidgeon of a smirk the semblance of authenticity, I had to conjure memories of Mila and me playing in the fields of wheat at the heart of the summer. I think it must have done the trick as the Beast went all soft-eyed and gooey. Whereupon he promised to procure other doses as soon as he could.

I flashed him another of my sickly smiles and said that I knew Wotan would look favourably on a union realized under the wonderful auspices of Winter. The fool is so gullible and childish he probably believes there's such as thing as Jack Frost. [43]

---

43 In Polish, *Dziadek Mròz* literally means 'Grandfather Frost'. The figure is a common in most European cultures.

36

Have been feeling elated all day. The magic medicine is doing its work! Ernst has been showing steady signs of progress for several days in a row—his temperature is down to practically normal and Herr Kolb says that he will be able to sew up the wound in a week if Ernst's health continues to improve. At least he is no longer talking about amputation!

But one worry pushed aside makes room for another. On no account must Ernst find out about my forthcoming pagan wedding to the Beast. The very idea would devastate him. He wouldn't understand that I am going to go through with it for both our sakes. I know he would see it as an unacceptable compromise. A sordid stain on my soul. If he knew how I obtain his penicillin, I'm certain he would refuse to take it and opt for death on the spot.

I hate having to deceive him in this way—I am now a deceiver of two men, one of them the arch-deceiver in person. The other is deceived out of love, for his own good. I try to convince myself that my decision is only a sin of omission.

In his suffering and weakness, Ernst is completely oblivious to the slight bulge in my midriff. It would no doubt aid him in his convalescence to know that he is going to be a father, but if I disclose that I am pregnant I will feel obliged to tell him the real reason why I must conceal the child and that would lay him low. He is so enfeebled that I do not think he will notice I am pregnant. Thankfully, the drop in the temperature allows me to wear concealing layers of clothing.

When we reach the winter solstice, the Earth will be at its furthest position from the sun. The darkest day of the year, a truly fitting moment for my marriage to the darkest knight on Earth. I feel the sun's ebbing presence in my heart at the thought of this seedy ceremony.

Himmler calls the December solstice *Julfest*, the ancient Germanic name for the season's foolish festivities. He says he wishes to dispense with Christmas entirely this year and replace it with *Jule* in honour of our secret wedding.

The celebration is to take place in the crypt of the North Tower, a place I have heard of, but never seen. When the ceremony is over, we will no doubt retire to his chambers—and that is when I will strike.

37

I was expecting the ritual to be harrowing—in the end, though, it was more laughable than dispiriting. My dress was relatively wearable, as far as wedding dresses go, a white lace affair with a headdress that resembled an openwork tea cosy pulled over my Gretel-like interlace of tresses. With the plaits pulling tightly at my scalp, my head felt like a clutch of conger eels caught in a river net, but I suppose I have to admit that overall it became me rather well, though I found it hard to recognize my usual self in the mirror.

I was festooned in runic jewels—primitive, pretty gruesome stuff, but I suppose it had its own sort of dramatic simplicity. I was mostly grateful I didn't have to wear a swastika pendant at the end of a necklace, or that unsightly pair of sig earrings he once mentioned he would love me to wear.

The crypt was rather eerie, though I was vaguely curious to discover it. Twelve stone bollard-shaped stools fringed the round chamber at regular intervals. In the centre of the dome lay a circular recess with a hollowed out circle of stone in the middle. Right above it, on the ceiling of the chamber, a carved ornamental swastika radiated outwards with an extra set of limb-like offshoots.

The Beast and I were made to stand face to face in the central circle of hell to pronounce our unholy vows. When we each spoke our piece (I was forced to rattle off an absurd little speech that I had to learn off by heart), our words seemed to fuzz and foam out of our mouths in deep cavernous clouds.

Something about the acoustics of the chamber seemed to give any utterance voiced from the exact centre an uncannily sonorous texture. The noise issuing from our mouths seemed to engulf us entirely in a sort of furry, reverberating woolly cocoon. It was so horrifying I was almost exhilarated by the experience.

By the time I had finished uttering my cow vows, it felt like my face and torso were padded in a kind of reverberating membrane.

Himmler didn't seem to find this phenomenon the least bit disquieting or unusual, quite the contrary. Being used to it I suppose, he revelled in the atmosphere it bestowed on the proceedings. The usually nasal timber of his voice made the eerie roaring resonance disturbingly insidious. Never before had I felt with more dismaying conviction that I was being wedded inside the very voice box of the devil.

The custom for SS officers who marry in the castle is to hold a long pointed dagger as they pledge their pagan troth. In this patriarchal order—there are no SS women of course—the parallel wife-to-be is given no dagger (presumably so that she will refrain from stabbing her spouse before the marriage is pronounced).

There was calligraphic writing etched all the way down to the tip of the blade Himmler was brandishing, but in the penumbra I couldn't quite make out what was inscribed.

Anyway, there we stood, both metaphorically and literally at daggers drawn. When we had said our lines, I saw to my disgust that a traditional Christian kiss on the mouth was expected after all. The Beast puckered up and pressed his pasty face forward like a cockerel coming in for a peck.

Not being able to move forward, so great was my revulsion in that moment, I just stared on in veiled nausea as he puckered. No doubt to avoid too much embarrassment in front of the twelve seated officers around us, the demon swooped in and I felt his cold moist membranes suction-cupping my mouth.

I managed to pull my lips into my mouth between my teeth the way I used to do when our over-frisky family dog used to lick my face as a child, so the Beast didn't get to deposit his saliva on any internal part of my cavity.

I don't know if Himmler noticed as he was closing both of his eyes. I imagine the congregation of officers perceived something of my reluctance despite the darkness, but no one uttered a word in the glacial silence that ensued.

When the whole sham was over and done with, Himmler took me down to his wine cellar—another cramped eerie round cell perforated with deep circular holes (everything was circular that day, including the art deco bedside table in Himmler's bedroom).

He made me dip my arm into the depths of one of the holes—it felt like I was putting my arm into a lair. Deep in the brick sleeve, my fingers encountered the neck of a bottle.

It turned out to be a transparent bottle of Riesling, one of the demon's favourites, and a necessary part of my plan.

The Beast retrieved another bottle himself from one of the holes in the wall and we retired to his private chambers. He poured out a glass of white wine for both of us into what looked like Bohemian-style glasses and we sipped at it, I a little gingerly. He seemed a tad irritated by my reticence. I think he is a little awkward with women in general, but my standoffishness probably didn't help to make him feel at ease.

I was gratified to see he swallowed his

glass down in one, after the initial sip or two. I
needed him to be a little tipsy to be able to pour
the granulated Pervitin tablets I had prepared
into his glass. The trouble was finding the
perfect moment to slip in the ground, powdery
substance.

As soon as he had emptied his glass, the
Beast poured himself another. Swallowing
as little as I could, I put my own glass to my
mouth to give him the illusion that I too was
drinking. Himmler happily flushed the second
glass down his throat, gave me a self-satisfied
lip-licking leer and started to stagger over to me
with open arms.

I was so alarmed and revolted by this
sudden pounce, I almost shattered the wineglass
in his face. I think I might have done so had he
lurched too close.

I imagine he sensed my hostility, despite
the alcoholic haze befuddling his brain, because
he kind of dance-waddled around me and
lurched back to where he was before his aborted
overture.

On edge, I held the wineglass like a potential
cudgel in my hand, my eye wandering to the
ceremonial dagger the Beast had deposited so
casually on the edge of the table.

Despite the alcohol in his blood, Himmler
caught the direction my eye was taking. It made
him grin right up to his jug ears. He started
shaking his head and wagging a loose, knowing,

slightly uncoordinated finger like a syncopated tail as if to say *none of those murderous thoughts now, it's time to seal our pact, you naughty little Polack.*

With that, he poured himself a third unsteady glass of Reich-approved Riesling and rivered half the liquid down his gullet. And then, to my utter mortification, he started shaking off his medalled tunic.

He began to loosen his tie and pull open the buttons of his shirt. Before I knew it, he had stripped to the waist and thrown all modesty and inhibition to the winds. As I had expected, his chest was pallid and unappealing, smudged rather than graced with the faintest wisp of grey hair.

I was beginning to wonder if I should have chosen death instead of parallel marriage. The thought of having to let any part of my body come in contact with this pasty-fleshed, withered-looking, middle-aged, moustachioed, round-spectacled furless walrus was more than I could stomach.

Not knowing what else to do to keep myself from trying to climb out the window, I put the lip of the wineglass to my mouth and swallowed the Riesling in three audible gulps.

I needed to be tipsy enough to bear what was about to happen and alert enough to make it happen smoothly, my main objective being to slip the powdered Pervitin into his drink without him noticing.

He had put his glass down on the round table in the middle of the room next to the knife, but how I was going to pour in the contents of my little vial unbeknownst to him was a practical conundrum I hadn't yet resolved.

It occurred to me that I should use a lady's prerogative to undress in privacy. Feigning modesty wasn't hard in the circumstances. The thought of his leering eyes gloating over my body was enough to make me as curt as a queen.

Treating him to my best glowering glare, I ordered the demon to turn around and he did so almost immediately, like an obedient child, chuckling and whinnying coyly all the while.

Once the Beast's back was turned, I came up behind him and pushed him forward with a firm hand so he was facing the wall and had his back completely turned to the glass and the knife on the table. I made him put his hands in front of his eyes and swear he wouldn't turn around until I was safely undressed and fully concealed under the bedclothes.

He kept nattering tipsily to himself so I had no difficulty making my move unheeded. In a matter of maybe two seconds, the full seven doses of powdered amphetamine were dissolved invisibly in the Riesling. I had no idea what the combined effects of alcohol and the drug would be, but I imagined the concoction could hardly be very healthy for the heart. Himmler himself had told me that some men's constitutions couldn't take even a single dose of Pervitin. Soldiers had died of it, stricken with instant heart failure. By my estimation, there was enough Pervitin in that glass to kill at least a horse or two.

If that didn't finish him off, I figured, there was always the dagger on the table, but of course using that would seal my fate. I would have no way of covering up a murder that obvious. There was also the complicating fact that I did not know if I had it in me to commit so violent an action as stabbing. Having to watch the Beast endure a massive heart attack was going to be trying enough.

The next step was a little trickier. I had to induce Himmler to drink my noxious potion and hide myself under the bedclothes at the same time.

I got undressed as quickly and soundlessly as I could to the clucking of Himmler's tongue as if he were a stallion approaching on cobblestones. I cast my clothes on the stout oaken chair by the round table, picked up the demon's glass and crept under the bedclothes spilling only a small quantity of the beverage on the sheet.

As soon as I was covered and comfortably installed on the plumped up cushions, I called out to the devil. Trying to muster a semblance of a smile and an alluring, Lorelei-like gaze, I held out the glass at arm's length and beckoned as invitingly as I could.

He didn't need asking twice. The Beast struggled to take off its shoes, toppling over three times in the process. Shedding his horsey stone grey Langhosen bunching out ridiculously at the thighs, he tottered in front of me utterly naked with a ghastly smirk of anticipated satisfaction.

Having to stare Himmler in the genitals was not something which I had looked forward to with unadulterated glee, but in the event it wasn't as much of an ordeal as I thought it would be. Himmler's penis seemed about the same length and girth as Ernst's. It wasn't as elegant by a long shot though and tended to veer to the side like a crooked stick with a rather graceless burr at the end of it.

Holding the glass in my hand and trying my best not to tremble, I felt like a cross between Judith and the big bad wolf waiting for little red riding hood to climb into bed.

As soon as Himmler reached the side of the bed, I handed him the glass, inciting him to drink with what felt like a smouldering look in my eyes.

To my relief, he swallowed the half-glass down in one go, smacking the emptied glass down with a bang on the round bedside table.

I was naïve enough to think that the drug would have an immediate effect. I had hoped — stupidly — that he would be instantly incapacitated, that he would just drop down dead on the floor before reaching the bed.

For the first few moments after he swallowed the drink, he looked exactly the same. I was so disgusted at the idea of having him paw me that I actually put out my hands to keep him at arm's length. I started pretending to massage his shoulders and arms so that he wouldn't move any closer.

It was only after about five or ten minutes that he started behaving out of character, though not at all in the way I had expected. The first symptom that caught my attention was a pronounced twitch in his nose and his mouth.

His lips started dancing around the lower part of his face as if they were performing some kind of lippy gig. His nostrils kept flaring and dilating and palpitating like a wild rabbit's nose. His eyelids started shuttering and opening widely in quick succession as if his eyes were trying to take stock of what was happening to his face.

It was really quite alarming to behold, though I welcomed every twitch. He started puffing like a grampus and sticking his tongue out and wagging it like the parody of a lecher I've seen in some films.

A few minutes later, he was practically

barking like a dog at the end of a leash.
Tethered to the cur by my arm, I had all
the trouble in the world in restraining his
onslaught. For some mindless reason, I hadn't
counted on the fact that the Beast's strength
might increase tenfold under the effect of the
drug.

Before I knew it, I had kneed him hard in
the testicles, the way my mother had done to
Paweł all those years ago in that disused school
cloakroom. I felt so much gratitude towards her
as I saw him buckle over.

Doubled up on the bed, Himmler started
emitting strange clucking noises like a hen with
a constipated egg lodged in its bowels. His head
started jerking forward in little spasms as if he
was trying to peck at the air. The veins on his
neck seemed close to popping.

I thought he was surely going to croak at
that point. He looked as if he was undergoing
the death throes. His eyes were all bulged out
and red. His face too was unspeakably veined
and congested.

But to my dismay, the Beast recovered
remarkably quickly from the blow to his manly
parts. The amphetamine must have counter-
productively inured him to much of the pain.
Glowering madly, he started thrusting himself
onto me with renewed determination. Beating
my arms away, he grabbed me by the neck until
I couldn't breathe or shout a word.

Within seconds he was astride me and had both my arms pinned back with his elbows. I closed my thighs as best I could, but there was little else I could do. I clawed at him as best I could. I tried screaming, but he just put his uncouth, brutish hand over my mouth.

Before I knew it he was inside my body, thrashing about like a demented fish, hacking away at my insides like a machine gone awry. There were moments when it felt like I was being raped by a man-sized cuckoo clock—in fact, it helped me to think that to endure the pain and the awful abject humiliation. Bearing the brunt of the Beast's onslaught, I focused my mind on my grandmother's horrid cuckoo clock. The brutality of its ejections, the deafening hammer of its assaults. The cuckoo bursting into my flesh.

I was so torn and distraught by his intrusions that I was ready to scream that I was Jewish in the hope that it might trigger instant heart arrest and deaden that sordid hater of all things Semitic, but the Beast's hand was on my mouth and I could barely breathe through my nose, never mind utter a sentence.

That men such as he can be allowed to prod and pry into our very souls.

38

My plan to wipe Himmler off the face of the earth has been an utter failure, but my cover up operation has not. My secret pregnancy is now safe at last. I won't have to hide it for much longer. Another few weeks and I'll be out of the woods.

As far as I could see, Himmler didn't notice the bulge on my belly when he crept under the sheets, not in his drug and alcohol-besotted state. He was so unhinged after swallowing the Pervitin he seemed scarcely human. I don't think he was up to noticing details of that kind. His body was nothing but a mindless, hell-bent machine.

After he finished pounding me, he got up with such a swift movement it rather reminded me of a cork flying out of a bottle. Bobbing on his feet, he sort of cantered around the room as if he thought he was running round in a circus paddock.

He snatched up his jackboots and swiped at his uniform. He had everything back on

faster than I've ever seen anyone get dressed —
bursting quite a few buttons in the process —
and then he literally bounded out of the room
without as much as turning his head to take
his leave. I'm not sure he even had in mind
that I was still there in the room. I wouldn't be
surprised to hear he bounced out of the castle to
sprint a marathon to Paderborn and back.

I've been feeling raw and ragged all day,
disporting myself like an aching combustion
engine forced to move forward in uncomfortable
shudders.
I feel like a hollow cylinder that's been
ramrodded by an industrial piston. Only the
thought that my secret is now finally safe
kept me going as I drudged in pain around
the castle, laying out the cutlery, mechanically
scouring the privies for longer than I needed to,
lost in hellishly recurring images of the Beast's
amphetamine-contorted face and the near-stran-
gulation he inflicted on my neck and mouth.
I was upbraided on several occasions by Frau
Whip for making the beds all too raggedly.
Even the handmaids who usually snub me
kept staring in bewilderment as if something
was gravely amiss with my behaviour. Perhaps
they overheard or have guessed what happened
to me. Anna kept asking me if I was alright, if I
wasn't feeling out of sorts. She looked a mixture
of worried and envious. Even she I am sure sees

the likes of Himmler as the catch of the century.
She might think differently had she felt him
machinegun into her body and seen him prance
about the room like a demented circus pony.

I wanted to go and see Ernst, but was so
worried he would see the destruction in my
eyes that I couldn't bring myself to his tent. I
hope he does not think I am neglecting him. I'm
sure his health would drastically decline despite
the antibiotic medicine if he knew what has
happened. It would probably kill him to know
I have been raped by the regime. And so I find
myself having covered up one secret only to
have to conceal another.

39

I have not seen the Beast all day. I do not
even know if he is still lurking within the
confines of the castle. Perhaps he has disappeared into the winter solstice. If only he and all
the rest of them could dissolve into the darkness
whence they came.

I keep fantasizing that the demented creature
has died on its frenetic sprint to Marathon.
I imagine the Beast galloping all the way to
Berlin to deliver his idiocy up on a platter to the
Führer. I suppose that if he had died or come
to harm, the whole castle would be up in arms.
The alarm bells would be ringing.

I asked the other handmaids if they had
caught sight of Himmler anywhere, but apparently nobody has. They all gave me very
knowing glances. I'm sure they're aware at least
to some extent of what has come about, though
Anna has been the soul of discretion and has
not uttered a word. Frau Whip walked straight
past me as if she was too embarrassed to
countenance looking into my face. Didn't even
bother to upbraid me for my sloppy sweeping.

I steeled myself to look as ordinary as I could before going to see Ernst. I took a long look at myself in the mirror to try to drain the horror from my eyes. I'm not sure that he noticed, though I had difficulty holding his gaze without blinking and letting my unsteady eyes flit to either side of his bed. He asked me if anything was the matter and I had to lie.

The upside is that he's looking a good deal healthier. At least the lividness has departed from his face. Doctor Kolb is confident he should be right as rain within ten days or so. He has told Taubert that prisoner 8 needs to rest so they don't send him back to work before he's able.

The rubble is entirely gone from the foot of the castle so at least the worst, the most strenuous, back-breaking donkey work is done. Hopefully, when Ernst is forced to go back into bondage they will put him to work on some menial task that requires minimal exertion like sandpapering or stirring mortar, although Ernst says that after an hour of sandpapering your arm feels as if it's about to fall off.

I can no longer stand the stink of waxing polish. The whole place reeks of it. Constantly we're asked to keep polishing the woodwork. I think they are afraid to leave us inactive. My sense of smell seems to have intensified, or else it's just that I've waxed enough woodwork to last me a lifetime. At least the pain in my nether parts is beginning to ease.

40

The parody of Christmas is already upon us. I almost forgot it after the ceremony, a mere two days ago. The whole castle is gearing up for festivity and another round of weary waxing.

We've been given express orders by Herr Taubert that there is to be nothing Christmas-like about Christmas this year. We are to prepare for Julefest and Julefest alone. There is to be no talk of Christ and cribs and crucifixes. Christmas carols are to be replaced with songs like "Hitler is the Noblest Person on Earth" —the most popular song of the year in this benighted part of the globe.

Even mentioning Krist with a spikey K is now apparently out of the question. We are to engage in nothing but pagan chanting and candle-lit processions in the dark. Decorated fir trees are allowed but the baubles must be nothing but blood red or black. Swastikas and straw versions of Thor's pagan rams are to be the only other objects hanging from the tree.

The Beast himself won't be present today or

even tomorrow. Not even for New Year's Day I am told. It seems he is alive and unfortunately well. The little hobgoblin has been called away on urgent matters pertaining to the security of the nation. It's a wonder he recovered so quickly. How can God in his munificence allow such putrid evil to prosper and prevail?

At least I won't have to kiss the Beast under the mistletoe and receive more runic jewels from his pale, pudgy fingers—reading over my last few sentences, I've noticed that anger makes me want to alliterate almost madly. What a meaty monstrous mind I have developed.

I think the demon was avoiding me in the two days before he left, I know not if it was out of embarrassment at his vile behaviour or if he wishes to indicate that my importance has now been considerably diminished. Whatever the case, I count my blessings that I do not have to countenance his ghastly face over breakfast.

Feeling cagey, I've decided to delay revealing the protuberance of my belly until well into January, to play it safe. I do not want anyone getting suspicious and nosey and I'm not particularly keen on having to bear people fussing or gazing at me as if I'm some kind of freak.

My main worry is how I will reveal my belly to Ernst. It's been easy to conceal the growth under the layers I have to wear to keep out the cold, but what will happen when it grows too large to hide in the spring or before? How harrowing it is to have to lie to someone who holds the unadulterated truth in such high esteem. I will have to try to make Ernst under-stand that I have to conceal his paternity.

But what if he discovers the truth? What will he do if he learns that I have married the devil?

41

As expected, Yuletide festivities were depressingly dismal—thanks be to God those are over and done with! Having to sit in front of the stately fireplace in the main hall all in a circle and sing horrid twisted little songs about the fatherland and how wonderful our Great Leader is and all the rest of the claptrap was more than I could take. Most of the men were sporting their best furry Hitler moustache and all the handmaids had their hair knotted into long Tyrolian braids. A pretty piece of sickliness.

The torch and candle procession through the snow would have been a bearable treat had it not been for the fact that the *Burgmeidens* kept giggling like a gaggle of geese, prodding and jostling and horse playing around. It was all screeching delight in crunching and balling up the snow to fling it around.

I was just watching on mirthlessly when Adolfa and Clara crept up behind me to stuff a whole armful of snow down the back of my dress, rubbing it hard into my back. I just wasn't in the mood for that kind of merriment. At least not with them.

With the drop in temperatures the domestic animals have all been dressed in the most hideous outfits. The SS steeds have been given death's heads equestrian wear which makes them look like a good impersonation of the horses of the apocalypse.

The guard dogs sport the double sig rune on their winter coats. They take good care of their animals alright. Being outside in their company was like being in a beast fable out of Aesop. The hounds kept yapping excitedly, snorting and snuffling in the snow. I saw them all gather round one of them who was munching a frosted piece of something, crunching away at it with a vacant expression as if it was nothing but a frosted brown carrot. It turned out to be a frozen piece of excrement on one of the guard's closer inspection, but the dog had swallowed most of it by the time the guards knocked the brown carrot out of its jaw.

The Julefest dinner was pretty tasty, though I have to say inescapably German on the whole. I hogged it all down as discreetly as I could. My appetite is more insatiable than ever. I took two helpings of a traditional seasonal currant and marzipan cake they call Stollen and a fat, very sizeable cream-topped piece of *Apfeltorte*.

I was able to make it out to Ernst with a few

slivers of roast duck and a slice of winter cake only long after it was all over. There wasn't a single sausage left on the table—I suspect the handmaids of sneaking food remains back to their rooms.

Still, it was wonderful to be able to feast on the burnt out gold in Ernst's eyes. His smile is still shaky but it's so good to see it back in the saddle.

Shortly after I got back last night, a blizzard started whisking and then whipping the air, wending its way up from the valley like a howling tooth-filled monster. A terrible swarm of snowflakes descended on the castle like a hive of whitened insects.

When I looked out the snow-caked window this morning, a powdery whiteness was still smoking over the snowdrifts, steaming up into the frozen air, gathering in whispering wisps over the walls and battlements.

42

All the silent silver snow has melted. It's rained so much there's a leak in the ceiling of my room—a single drop at a time in exactly the same place like a clepsydra pattering out the seconds as they plop and piddle onto the floor. The damn thing keeps me awake into the darker reaches of the night. I lie there wondering how many drops it would take for the water to tap a hole into the stone.

I have to inquire of Herr Klamm and his sooty eyebrows if he will have the leak fixed, but the thought of having to coax that sluggish, dewlap-decorated man out of his lethargy is too soul-defeating to contemplate. I think I'll just have to wait it out until the weather clears up.

My new anxiety is that Ernst will be placed in the new camp at Niederhagen. I've heard some of the officers referring to the prisoners as *Stück* again, as if they are pieces of wood. It doesn't bode well for how the inmates are being treated at the new camp. One of them spoke of certain prisoners receiving special treatment and cackling—it wouldn't surprise me to learn that this *special treatment* is code language for a form of grisliness.

Now that the outer layers of the castle have been refurbished, over half of the prisoners have been sent down to Niederhagen. I really fear that Ernst will be cooped up in there as well, as soon as he is able to stand on his feet. I have warned him against showing too many signs of recovery. As long as he is convalescing, Dr Kolb has said that they will let him remain at the infirmary.

How I will keep him there is to be my next task. Himmler made it clear when he was here the last time that he is already wary of my tending what he calls "my ward". I think he rather suspects that there may be some kind of romantic attachment between Ernst and me. I caught a glimmer of jealousy nettling the Beast's eyes. I do not know how he will be disposed when he returns next time. Now that I am "married" to the man, I think he may expect me to stay tightly tethered to my leash.

43

The demon is back from God knows where, much sooner than expected. The moment I saw his black SS1 Mercedes enter the gate house late in the morning, I made my way over to the west wing.

But he was again without news of Mila. His commanding officer in Poland, the man known as "the pig of the trenches", is still at logger-heads with Hitler's henchman, the one called Herr Hans Frank. I suspect both of them to have killed and deported a countless number of Poles in the course of what the demon calls "the pacification of Poland". So what is one little girl to them? Surely nothing more than a dispensable *Kleinigkeit*.[44]

To hear men like Krüger spoken of with warmth and affection makes me want to scream

---

44 *Kleinigkeit* means 'a little thing of little significance'. Himmler is on record as having said that the extermination of the Jews was also nothing more than 'a trifle'.

with horror, but I keep my emotions in check.

Himmler doesn't seem to care anymore than I imagine Krüger does that I am in deep-seated dismay over the loss of my sister. He says he is sorry, but I feel that under this word there is little, if any, heartfelt commiseration. Every time he says he is sorry it just feels like he is mouthing nothing more than a pretty piece of politeness. Mila is for him hardly more than a pawn, useful to waylay his captive queen on her pyrrhic pedestal as he takes advantage of my position.

There are times when I wonder if the devil isn't pretending to be unaware of my sister's whereabouts. Perhaps he thinks that if I knew I would try to seek her out or demand that she be brought to the castle. She would be an encumbrance to him, I suppose.

If I didn't loathe my adversary so much and find his thoughts and ideas revolting, I would probably find him reasonably engaging. It's hard to imagine that I would actually warm to him, but I can see why someone amenable to his convictions might find him affable enough.

Today, just after lunch, the Beast brought me down to another locked room, yet another of his concealed Bluebeard chambers. He called this one his *Schatzkammer*.[45]

At the back of the room, he opened a safe

---

[45] *Schatzkammer* means 'treasure room'.

that was longer than he was, confiding that I
was the only other person allowed to see what
he hid in there.

He made me close my eyes as he rummaged
inside. I heard a brief clank as he came up
to show me his loot. I opened my eyes on
his urging and there he was, looking solemn.
Beaming with pride, despite the fact that he
looked ludicrously incongruous. A moustachioed pudge holding a time-honoured historic
artefact.

The Beast claimed that the weapon he hefted
in his hand was the actual 'Spear of Destiny'. I
have to admit I had never heard of it before.

The lance's tip was equipped with a long
winged blade encrusted with an inlaid nail,
partially covered in gold and silver sleeves.
It looked too recent to be the Holy Lance he
took it to be, the spear that is supposed to have
pierced our Lord's side on the cross.

Himmler claimed that his *Ahnenerbe* scientists had determined that although the wood
of the lance was not the original Roman-era
material used in the making of Longinus's
spear, all the metal parts were consistent with
the designs prevalent in the first century A.D.

I had trouble believing that the artefact he
brandished before me was genuinely the Lance
of Longinus, the weapon that killed Christ, but
the Beast was very insistent. He kept making me
whisper, as if anyone could hear us through the

four-metre-thick walls of the castle.

He confided that he had had the lance removed from the *Kunstbunker*[46] underneath Nuremberg Castle for safekeeping in his private collection at Wewelsburg. Not even Hitler was aware that he had it secreted away. In doing so, he assured me that he had acted in the interests of the nation. He looked like a little boy afraid of chiding when he whispered this. He is so self-deluding and childish I would find it almost endearing were circumstances not what they are.

He's convinced that the nail embedded in the Holy Lance is one of the nails that pierced Christ's body. He really believes it. You could see it in the fanatical glow of excitement in his narrow pagan eyes as he said it.

He sees the lance as some kind of magic relic that will guarantee Germany's victory in the war. According to the legend (which he takes as fact), the man who possesses the Spear of Destiny is fated to overcome all his enemies.

When I asked him why Hitler didn't keep it for himself, he adopted a hangdog expression of disappointment and said that although the Führer was the greatest man who ever lived, he had a tendency to be a little out of touch with

---

46 A *Kunstbunker* is a bunker previously found in the dungeons of medieval castles. Its purpose was to house and protect art collections from being pillaged.

the occult. Himmler seems to perceive himself as a kind of necessary complement to what he views as his slightly over-rational master.

The irony of viewing Hitler as rational is completely lost on Himmler. I didn't bother to point it out, not wishing to antagonize him pointlessly and lose my foothold on his mind. The Beast brooks no criticism of the Führer, speaking of him always in the hushed tones of hero-worshipping reverence.

Himmler then let me in on his future plans for the castle. As soon as the war is won, he aims to have the whole of Wewelsburg remodelled so that the outline of his new Nazi city will look like a lance from the sky. He believes that the triangular shape of the castle was intended by its original architects to represent a spearhead and that the Germanic peoples of the time considered it to be the epicentre of the world.

As soon as Germany is rich and victorious, he plans to pour millions of Reichsmarks into the construction of the new spear-shaped Wewelsburg. He fantasizes that I will reside there and grow and prosper like a fatted queen bee, having at my disposal everything I could possibly wish for—except freedom and the possibility of being rid of him forever.

44

I should have guessed they would do it.
Himmler — or perhaps it is Taubert's doing —
has had Ernst promptly removed from the
infirmary. When I went there this morning, I
found the tent stretcher empty. I have searched
through the castle grounds and found no
prisoners around. He has surely been sent to
Niederhagen concentration camp, which means
it will be hard for me to get within a stone's
throw of him.

I fear they will put him to work on some
futile burdensome task before he is able to take
the strain. I also fear that they will underfeed
him at a time when he is still so weak. If he has
been sent there, I will no longer have a way of
smuggling in extra food to bolster his defences.

I imagine I will have to bargain with the
Beast and be forced to accept more of his crass
overtures if I am to get to see Ernst again. The
thought of having to do this again is simply
revolting, but I'm resigned to the idea that there
is no other way for me now.

45

When I inquired about Ernst, I saw another glimmer of jealousy steal over the Beast's bloated face. I think the Beast believes he is "in love" with me and I think he knows that I love Ernst.

When I asked to have Ernst brought back to the castle infirmary, he said there was a far more efficient dispensary at Niederhagen and that prisoner 8 would be promptly taken care of. He spat this at me with a kind of cold venom I had not noticed in him before.

The Beast warned me against pampering what he called "hangers-on and useless feeders". He claimed to my face that some people were "unfit for life"—whatever that means. Again, he spoke of strengthening the nation's sinews of racial hygiene as if it was some kind of acrid detergent. He argued that I should take the camp as a test of Ernst's inner worth. If he survives, it means he is worthy; if he does not, it means he belonged to the weak, a condition that the Reich cannot tolerate.

When I informed the Beast in no uncertain terms that I would never let him touch me again if he did not let me see Ernst, he visibly coloured and began sputtering about Odin and the whole pack of Nordic gods and how they shared their goddesses. Having calmed down and composed himself a little, he said he would consider my request but that I was not to expect any weakness coming from one such as him.

46

I was granted a short hour with Ernst earlier this afternoon. Himmler came up to my room to announce that he would come to escort me to the camp and that I was to see Prisoner 8 in his company. When I declined to have the Beast hover around us, he said that he would keep his distance and remain out of ear-shot, but that he would on no account leave us together alone.

He took me down to the camp in his black coffin of a car. I felt leaden and full of foreboding, expecting Ernst to be barely standing on his feet.

I found my sweet man waiting next to a guard by the entrance to the camp, looking rather pale and forlorn, but his stare was pretty unvanquished.

They have given him a new uniform that is a little longer and broader at the shoulders so he doesn't look compressed the way he used to in the old set of linens. His face lit up when he saw me wave to him from within the automobile. He didn't move towards me, though, presumably having been ordered not to budge.

Himmler almost frog-marched me over to him, depositing me like a prized possession into the hands of a slave. He treated both of us to his best mustachio-rimmed scowl and wandered off a few paces in the direction of the forest, muttering a sentence to the guard who moved away to leave us in peace. As far as I could tell, they were both more or less out of earshot.

Himmler had expressly enjoined me not to engage in any physical contact, but I could not help but take Ernst in my arms when I found myself standing in front of him with my arms dangling uselessly by my side. I felt his frail frame tremble against me, it was like embracing a tall bony child. He has lost so much weight he is almost frightening to behold. Lying on his stretcher for some reason he had not seemed quite as skeletal.

Ernst says that the rations they are being given at Niederhagen are little more than scraps and fetid leftovers. Each prisoner gets one single stale wrinkled sausage, a small bowl of gloopy soup, a handful of half-hardened bread and a little smidgen of margarine in the morning, and that's it for the day.

Conditions in the camp are horrendous and far worse than the treatment that was meted out to him at the castle. He told me the dormitories are so overcrowded and cramped the workers have to sleep on their side to make room for new inmates. Those who renege, disobey orders or fail to comply in any way are forced to hold up their arms and maintain the Nazi salute until their bodies drop to the ground from exhaustion. Others are hanged by the wrists from trees or whipped on the box.

They're all lined up naked for roll call in the morning, despite the cold. Once all the names have been tallied, they're allowed to cover themselves up and have breakfast. Ernst told me he tries to save a piece of bread for the afternoon so that he can stand the brunt of the work, but he often gives in and swallows the last morsel of his meagre ration around midday to avoid collapsing from inanition.

I was so shocked to hear all this that I didn't speak to Himmler on the way back in his motorized coffin. I think the silent treatment did its work. I noticed the Beast's fingers twitched a little nervously on the steering wheel. He looked sort of hangdog and lippy when I turned to give him a glare as we parted. As a parting shot, I told him that if he wanted me to act the part of his wife in future he would have to triple the prisoners' rations. He looked at me blankly, but I could see the words sink into his eyes.

47

The girls are all edgy and lovelorn. Many of them fear they will be sent back to their homes by Frau Whip and exchanged for another set of handmaids without having had a fair chance at maintaining their seat at the love feast because of the war.

No longer receiving letters from her courtier, Anna is peevish and sad most of the time. She fears her suitor has either forgotten her or met his demise. Believing that I alone will be allowed to remain at the castle, another three girls have joined Adolfa in spitefulness.

Klara and Rozmonda have told me they have overheard Taubert say that the inmates at Niederhagen are being deliberately starved and worked to death so that they won't survive to tell the secrets of the castle. Those who have worked here are being singled out for whippings and beatings on the slightest whim.

Bettina says she heard one of the guards say to another that they've started sterilizing the criminal elements at the camp, by which he seemed to mean more or less every prisoner. But Bettina is a bit of a fibber. She tends to invent all sorts of wild statements to create a bit of drama. Why would they bother to sterilize someone they are going to work to death anyway?

I have asked Himmler to cease any mistreatments he may be allowing immediately. He is turning out to be more of a monster than I thought he was. I told him so to his face and he didn't take it very well. He may not believe in Christ anymore, but I've noticed that his conscience can be prodded. Something in his brain still responds to ethical appeal.

The demon tried to take me into his arms but I managed to keep him at arm's length this time. He's not that strong without the Pervitin. I think he's beginning to lose his patience, though. Sensing this loss of ground, I decided to lay down my trump card. Almost offhandedly, I told him I was now certain I was pregnant. The look on his face was rather comical to behold: something like a bullfrog achieving ecstasy.

He wanted me to show him the skin of my midriff so I said I would show him if he stepped away. Once he was satisfied I wasn't bluffing, we talked a little more about the conditions at the camp. He was so elated by my announcement I could tell he would have been open to the suggestion whereby each prisoner be given a big slice of Apfelstrudel.

In the end, once I had plucked on his
vibrating heartstrings, he merely promised to
limit the number of floggings and increase the
prisoners' rations by half—not nearly enough
by a long shot, but at least it is something.
He refused to make an exception for Ernst,
however, so I treated him to a bit of a scowl.

When I had finished a round of sulking,
I made it clear to him that if anything ever
happened to Ernst I would throw myself and
the baby out the window. If Himmler knew that
I was half a Jewess and carrying the child of a
Jehovah's Witness, he would in all likelihood
cast me out the window himself this very
minute.

48

How mercifully good to be writing again after a full four long months of being deprived of my diary. I wasn't sure at first who had stolen it, though I had my suspicions. The initial shock of not finding my precious booklet in its usual place under the mattress sent a stinging chill right to my womb. It felt like my child and I had just been sentenced to the gallows.

My first intuition was that one of the handmaids had purloined it, either Adolfa or Olga. They both resent my Polishness and are jealous of my proximity to the *Reichsführer*. I also suspected Ulrike for a while, but she seems too guileless.

As the weeks passed, I began to turn my suspicions on other members of the keep. I thought of Klamm and Frau Whip, but had trouble picturing them snooping around. I even suspected Taubert and his henchmen.

I was terrified for days when I considered the consequences of anyone discovering the contents of the diary. I suppose to even start writing in this book was a thoughtless folly to begin with, and yet would I have survived this far without its soothing at dusk?

To write down that I am a Jewish Catholic was dangerous enough. But to have it known that I attempted to dispatch the *Reichsführer* SS would no doubt be deemed a count of high treason and punishable by death. The fact that this log is couched in Polish, a language that no one at the castle understands, is of course by far too thin a barrier between me and execution. I should have invented my own coded language.

I have come up with a new much better hiding place for the diary, though if a thorough search is conducted again it will no doubt be found. I have nevertheless decided to continue writing, come what may. The individual who removed it in the first place already has enough incriminating evidence to have me put away and probably executed too so it won't make a difference what I write now.

I got used to not writing, but what a loss it was in the evenings, especially when I found myself worrying about who might have stolen my log. All those weeks of waiting in utter fear of being summoned.

Writing does comfort one so, especially when one has no one else to confide in. It's such a delight to hold the pen between my fingers and watch the inky squiggles appear almost by magic on the page. Almost as wonderful as cupping my bulge between my hands.

I soon figured out it was Himmler himself
who had my room searched. He left three days
after it was taken and came back over three
months later.

When he handed it to me with a propri-
etorial flourish over the desk in his office, I was
only mildly taken aback. He had had the most
leverage to gain by reading it, so I was pretty
sure he was behind its disappearance. None of
the others looked remotely guilty and Adolfa
gave me the most clueless look I've ever seen
etched on her thick-cheeked Ruhr face.

I'm still not sure if Himmler has had it translated. He slid it to me over the desk without
batting an eyelid, as if it contained nothing but
the most insipid dross. I imagine he has had
parts, if not all of it translated, though perhaps
he has not. It was impossible to tell from the
look on his face. Was it now laced with a
compound of attraction and repulsion?

In any case, he hasn't betrayed the slightest
air of suspicion concerning its contents, as
if all he had done was take a look at my
handwriting. Or else he is saving the pounce
of his indictment for later, when I least expect
it. Perhaps he aims to use this evidence against
me as a form of blackmail to keep me in check
in case he feels he is losing his grip, not that
he needs to blackmail anyone with the power
vested in his executioner's hands. Perhaps he

is merely in love with me and cannot bear the thought of having me put out.

If he's aware that I tried to kill him, if he knows that the child in my womb isn't his, then surely he would have me taken out and had me interned or shot in the back of the head. When I saw him take the diary out of his drawer, I half expected him to pull out his Walther PPK and shoot me dead in the armchair.

49

It sometimes occurs to me that the Beast is just preoccupied by the upcoming summit he keeps mentioning. This looming grandeur has perhaps eclipsed the *Kleinigkeit* of my treachery for the time being. It is to be such a momentous conference, held in the company of his twelve most high-ranking officers. When I asked why they were convening, he brushed the question off, saying that it should not concern me for the moment and that I would find out in due course.

He wishes me to be present at the meeting so that I may meet his coterie of knights in shining navy-black starch. As the bearer of the nation's upcoming generation, I am to act as a seated muse of our glorious future. Since my belly has swollen out to what seems like more than full capacity, he tends to speak of me as if I am some kind of icon of fertility. He once laughingly called me his Venus of Willendorf, as if I could take it as some kind of compliment. He showed me a picture in a book of a grossly distended mountain of stony flesh.

There are times when he calls me The Mother Goddess, something which triggers peals of laughter deep within him. It causes the grease around his chins to wobble around like jelly flesh.

It's true I've put a lot of weight on with this almost unquenchable hunger I've developed since the start of the pregnancy. No longer able to bring my evening cakes to Ernst, I started consuming them myself and the hot chocolate brought by Artus along with it.

I've taken to calling our child Mila, in remembrance of my sister. Ernst has agreed to call our child by that name. If it turns out to be a boy, we will call him Milo, even if Himmler names it something else. It will be our secret and I will whisper it into the child's ear whenever we are left alone so that it will know its true name.

50

My breasts have started leaking. A kind of creamy beige liquid. My new loose-fitting dress was all smeared and stained with the substance.

A little worried, I went to consult Doctor Kolb.

He said it was only 'colostrum'—I have no idea what the Polish word for that is. With his usual sage manner, he informed me that this kind of leakage tends to occur before parturition. It's simply the breast test-running its milk in preparation for lactation.

Only a week left before the conference. The whole castle is in a state of turmoil. The handmaids are all skittish, a gaggle of gigglers, still nervously fearful of being replaced in the love nest, despite the fact that Frau Whip has informed them that she will not be sending them home due to the special circumstances of the war and the need to groom the castle for the upcoming event.

We've been swept off our feet so much in preparation and endless errands that I haven't had a moment to myself in weeks. All you hear in every conversation is *Gruppenführer, Gruppenführer.*

The most notable of all the bigwigs is expected to be Reinhard Heydrich. The girls seem to consider him as the ultimate lodestar in the constellation of the heavenly Hs. Tall, young, blond, skilful and powerful, he is all they have ever aspired to. Even Himmler pales in comparison with the renown of his protégé.

In tones of veneration, Bettina told me that even Hitler himself refers to Heydrich as "the man with the iron heart", a phrase which no doubt sums him up in a neat and tidy nutshell. Olga claims that Heydrich is supremely intelligent, that none can hold a candle to his lofty Aryan mind. It's said that in the upper ranks of the Nazi party he goes by the name of Himmler's Brain. His other nicknames include The Blond Beast. I've also heard him referred to as The Hangman.

Heydrich is reputed to be an expert swimmer, as well as a consummate fencer and musician. The handmaids are thrilled by the idea that he is supposed to be an extremely talented violinist. They can't stop talking about how romantic that is; I personally find the cranky string instrument as squeaky and nerve-wracking as an unoiled hinge, but perhaps I have never heard it played with great skill. Still, I doubt Heydrich's playing could awaken

anything within me other than the contempt
and disgust I already feel for all the men of his
ilk.

He also has the infamous reputation of being
a somewhat callous womanizer, a rumour which
triggers no end of merriment and excitement
amongst the Burgermeiden. The fact that he has
apparently been married for ten years makes no
difference to their fantasies of liaising with the
ruthless Reinhard.

It is said that when RH looks at you, you
feel cloven and sundered, pierced to the core. It
is like being gazed at by a man-sized iron hawk.
It is said he never smiles in public. As head of
counterintelligence, he knows everything about
everyone, Himmler and Hitler included, or so
it is rumoured. Hearsay has it that he possesses
the power to arrest anyone on the mere
suspicion that they might perpetrate a crime in
the future. It is said he carries out these arrests
so discreetly that no one notices anyone is
missing. People just disappear under the cover
of night and are never seen again.

I am told that he, just as much as Krüger,
is responsible for the annihilation of Poland's
intelligentsia—all of my future teachers crushed
to nothing like flies in the clap of his hands. I
suppose it is sinister to long for this, but I sort
of look forward to staring Krüger and Heydrich
straight in the soul.

51

Oh what horrors I have heard. Such
horrendous things that I have not been able to
put them down in writing now for three consec-
utive days. Even after they left, I could not
bring myself to place such dismaying things on
the page.

The *Gruppenführer* arrived early on the
11th of June accompanied by the usual fleet
of black limousines. A slow, black caterpillar
of automobiles, entering in oozing segments.
Every single one of them was a near-identical
Mercedes-Benz. Twelve cars, twelve chauffeurs,
twelve black knights in peaked caps. From the
corridor window, we saw them dismount in the
triangular courtyard, all stiff and self-important
and grim as a rookery of starched crows.

The handmaids were so excited to be able
to contemplate so many triple Oak Leaves at
once they started emitting barely suppressed
squeaks of awe. In hushed, piping tones, they
pointed out Heydrich to me and then Karl
Wolff, Friedrich Jeckeln, Hans-Adolf Prützmann,

Theodor Eicke, Erich von dem Bach-Zelewski, the stars of their firmament. And last, but not least, Wilhelm Friedrich Krüger, the other slaughterer of my compatriots.

The handmaids didn't know the names of the other five dark knights filling the courtyard, but they were prolix about the cynosures they knew. They were eager to tell me about Erich von dem Bach-Zelewski because his father was apparently Polish, a fact he is thought to be embarrassed to acknowledge in public.

Despite his Slavonic ancestry, his repression of Poles is legendary throughout the Western hemisphere. He's also supposed to be particularly brutal and heartless in his treatment of Jews. He looked a bit Polish alright, though rather germanised by his Brill cream-lathered haircut and wire-rimmed gold glasses.

Friedrich Jeckeln is supposed to be a real Jekyll. He's in charge of the largest Einsatzgruppe, one of those divisions tasked with suppressing undesirables in the territories Germany has annexed to the east.

Theodor Eicke is head of the Totenkopf division. I can't remember what the handmaids said about the other *Obergruppenführer*, but they are all top-ranking dignitaries of the regime. And they all have some connection to the eastern territories.

After they disappeared into the castle, we didn't see them emerge again until the next day.

In the course of the early afternoon of the 12th, I heard a knock on my door.

In his brisk, efficacious mode, Himmler barged in straight after knocking to rattle out my marching orders. He was all jittery and brittle, the real commander-in-charge in nervous mode. Gone was the soft-toned, crooning wooer I'd got used to.

He said he wanted me to grace the afternoon officer meeting with my presence. He wished to show me off to the generals to give them courage and might in the ordeals that lay ahead.

So I complied, of course. At the appointed hour, I took my womb-heavy body down into the triangular courtyard and strained up into the North Tower to where the meeting was scheduled to take place.

When I entered the circular chamber, they were all there sitting solemnly at the rotund table in the centre. Himmler was pacing about, his standing position denying the symbolic equality of the round table.

Thirteen pairs of eyes turned to scrutinize me as I walked in and the hubbub around the table subsided momentarily. Himmler stopped stalking and introduced me to the generals with a starchy smile as "the future of our nation". There was something distinctly ominous I thought about the way he said it, but perhaps he was just deepening his voice for rhetorical effect.

In any case, they took his word for granted.
I saw a few heads nod in polite approbation.
The man who had been pointed out to me as
Heydrich was sitting, long-faced and wolfish,
at the table with the others next to Himmler's
empty chair. Even seated, he seemed to carry
himself like a reptile poised for the pounce. His
gaze latched onto my face as if he was trying
to decipher a hieroglyph. They all seemed to be
aware of who I was. Nothing further was said
of my gravid appearance though I caught Karl
Wolff and Krüger eyeing my bloated body with
what looked like a mixture of surprised awe and
not a little distaste.

Pointing to a nearby table laden with
cups and various pots, Himmler asked me if I
wouldn't mind serving a bit of tea and coffee,
I suppose so I would know my place and not
presume to engage in any pointless trivial small
talk with the officers. He got a few stares for
asking a pregnant woman to do that, but none
of the seated officers so much as uttered a word
of protest. I also got a few sardonic stares too,
the kind of glare that makes you want to hide
your face and cry. I find myself getting inordinately emotional, as if I am feeling twice my
usual levels of feeling—I suppose carrying a
second person within me has done that.

So there I was, being groomed as a fertility
object of both reverence and scorn, a pedestalled
dispenser of drinks. I could tell that to some of

these snobs I was little more than a flesh-engorged statue, a Germanic horn of abundance.
An ornamental canister repurposed to pour out
caffeine bounty to the nation's top brass.

Although I felt about as graceful as a bloated
ostrich in the company of this rookery of ravens,
I did my best to manoeuvre my bulk around the
table with as much grace and dignity as I could
muster, having to ply the base of my belly onto
the table in order to pour out the coffee-black
beverage to the knights.

To keep myself from sinking into sadness, I
tried to imagine the look on their fatuous faces
if I had bared my breast to squeeze out a few
drops of creamy colostrum into each of their
coffees.

Before I had quite finished serving their
drinks, Himmler began holding forth again.
There seemed to be a little dissent among two
or three of the generals though it was hard to
catch what they were muttering as Himmler
kept pounding out his loud-mouthed speech
about the necessity of attacking Russia before
overcoming England. I thought it sounded
utterly insane to be taking on an extra enemy of
that calibre.

The Beast conceded that he understood there
was some disappointment about abandoning
the conquest of Britain, but that the Führer had
decided that crushing Soviet Russia first would
send out a strong message. Confrontation with

Germany's most powerful ally was in any case inevitable in the long run. It was paramount to attack first to preserve the element of surprise.

I was rather taken aback that Himmler was discussing such key military operations in my presence, but kept my head suitably lowered on the crockery as if I had heard nothing out of the ordinary. I made myself as transparent as I could, a kind of deeply pregnant anonymous butler, a mountainous tea-and-coffee fountain, a silent pourer of drinks.

It was necessary, Himmler pursued, to vanquish communism for good. He kept hammering out the necessity of "cleaning up the east". Taming the Soviet Union would also confer on Germany an immeasurable tactical advantage for future operations in the east. What he called Operation Barbarossa (God knows why) would take no more than four months. Although the Soviet Union's territorial expanse was colossal, German troops would inevitably prevail.

The Soviets were only bluffing when they claimed that their army was vast. He said it was nothing but a groundless scare tactic and that Germany would crush the Soviet army in a matter of weeks. Hitler had said he wanted to raze Moscow to the ground and turn the entire city into a lake.

No less than four million soldiers are to be sent in to lay Russia low, which means the

German army will greatly outnumber its Soviet counterpart. The Panzer division is to take care of the rest.

Once they gain ground in the Baltic tribes, Bielorussia and Ukraine, hammered the Beast, looking intently at the one who had been pointed out to me as Adolf Prützmann, it would be the task of the generals in charge to train local populations to fight in Germany's name and "wipe away any remaining communist scum".

Himmler kept pounding away at his open left hand as he said all this, as if he could picture a piece of Bolshevik filth being beaten to a pulp in his palm.

Germany needs to create room for its settlers, he almost yelled, so that enough Aryan farmers could till enough soil to raise large families and increase the size of prime quality human beings. He kept citing two-hundred million as the figure to be achieved, as he had told me in confidence before. With two-hundred million Germans in the world no other nation would be able to assail the sovereignty of the German folk, he cried. Germany would achieve its destiny, it would become invulnerable forever.

For this to take place, he had calculated that approximately thirty million Slavs would have to be erased.

He stated this as if it was a reasonable sum,

a modest estimation, pressing the table top next to Heydrich's hand with a compressed yellowed finger.

I had been serving Erich Von dem Bach-Zelewski when he uttered the astronomical figure. I started visibly, upsetting my hold on the rather unwieldy pot of coffee and sending a small puddle of darkened water into B-Z's overflowing sig-stained saucer.

The Beast was so busy kneading the table with his mercilessly mechanical finger that he didn't notice my faux-pas, but Zelewski glared up at me with fiery irritability darting out of his pupils. Had it not been for the deathly silence provoked by Himmler's startling statement, he would probably have grunted his distaste of me more openly and I might have been dismissed from the chamber as a dysfunctional allegory.

Himmler continued to set forth what he called the Battle of Annihilation. Still pacing the room in measured steps, he stared them all one by one in the eye to get them into the mood of the moment, so that each of them would be ready to react with great promptitude and vivacity.

The operation should take no more than four months and should be over well before the Russian winter could set in. It was paramount to be quick and ruthless.

The Russians reproduce like vermin if left to their own devices, he continued. They need to be removed to make room for Germany. The invasion was set to begin before the end of June and the German army would reach Moscow in early autumn at the latest.

"We must wipe the table clean!" he raged, "so that the royal race can prevail again, at last. From our hearth, we will clean away all the dirt!"

Once the ground is cleared, affirmed the Beast, there should be a minimum of four children per family. There will be monitors put in place to make sure that these high standards of fertility are upheld in all households. If the head of a household is incapable of increasing his offspring, it will be the duty of German officers to stand in to make sure that the women of the household are sufficiently fertilized. Infertility will become grounds for divorce, the only grounds admissible, and women will be encouraged to conceive outside marriage.

"Your sexuality, your children", said the Beast in even tones, pointing at Wolff with grim determination in its eyes, "will no longer belong to you alone. They will belong to the greater good of the nation."

52

The heinous act they are about to perpetrate against all remaining Slavonic people left on Earth has scorched my mind and left it black. I have finally come to realize what they have no doubt already done.

If they intend to annihilate Soviet Slavs with such careless, callous, blithe indifference, it means that in all likelihood they have already wiped Poland off the face of the map. I am certain they have laid waste to it.

My parents are doubtless deceased or deported. Dead and buried in a pit now seems more likely than ever.

And yet, although this seems like the lowest possible ebb, I know that things can sink even lower.

What the Beast plans to do with the little Mila growing in my belly appears in perfect clarity. If he is aware of what I have written, but even if he is not, in both cases she will be shucked like a nut. She will be husked of me and I will be left as dross without a kernel. They

will either throw me out or have me impregnated once more like the fake golden cow I've
become.

At least one thing is clear: once Mila is born,
she will be taken away from me as everything
else has been taken from me and my people.
And that is something to which I simply cannot
concede. I cannot allow it to occur.

I have to see Ernst on the instant about this
and other matters before we run out of time.
We must be granted one more meeting. It is the
only way.

Outside the window, the new spring
sparrows shoot around like axe heads through
the evening. I see them pit their pointed bodies
through the air. What do they fly so low?

My grandmother told me once that it is not
that the birds fly low when storms are brewing.
They skim the grass because it is the winged
insects that go down before the tempest.

Epilogue

With these unresolved, enigmatic words ends Ewa's story. I was myself afflicted to see her diary come to a close so abruptly, without a word of closure, over a third of the way before the end of the diary, the empty pages almost crying out to be filled by more life, more hope, more everything. Aghast, I flicked through the last thirty blank pages of the notebook, almost desperate to find another word of consolation.

All those pages white as snow, blank and empty as the never-to-be-filled gaps in history. I cannot say how much it aggrieved me to be torn away from the balmy presence of Ewa's prose without a single note of valediction.

I can only attempt to alleviate the loss for the reader by adding a few appeasing (and not-so-mollifying) words of my own. My first thought on reaching the end of her narrative was that Ewa must have fled Wewelsburg in some kind of hurry, on the wing, unexpectedly, in the dead of night, with or without Ernst.

But where would they have fled to? And how could she ever have successfully effected

Ernst's prompt release from the prison camp?
Himmler seems to have given her reasonably
liberal amounts of money: could she perhaps
have put some of that aside to bribe a prison
guard?

My second darker stream of thought soon
replaced these no doubt over-optimistic hopes
to settle like wormwood in my chest. I cannot
shake from my mind the stomach-churning
intuition that Ewa was summarily arrested and
thrown into a camp. Either Ravensbrück, the
Reich's all-women's death camp, or else the
almost as deadly Niederhagen.

The fate of Ewa's child is hardly easier
to come to terms with. I sometimes think the
distress caused by her sudden panic after the
conference made her go into early labour.
It is possible that she died in childbirth or
else that she was conveyed to the nearest
Lebensborn facility after having delivered the
child. She would in that case at least have
been in the company of her new born infant.
I have however been unable to trace her in
the remaining registers of the Third Reich's
child-care centres.

I have been given comprehensive access
to all extant archives at Wewelsburg. While a
number of prisoners are mentioned by name
in miscellaneous documents, no exhaustive list
of detainees survived the fire that ravaged the
castle after Heinz Macher, Himmler's military

henchman, was ordered to destroy the edifice in 1945 to ensure that its secrets and treasures would not fall into enemy hands.

When they laid siege to the fortress, the Allies opened Himmler's treasure safe thanks to the use of dynamite. Local Buren authorities later found the safe blackened and empty after the withdrawal of these troops. Whatever else was in there has disappeared. The Spear of Destiny is, however, now safely housed in the Völkerkunde Museum in Vienna. Suffice it to say with some historic irony that it brought its unlawful purloiner no passage to victory.

What other fates can Ewa, Ernst and their child have met? My spirit quails to imagine that she was subjected to the soul-and-body-devastating horrors of the death camps. What inhuman brutality she may have experienced is thankfully not documented in her diary, nor will I adumbrate the reader's soul with too vivid an account of the horrors that took place in those places of perdition.

How Ewa's diary happened to survive the castle fire will have to remain an unexplained mystery. How it managed to survive History's scouring blaze is even more of a conundrum.

In my more hopeful moments, I imagine her hale and healthy. It is after all possible that she lived to see the end of the war: the Lebensborn facilities were strict, but in most respects they were the exact opposite of concentration camps.

Their main aim was to nurture the frailest
Aryan-looking babies and their mothers. While
many Germans suffered from hunger during
the last years of the war due for the most part
to the paucity of available food, the Lebensborn
centres never experienced hardship, dearth
of produce or any deprivations whatsoever.
The babies there were overfed, so were their
mothers. Even the nurses working at the facilities were plied with thrice daily meals and
protein-rich milk. They were considered by the
Reich to be the future of the nation. Every effort
was thus made to keep the facilities running at
the same high-living standard until the very end
of the war, when the rest of the country lay in
ruins. For obvious reasons, few of them were
bombarded by the Allies.

The other Mila too may have survived,
especially if she was placed in Lebensborn
though there is no record of that as far as I have
been able to ascertain. In my more sentimental
moments or when I think of what misfortune
may have afflicted them, I imagine the two
sisters reunited.

I sometimes indulge a fantasy. I picture
the two of them returning to their land in the
dusty rubble, in their war-sodden clothes, the
new mother cradling the child in her arms,
her sister standing staunchly by her side. I
see them wading through the Polish ash in
dimmed but dainty garments. I see them enter

their untouched, empty house. The door creaks slightly on its hinges. I see the grown up child run past fresh fields and golden wheat. I see her traipse around a courtyard strewn with milling hens and goats and milk-fat cows. Wishful thinking, of course, a thought for sore eyes, but it helps me to sleep in the evenings.

Addendum

And then I received that email.

About three months after the release of our first translation of the diary into German. The book had taken a few weeks to climb onto the best seller list but I had already started receiving a few dozen letters a week by the time I received that email on the inbox of my institutional address.

Needless to say, my natural inclination was to suspect a hoax of some more or less fraudulent kind. Most of the correspondence I received was run-of-the-mill fan mail, most of it for Ewa who could no longer receive it. In some of the more naïve cases, I had to write back to say that no I was afraid I could not pass their letter onto Ewa as I had no idea of her whereabouts.

I was generally so delighted in those first few weeks that the book had triggered such interest that I replied to every letter (none of my own history books had received as much as a single enthusiastic email in over forty years of publishing).

The flood of letters I subsequently received soon made it impossible to respond.

My email inbox too was chock-a-block with messages. I would find my locker at Humboldt literally crammed with white envelopes. When the book hit the German top ten bestseller list, I would find my locker so jam-packed with post it literally disgorged out of the slit—I had to proceed by removing a few dozen envelopes before opening the locker and had got into the habit of bringing a sizeable zip bag along with me that I had to position under the locker so that most of the avalanche would flow into the bag when I opened my pigeonhole.

Although I was unable to respond to all letters, having nothing better to do with my time, I tended to single out a weekly handful of the most engaging or moving ones. It kept me busy and accompanied in those otherwise lonely evenings.

I received the email I have mentioned rather late in the evening as I was browsing through my daily onslaught of electronic messages. The usual email subject title was "Your Book" or "Himmler" or "Ewa"; this one was titled "Eva Kaufmann".

I had received quite a few emails entitled "To Ewa" with the Polish spelling, but none with the German, and none at all with her Nazi-endowed surname. It rather alerted me and piqued my curiosity.

For obvious reasons, the email address, however, seemed more than a little untrustworthy. The sender address read *peter.lorre@hotmail.com.*

Of course chances are there is probably more than one Peter Lorre in the universe, but the happenstance seemed too much of a coincidence.

When I clicked to open the email, I half expected my anti-virus protector to start sounding one of those horribly noisy alarms that transform your computer into a beeping time bomb. But nothing happened. There was no further attachment to download, no tab, no Trojan horse malware to click on. Without a word of introduction, the unsigned message simply read

"I KNOW WHERE SHE IS."

You can imagine that the heart of a man of my age and sensitivity was set racing by so blunt and direct a message of hope. After my first paranoid intuition that this was nothing more than a lame hoax, I was unable to refrain from entertaining the wildest of surmises, not least of which was the most groundless hope that the sender was Ewa's direct descendent.

Ewa had been convinced that the child she bore in her womb would turn out to be a girl and that it was Ernst's and not Himmler's, but these intimate intuitions are often mistaken.

She could well have delivered a boy and named
him Peter and ended up marrying a Mr Lorre.
It seemed a slightly improbable supposition,
but for some irrational reason it clung to my
thoughts all day long.

I waited a few hours before answering
the email to let the turmoil in my mind settle
down. The wary side of me was more inclined
to believe that the email was merely a piece of
deception, perhaps even Jew-bait.

It occurred to me that this might be one of
those dark operators who now knew from my
prologue that I was Jewish and black-market
streetwise but eager to acquire any information
whatsoever about the manuscript and its author.

Above all, Peter Lorre put me in mind of the
Otto Bismarck who had given me the original
manuscript. It occurred to me that he might
now be regretting having ceded the item to me
and that he might be desirous to obtain an extra
cut from the proceeds of the book.

Before answering, I googled Peter Lorre just
in case, but all I came up with was a stream of
information concerning the Hungarian Jewish
actor whose real name I discovered was in fact
László Löwenstein.

Drawn in as one always is by the thirst for
miscellaneous knowledge, I read a little about
his Comedy of Terrors, The White Demon, M,
The Man Who Knew Too Much, Crime and
Punishment and Invisible Opponent.

I then googled Lorre Facebook to see what would come up. There was a Chuck Lorre, a Lucie Lorre, a Liliane Lorre, a Ludovic Lorre and quite a few others, but no Peter.

Twitching with curiosity, I finally wrote back the following cautious message:

> Dear Mr. Lorre,
>
> Thank you kindly for your email. Could you perhaps provide me with some credentials and tell me what you know about Ewa Kaufmann and her whereabouts?
>
> Yours sincerely,
> Kaspar Blumenfeld

The answer came back within the hour:

> "I do not wish to divulge any further details about myself. If you wish to know more about Eva Kaufmann, we can meet and I can explain."

It sounded like Peter Lorre was so wary about giving up anything that he was disinclined to provide even the conventions of polite correspondence. It reassured me that the writer didn't seem to want any money. It suggested Peter Lorre was no avatar of Otto Bismarck. But he could equally well be biding his time to address the issue of financial compensation at a later stage.

I wrote back post haste saying that I would indeed like to know more and where would he

like us to meet. Not wishing to be identified
even as the denizen of a specific town, he
offered to come and meet me in Wolfsburg.

I was immediately thrown into a state
of some alarm at the idea that he wished to
encounter me in my city of residence, but
agreed, suggesting we meet in broad daylight
in a pleasant popular park on the other side of
the city. I thought that if he wished to remain
anonymous, he might balk at the suggestion of
a café.

To my relief, Lorre wrote back saying the
assignation suited him perfectly. The next day
was equally convenient. He would be wearing a
black hat and a brown scarf and we could meet
at the western entrance to the park. He was
either familiar with the park already or had it
google-mapped.

My trepidation the following day even
before breakfast was almost greater than the
excitement that had accompanied me that fateful
day when I had first found the website adver-
tising Ewa's diary.

I didn't bother donning my Himmler-black
leather as I figured that Lorre had already
read my introduction to the book and knew
my exact identity, down to the fact that I carry
a sharpened screwdriver for protection in my
pocket when meeting with shady strangers.

It was the only time I ever rued having come

out of the closet in that foolhardy prologue of
mine—I had for the most part received encouraging praise for having penned it so candidly.

Much as I would have liked to I had not
asked what age he was. I was hoping he would
say about 80 as that would be the age Ewa's
descendent would have been. Asking him if his
scalp harboured hair or not was of course out of
the question. I had to make do with the hat-and-
scarf description.

Although I am rather fit for one my age
(having avoided wearing my body out with
sport), I did not fancy the thought of having
to wield the pocket screwdriver. I was rather
hoping Lorre would be of a geriatric nature and
of a hairy disposition.

Foremost in my mind of course was the hope
that he would turn out to be Ewa's boy or that
he would at least know if she had carried her
child to its final term and survived the delivery.

For good measure, I decided to bring a
hand-held hardback copy of the published
version of Ewa's diary. It was a sturdy volume
and would heft nicely in case I had to push back
an assault. I have always believed in the power
of books, viewing them as ideal, non-piercing
weapons. They can serve as both shield and
blunt instrument in case you need to knock
someone out—I once read a novel in which the
hero defends himself from a knife attack with
an art book. If I did not need to knock him on

the head with the book, I was sure he would be pleased to receive a signed copy.

I set out for Allerpark at 2pm in the aim of getting there well on time. As I live twenty minutes away from the park that meant I would have to wait forty minutes, but being nervous I preferred an extra walk about in the park to walking around in circles in my study.

Arriving at 2.20pm sharp exactly as planned, I took a stroll around the park, pausing in front of the milky white sculptured sphere squatting on the lakeside shore known as Planetenweg. I ambled past the rollerblade and skateboard ramp installation and took the long way around the pond past the Wolfsburg stadium and the Volkswagen Arena.

Having a few minutes to spare, I took a few steps down onto the artificial sandy beach they've installed on the eastern shore of the lake.

I got a little lost in thought at the sight of the water and had to rush back towards the western entrance to the park. I was worried Peter Lorre would lose patience and leave if I were more than five minutes late.

I reached the western entrance to the park in a lather of sweat despite the early March wind that was blowing. There was a rather tall-looking man in a hat wrapped in a dead-leaf-brown scarf loitering by the entrance. On approaching, I was relieved to see he was of only average build and well into his eighties, if not spilt right into his naughty nineties—an old-fogey like me, nothing too strenuous to grapple with. He looked wizened and rather frail, as if old age had whittled the sinew off his bones, and yet despite the frailness of his frame, his stare exuded a certain solid sturdiness.

His face was as wrinkled as a cobweb and he carried a steel cane in his left hand. I figured by the ancient look of the stick that it could conceivably contain a cane-sword, but the look of geriatric weariness writ large in his features suggested I would not have to deal with any unwanted belligerence on his part.

I tightened my grip on the hardback of Ewa's diary nevertheless, but didn't bother to slip my hand onto the screwdriver grip in my pocket.

Slowing down a little, I paced up to the gate and extended my free hand. He seemed a bit reluctant to shake it, despite the recent dropping of barrier gestures. Finally, he extended a gloved hand and took my leather paw.

I realized on the instant that he was going to be a man of few words, but he had a good smile and I warmed to him. We took a walk back in the direction of the lake. I had spotted a place or two where I could ably push him into the water if he proved to be a threat, a ludicrous precaution which turned out to be quite unnecessary.

The first thing I asked was if he happened
to be Ewa's son. He looked a bit taken aback
that I would venture to ask such a question. He
smiled a melancholy warm smile and shook his
head.

And then he told me his story, how it
happened that he knew of Eva Kaufmann.

According to Peter Lorre, Ewa and her
child were admitted to the Lebensborn centre
in early July of 1941. He averred he was the
director of the facility—although he demurred
at giving me his real name, he has agreed
under my insistence to feature in this annexe
under his alias. Dr Lorre has declined to tell
me the name and location of the Lebensborn
he ran. Although I pointed out to him that at
the Nuremberg trials, all personnel involved in
Lebensborn institutions were formally acquitted,
the centres having been somewhat controver-
sially deemed "humanitarian organisations",
he was apprehensive about having his name
associated with this period of history. While Dr
Lorre has vowed that as a doctor under the Nazi
regime he was never asked to put any Jewish
children to sleep with a needle, he wishes to
protect his reputation from malicious rumour,
despite having retired two decades ago from the
profession.

Dr Lorre was unable to tell me if Eva
Kaufmann had gone by any other name at the
Lebensborn. He says he never thought to ask.

He was only able to tell me that Ewa remained at the facility with her child until the end of the war.

When the Allies entered the town, she was released along with the other mothers and their children. Having talked with Ewa and monitored her child's progress for the first years of her life, Dr Lorre availed of many opportunities to talk with her. He recalled that during her protracted stay, she repeatedly asked him if he could discover the whereabouts of her sister. She also inquired many a time after a certain prisoner at Niederhagen.

As a mere director of Lebensborn, Dr Lorre was unable to ascertain the information she required though he says he tried his best to obtain it. He had Heinrich Himmler on the telephone on more than one occasion, and yes, the Reichsführer SS asked after Eva Kaufmann's well-being and the child's. Himmler stated each time that he would come and visit the centre in person, but with the complications ensuing from the increasingly unpropitious outcome of the war, these visits had never materialized.

Several months before the Allied forces entered the city, when it was known that Germany had been defeated, Peter Lorre had asked Ewa what she would do once the war was over.

It appears she confided that she would return to Wewelsburg in the hope of recovering

the man she believed was the child's father in
the nearby prison camp. She had then resolved
to travel to Berlin in the hope of finding information regarding her sister. If her sister's
whereabouts could be ascertained, she would
take the necessary steps to find her.

Accompanied by these two people if
possible, she would endeavour to find her
way back to her homeland to see if she could
locate her parents and recover her childhood
home. If all else failed to work out, she said
she had always nurtured a longing to visit the
Scandinavian countries, in particular Sweden.
If none of her family could be located, it was
possible she might emigrate to Scandinavia.

And that was all Peter Lorre had to offer. I
must say I was rather disappointed that he had
nothing more substantial to give me. I had been
led to believe that he knew of her exact location.
All I had to go on was at best southern Poland
or the whole of Sweden.

And yet having met someone who had seen
Ewa in the flesh brought her back to life for me.
Within days, I was rearing to go again, hot on
the heels of history. I had already conducted
some research to locate Ewa in Cracow and
Katowice and a number of other neighbouring
cities to no avail. I had checked in remaining
town hall registers, but for some inexplicable
reason it had not occurred to me to sift through
the archives of the emigration bureau.

Three days after meeting with Peter Lorre,
I took a day train from Wolfsburg to Cracow. I
hate taking night trains as I tend not to sleep a
wink in them—the darkness, the bunk berths,
the feeling of being trundled like a bag of
potatoes being sent into exile remind me too
much of that train my parents and I once took
to Auschwitz.

So I took an early express train that day to
Dresden and from thence a rather slower one
from Dresden to Wroclaw and on to Cracow.

For days, I scoured the archives of the cities
of Silesia, finding nothing whatseoever. I had so
little to go on, just two girls' first names and the
faintly absurd hope that Ewa's Polish surname
had begun with a K—it had said in the diary
that her real surname was vaguely related to
Kaufmann, but how close I had no idea.

I found a number of Ewas who had
emigrated to the Czech Republic, to Hungary,
Bulgaria, France, England and the Netherlands.
I even spotted a few who had apparently
headed for Scandinavia, but no sign of an Ewa
with Mila as a daughter.

Most of the Ewas registered were accompanied by husbands and little boys and little
girls. There was no Ernst Meier to be found, no
Ewa Meier either.

But then it occurred to me that it was
possible Ewa had not registered her departure
in Silesia. It was possible she had either taken

a train or a boat up to Sweden or Norway or another part of Scandinavia.

I figured the ferry seemed a likelier option, Ewa no doubt being disinclined to travel through Germany, the country of her captivity, in a rather roundabout train journey up through Denmark and on to Sweden.

And so I journeyed straight up to northern Poland, establishing my base in the wonderfully rebuilt city of Gdansk. From there, I rooted out every shred of information I could find, in every subsisting archive.

And finally, I found her.

I wasn't entirely certain it was her of course, but my heart almost failed me when I read the document: Ewa Kowalska, aged 24, and her daughter Mila Kowalska, aged 5, had embarked to emigrate officially on a liner set for Stockholm on the 24th of March, 1946.

It gave me a queer kind of thrill to notice that Mila Kowalska had been born the same month as me in August of 1941. I checked to see if an Ernst Meier or Ernst Kowalski had emigrated on the same date, but there was nothing. I also tried to hunt down a second Mila Kowalska, but met with no other girl of that name.

You wouldn't believe the state of excitement I was left in with that sheet of paper in my hand, after all those weeks of going bleary in the eyes and slightly crazy and asthmatic from sifting through the flurry of dust on those endless reams of musty paper.

Having contacted the emigration office in Stockholm to see if I could carry out some research on their archives in my capacity as a historian, I received an email within the hour from a certain Torsten Falk granting me full access to the archive.

I booked a Scandlines ferry ticket to Stockholm for an inevitable night crossing from Gdynia the very next evening and arrived in the Swedish capital after a relatively smooth, seasick-free journey. As soon as I got there, I checked into my hotel and took myself off to the bureau of emigration.

The filing system for early archives was all very efficiently online so I had no trouble at all in locating the relevant records. Within less than an hour of research I was able to locate Ewa and Mila Kowalska on the day of their arrival.

I contacted the services of the Stockholm town hall to see if they possessed any further information, and lo and behold, I found what I was seeking. A beautiful, pristine, updated address.

It seemed that the two Polish immigrants had travelled from Stockholm to Gothenburg and had registered as permanent residents near Uddevalla, on the western coast.

My heart sank to the bottom of the ship though when I read on the town hall clerk's

screen that Ewa Kowalska's death had been
registered in 2014 at the age of 91.

But her daughter Mila Kowalska was still
living in a coastal hamlet that went by the
heavenly address of 9, Amundsväg, Ammenäs
in the administrative district of Uddevalla.

I even found a phone number tagged to her
name when I typed it into the server. I jotted
it quickly down as if it was about to disappear
and went back to my hotel to grieve and rejoice
in equal measure.

Before going to bed, I dialled the number
on my cellphone with trembling fingers and
trotting heartbeat. I heard an elderly woman's
voice answer, an elegant, distinguished sort of
voice that conveyed a sense of beauty to the
mind.

Having ascertained that she was the Mila
Kowalska I was seeking, I told her in my most
controlled quavering voice that I possessed
something that belonged to her mother. I could
tell from her manner of speaking that she was
rather stirred when I told her about the diary.
She had not heard of the published book. It
hadn't yet been translated into Swedish. My
publisher had only ceded the translation rights
a month before that fateful encounter with Dr
Lorre.

Having agreed that I would come and visit
Mila Kowalska, I took the morning express
train to Gothenburg, and then a local train to

Uddevalla. From there, I had to take a taxi out to the coastal town of Ammenäs.

Having reached the swaying golden wheat around the hamlet, I asked the taxi to drop me off at the foot of the hill as he began to ascend the serpentine road that wended its way up through the forest.

I was keen to walk up the steeply winding road to Mila's house. It seemed somehow appropriate to walk the last lap of my pilgrimage up the hillock, as if I were some kind of Romeo that needed to climb the forest balcony up to her feet.

I got to Amundsväg in a bit of a sweat though the spring breeze wafted freshly onto my face. I took my coat off and hung it on my arm, removing Ewa's booklet so that I could have something to hold on to.

In my precipitation and excitement at meeting Mila Kowalska, I had quite forgotten to bring a bouquet or a bottle of wine or even chocolates. I was thankful to be able to gift something that would trump all of those.

Mila's house was different to the other houses in the vicinity which tended to be either traditional red in the style of nineteenth-century Swedish housing designs or white or bright yellow and pale blue.

It was a sizeable dark-hued log cabin set in a kind of Walden-like wilderness of densely growing trees and ferns and low-lying blueberry bushes. In marked contrast, the other houses tended to have well-behaved lawns with automated lawnmowers almost incessantly doing the rounds to track down and clip any last blade of recalcitrant grass.

There being no doorbell on the glass and pinewood front door, I knocked.

The woman who came to greet me was exactly my height. Gracing me with the most winsome of smiles, she opened the door and let me in.

On the round pinewood table lay an assortment of Danish pastry. The combined fragrance of cardamom, cinnamon and marzipan wafted up to my face like the heat from an open oven. An outsized chick-yellow teapot sat in state in the centre of the table.

The sun had pushed its fingers deep into the open-ceilinged living room. With her loosely hanging silvery white hair, Mila was so utterly beautiful I couldn't take my eyes off her.

Taking my coat, she asked me to sit down on one of the plush upholstered chairs so I sat down. She inquired if I would prefer tea or coffee. Gesturing mutely towards the stately yellow teapot, I murmured that tea would be lovely.

Holding the massive teapot with two sturdy, unwavering hands, she poured out an amber stream of English Breakfast into my Swedish-looking cup. Over the most delicately exquisite cinnamon and cardamom rolls, we talked a little about her life and then a little about mine.

After my third roll, I wiped my hands on the paper napkin by my side and with a little surge of emotion showed her Ewa Kowalska's diary.

Mila handled the time-weathered booklet with such reverence, with such a dainty touch, opening the cover ever so delicately with the tip of her fingers that an unexpected wave of bedrock emotion rose up inside me and I started shedding uncontrollable tears like a boy.

Mila reached across the table, placed her hand on mine and smiled me back to calmness. She seemed moved, though not to tears. I think I was shedding enough of those for both of us.

The reader will have guessed how this all ends. You may be happy to know that since that day I have been in regular correspondence with Mila Kowalska, both on the phone and in letters, and that I plan to move to Sweden in the autumn, as soon as I can sell my house and auction off most of my collection.

Erik Martiny (born 11 June 1971) is a Franco-Irish-Swedish novelist, academic and journalist who teaches at the Lycée Henri IV in Paris. His reviews on art and literature have appeared in *The Cambridge Quarterly*, *The Times Literary Supplement*, *Whitewall Magazine*, *The London Magazine*, and *Aesthetica Magazine*. He is the author of eight previous works of fiction, including *Night of the Long Goodbyes* (2020), *Crown of Beaks* (2021), *Waiting for Gaudiya and Other Stories* (2021), *The Moose, the Mouse, and the Little Irish Boy* (2021), which he co-authored with his son, and *Cocteau's Invitation* (2023).

www.ingramcontent.com/pod-product-compliance
Lightning Source LLC
Chambersburg PA
CBHW060243030726
47493CB00025B/1578